Your Endless Love
(The Bennett Family, Book 9)

LAYLA HAGEN

Dear Reader,

If you want to receive news about my upcoming books and sales, you can sign up for my newsletter HERE: http://laylahagen.com/mailing-list-sign-up/

Cover: RBA Designs
Cover Photography: Sara Eirew Photographer

Copyright © 2018 Layla Hagen
All rights reserved.

Chapter One

Summer

"There are too many options." I flick my gaze from the Cinderella figurine to the carriage on the shelf below. Next to me, my brother Daniel seems to have as much trouble deciding as I have. We're shopping for presents for our niece's birthday. As we head to the next aisle, his phone chimes.

"Great news," he announces, his attention on the small screen. "Alex Westbrook's team just informed me he can drop by St. Anne's next week."

"Thank you, thank you, thank you." I clasp my hands together, grinning. St. Anne's is a group home where I often volunteer. Nothing makes the kids' day more than a celebrity visiting, and Alexander "Alex" Westbrook is playing their favorite superhero on the big screen. Daniel owns an adventure center, catering to a famous clientele. Ever since I found out Westbrook is his client, I pestered him about this. "You're my favorite brother."

Daniel shoves his phone back in his pocket, elbowing me conspiratorially. "Don't play the favorites game. I know you say that to all our brothers."

"How about, you're my favorite brother right

now?"

"Ouch. Hurtful, but honest."

I sigh, tilting my head to one side. "We have seven siblings. You can't monopolize the favorite spot all the time."

I *love* being the youngest, and I take thorough advantage of it. As a kid, I could get away with anything.

As we step into an aisle displaying miniature musical instruments, I ask, "Does Alex have any special requests?" I've organized quite a few celebrity visits at the group home and know stars can be high-maintenance. Since Alex is leading the A-list in Hollywood, I imagine he'll have some requests.

Daniel nods, inspecting a miniature saxophone. "Yeah. He doesn't want press or PR communication. No photos on social media."

That's not what I expected. "Sure, no problem."

"He's not one of those celebrities boasting about their charity work," he says, as if reading my mind. "And since his split from Amy, he tries to keep an even lower profile."

"I don't blame him. What a mess." I'm not one to keep up with celebrity scandals and tabloids, but as Hollywood's darlings, their split is so highly publicized, there's no escaping it. The official reason for the split was that they simply grew apart, which the tabloids don't believe. As such, the speculations run wild.

I can't imagine how dreadful it must be to

have your heartbreak splashed all over the Internet and printed media. A breakup is bad enough in itself. I usually go through them by consuming copious amounts of sugar—or wine—and watching bad rom-coms with my sisters commiserating with me. But having the whole world watch your every move when you're at a low point? That has to be a special kind of hell.

"Audrey would love a saxophone," I tell my brother.

"I'm buying this one then," Daniel announces, grabbing one of the miniature saxophones.

"I think I'll buy her that treasure-hunting set we saw right next to the entrance."

"That's what I call an efficient shopping trip."

"The power of experience, brother. The power of experience." Since all my siblings are married, and most have kids, I developed quite a knack for buying gifts.

"Just so I'm mentally prepared, will it be one of those over-the-top parties?"

I bring both hands to my chest theatrically. "I'm shocked you'd think otherwise. Of course it will be." I smile sheepishly. Yeah, I might go a tad overboard when it comes to organizing our nieces and nephews' birthday parties, but I can't help myself. The kids love it. And so do my siblings. They just like teasing me about it. I point my forefinger at Daniel. "And don't think you can get out of me what the theme will be. It's a surprise."

"I made the meeting with Alex happen and I don't even deserve a heads-up?"

I narrow my eyes, recognizing one of my own tactics for luring out secrets: inducing guilt. "Nope, you don't. And speaking of Alex, is he flying in that day from LA? Should I arrange for a car to pick him up from the airport or the hotel? I can pick him up too."

I can't hide my excitement at the prospect. There's no point lying to myself; I swoon every time I see him on screen, along with every woman in America.

"I'll tell you all the details as soon as I have them. But he's moving from LA to San Francisco, so he won't be staying in a hotel."

"Oh, okay."

I nod, my mind back to Audrey as we reach the row of treasure-hunting games. I choose the diamonds-themed one, and then we head to the cashier line. The stack of magazines next to the counter catches my attention. Two gossip magazines show Alex on the cover, looking very low-key, even sporting an unkempt beard in one. The titles underneath are as speculative and cutting as ever: *"No real-life superhero. Why did Amy leave him?"* And *"Lose the hobo look, Alex. No wonder Amy left you."*

My stomach sinks. I hope Alex isn't seeing everything that's being written about him. Next to me, Daniel shakes his head, his gaze on the headlines as well. We pay quickly, heading out of the store. We parked next to each other, and as we reach our cars,

Daniel says, "Just one thing. Promise you won't be starstruck around Alex."

My brother knows me all too well. Among my many, many faults, the top are: only realizing a guy is an ass too late, a chronic inability to stop after eating one muffin, and… being starstruck whenever Daniel introduces me to one of his clients.

"I promise I'll try," I say truthfully, pushing my hair out of my face as a gust of wind ruffles my shoulder-length dark hair.

Daniel presses his lips together, smiling. "You're lucky I love you so much."

"You have no choice. I'm your baby sister."

Even though I'm twenty-eight, I still love the sound of *baby sister*. So much sweeter than *youngest sister*.

"And thanks again for getting him to agree to the visit," I add before Daniel can admonish me more. Plus, I really do intend to keep the fangirling to a minimum. I have a feeling Alex needs peace and quiet. The guy agreed to visit St. Anne's when he could have easily declined, so I'm determined to make an effort.

"No problem. Do you want to go grab dinner?"

"Nah, I have to go back to the gallery. I just wanted to get to the store before it closed."

"Okay. I'll send you all the details about Alex's visit as soon as possible. And remember your promise, okay?"

Sighing, I stand on my tiptoes, kissing my

brother's cheek. "Yes, yes. No need to be insufferable about it. Kiss Caroline and the kids for me."

"Will do."

As I climb into my car, I'm mentally planning the party. I arrive at the gallery after closing time. All the patrons have left, and my colleagues Jacob and Diana are already wrapping up the Monet collection. We're shipping it back to Paris tomorrow.

"Olivia's already gone," Jacob informs me, mimicking the act of wiping sweat from his brow. Our boss isn't the easiest person to work with. Grabbing the Bubble Wrap, I help him cover one of the larger paintings.

"Hey, don't be so brusque," I admonish when he turns the painting so abruptly it nearly slips between his fingers.

"I have a date tonight, and I don't want to be late. New girl, first impression counts."

I point a finger at him in warning. "Not a good enough reason to do a half-assed job. The paintings must be handled with love and care."

Diana narrows her eyes at him. "Summer, I suggest you and I finish the job before Jacob mucks it up because he's hurrying."

Jacob grins. "That was exactly my plan."

"Go, go, go. Don't unleash your non-humor on the poor girl right away," Diana says, shooing him away. Then she pouts in my direction. "Why is it that he gets more romantic action than we do?"

I bite back a laugh. "Must be his non-humor."

I don't remember the last time I went on a date, and it doesn't look like my luck in the dating department will change anytime soon, but I'll be seeing the one and only Alex Westbrook in the flesh. How is *that* for a silver lining?

Chapter Two

Alex

"I can come straight to your house after the viewing and deal with the movers," my sister says into the phone.

"Sophie, stop fussing over me. I'll deal with them."

"Are you kidding me? We're in the same city for the first time since we were kids. Of course I'll fuss about you. If I don't, who will?"

I chuckle. "I'll call you if I need anything. What time are you bringing Drew tomorrow?" Drew is her seven-year-old son. I can't wait to spend the day with my nephew.

"Does nine work?"

"Yeah."

"He's so psyched you're here. Oh, shoot, I've got to go. My clients are here."

"Good luck at the viewing. See you tomorrow."

Sophie is a real estate agent here in San Francisco, and she found me this house. I used to fly here between movies, but I still saw her far too seldom for my taste. We're from Portland, but she moved here after college. I've wanted to move out of

LA for a time, and now is the perfect moment for a change of scenery.

When my sister asked what my requirements were for the house, I just said I wanted privacy, space, and the ocean within walking distance. She found me the perfect place. She took care of furnishing it for me too. I didn't take any furniture from the home I shared with Amy in LA, but I still had so much crap lying around there that I hired a moving company to pack it in boxes and bring it over.

Filming of my last movie wrapped up two days ago, so I have the delivery scheduled for today. Sophie offered to take care of delivery and unpacking for me, but I want to do it myself. While on set or promoting a movie, everything is being done for me. I want to do things myself in my free time, regain some semblance of normalcy.

I check my watch, deciding to wait five more minutes for the delivery company to show up before calling them. If they're not on time, I'll have to call Summer Bennett and ask her to pick me up later for the trip to the group home, and I don't like being late.

While I wait, I finish reading the e-mail I received when Sophie called. It's from my manager, Preston.

Alex,

I've updated your schedule. We booked you for two events. It goes without saying, but you're only allowed to answer any questions about Amy the way we discussed. The studio is antsy about this. You know what's at stake.

Antsy is an understatement. They produced the romantic comedy Amy and I starred in, and part of the marketing for the romantic comedy was relying on the real-life romance between us. They're also producing the superhero franchise I'm part of, and we're in talks about developing a spin-off for my superhero character. Now is not the time to make them antsy.

I check my watch. Where is the delivery company? They should have been here five minutes ago. As if on cue, my phone rings, the company's number flashing on my screen.
"Mr. Fulton, we're sorry, but we're stuck in traffic five blocks from your house. We'll be fifteen minutes late."
The guy will realize who I am the second he sees me, but revealing my real name over the phone sometimes leads to unwanted paps visits.
"Thanks for letting me know, but hurry. I have an appointment in twenty-five minutes."
After hanging up, I immediately pull up Daniel Bennett's e-mail on my screen.
Hey Alex!
Talked to my sister Summer, she'll pick you up at five o'clock sharp. Here's her number in case you need it.
Bingo. I knew he'd sent me her number. I dial it, and she answers right away.

"Hey, Alex here."

"Hi!" she answers in a high-pitched tone.

"I'm sorry, but I'm going to be about fifteen minutes late. The movers bringing my things from LA should have been here by now, but they're stuck in traffic."

"Umm, okay. No problem. I'll just wait in my car."

"You're here already?"

She laughs nervously. "I didn't want to be late, so I hit the road a little early, and there wasn't much traffic. I parked just in front. Hang on, I'll move the car so the moving truck can access your gate. I'm blocking it."

Instinctively, I look out the window, but I can't see the street, obviously. Eight-feet-high evergreens surround my property, forming a thick wall.

"Come on in after you park. You don't have to wait in the car."

"Are you sure? I don't mind."

"I'm not going to make you wait half an hour in your car, Summer."

I asked to be picked up because the new car I ordered will be delivered next week, and I avoid cabs if I can.

"Okay."

Clicking off, I head outside and open the door next to the double gate, just in time to see a woman climb out of a red Ford. The moment she sees me, her eyes widen, and she presses her full lips together.

I switch on my camera smile, motioning with my head toward the house.

"Come on in."

Nodding, she rushes forward, smiling and fiddling with her thumbs. I've seen this behavior before, when it's clear someone is trying to hold back from squealing or jumping in my face and taking a selfie. I appreciate the effort.

I close the gate the second she's through and hold out my hand.

"I'm Alex."

"I know. I mean, obviously you know I know." She closes her eyes and breathes in. "Sorry. I'm babbling. I'm Summer."

Grinning, I shake her hand, then lead her to the house on the path of cobbled stone. "How long have you been waiting out there?"

"Ten minutes. I left the gallery early because I didn't know how the traffic would be."

"What do you do at the gallery?"

"I'm a curator, but I do a bit of everything," she explains as we step inside the house.

I'm close enough to see she wears no makeup. She's biting on her plump lower lip, her hands crossed over her chest. She's a petite woman, but the simple black dress and wide belt she's wearing shows off her beautiful curves. When she's done inspecting the room, she focuses on me. Her eyes hold a mix of curiosity and excitement, but there is also unexpected warmth there.

"Sorry, I'm staring," she says when our gazes

meet. Shifting her weight from one leg to the other, she looks at the hardwood floor.

"I'm used to it," I say honestly. Plus, I was checking her out, so I can't exactly point fingers.

"Now, Daniel's told me you're very chatty."

She smiles sheepishly. "Usually, yeah."

"He also said you can be pretty wild when you unleash your inner fangirl."

"He did not say that!" She stands up straighter, her cheeks turning pink. Then her ears turn pink too. Fuck, she's cute. "Did he? Did he?"

"Sort of. But seeing your reaction, I think the question warrants more digging."

She offers me a firm shake of her head. "Nope." Then she sighs. "I might have embarrassed him once or twice when I was dying for an autograph."

"I'll gladly give you one, Summer."

"What makes you think I want one?" She narrows her eyes and plants her hands on her hips. I get the feeling she can be a downright little minx.

"Touché. Want anything to drink?" I motion to the leather couch on our left. "You can sit if you want."

"Thanks. A glass of soda would be good. By the way, this is a very nice house."

"I like it too. My sister found it for me, furnished it too," I explain while I head to the small bar in the corner and pour soda in a glass.

"Oh, your family lives in San Francisco? Sorry, I'm prying."

I chuckle. "You don't have to walk on eggshells around me. I don't mind curiosity, as long as whatever I say doesn't get to the press."

Her smile fades as I hand her the soda. "I'd never do that."

"I meant in general, not you specifically."

She takes a small sip from the glass. "Okay. I didn't get to thank you for agreeing to visit the kids at St. Anne's, by the way. It means a lot to them."

"Sure, no problem. That's one of my favorite parts about this gig. How did you get into volunteering there?"

"Well, Daniel and his wife adopted two kids from there. One thing led to another…." She lowers herself on the couch while she explains to me about St. Anne's, and her skirt lifts a few inches. Nothing indecent, but enough to reveal beautiful, toned upper thighs, making my mouth water. Christ, she's pretty, sitting there, legs crossed, her rich dark hair pulled to one side, baring her neck. Swallowing hard, I look away.

A honk resounds from outside, startling Summer. She nearly spills the remaining soda on her, but catches herself in time.

"That'll be the movers," I say. "I'll just ask them to unload the boxes, and then we can go. It'll take five minutes tops."

"Okay."

"Mr. *Fulton*," one of the guys says five minutes later. His voice drips sarcasm. He recognized me right away. "I need you to sign extra for this last box. It contains valuables. You need to open it and confirm that all items on the list are inside."

They've offloaded all fifteen boxes, and the guy just laid the last one at my feet, holding a list.

"What valuables?" I ask.

He glances over the list. "Philip Patek watch, Omega watch, eight-carat diamond ring encrusted with emeralds."

I freeze, feeling like someone punched me straight in the gut. Amy sent me the engagement ring with the movers? Jesus Christ. I didn't even want the damned ring back.

"That's fine, you can go," I say in a composed voice.

"I need you to open the box and sign the list before."

If he realizes the ring is our engagement ring, he doesn't let on. Crouching down, I open the box. Two watches, a ring box. I don't bother opening up the box. Standing up, I sign the damned list. "Everything's here. You can go now. Thank you for your business."

I feel a vein pulsing in my temple as the movers' truck pulls out.

"We should go," Summer says quietly, stepping past the boxes in the living room. When I meet her gaze, I realize she knows exactly what was in that box. Women put two and two together much quicker than men, and she's looking at me with pity.

"Yeah. Let's go." My voice comes out low and

harsh, making her wince.

"I'm sorry. That... that was the engagement ring, right?"

"That's none of your business."

She flinches again, harder. Fuck, what am I doing? This isn't her fault.

Rolling her shoulders, she juts her chin out. "That's a shitty thing, what just happened, but I'm not the one who sent you the engagement ring with the moving company, so don't bite my head off. If you want to reschedule the trip to St. Anne's, I can arrange that. Don't want you blinding the kids with your sunny disposition right now."

Well, well. It's been a long time since someone called me out on my shit.

"I'm going to wait in the car for ten minutes, give you some space. Call me if you want me to reschedule."

And without another word, she walks out of the house and slips out through the gate. I scrub my hands down my face and take a few deep breaths to calm down. That was a dick move. But rescheduling would be an even bigger dick move. I know how much kids look forward to these things, and I don't want to disappoint them, or Summer.

I'm an actor. It's my job to smile even when I don't feel like smiling. So I grab my leather jacket from the hanger and head out.

Summer is looking pointedly out her window when I climb into her car. We sit in uncomfortable silence for a few seconds.

"I'm sorry, Summer. I was out of line."

"Yeah, you were."

I touch her bare forearm, and the contact zings me. Her skin is soft, enticing. Damn, I have no business being enticed. I let her go as she snaps her head in my direction, looking a little wary.

"I was taken by surprise," I continue, needing to explain myself. I want her to know I'm not a dick, someone who treats others badly whenever he's in a funk. "I don't usually act like this. The ring was just… unexpected. I'm really sorry for jumping down your throat."

She sighs. "Fine, you're forgiven."

That makes me smile. "Just like that?"

"It's one of my many faults. I forgive easily. Staying angry takes up too much energy. And well, that was a shitty thing. Anyone would snap. Are you sure you don't want to reschedule?"

"Nah, I don't want to let the kids down. I can entertain people even when I don't feel like it, I promise. Acting's my job."

She narrows her eyes, as if considering something. Then she reaches in her back seat. That's when I see the huge box with a cake as a label, with an identical smaller box on top. She takes the smaller one in her hands, opening the lid, revealing three cupcakes.

"Here, have a cupcake."

"What?"

"It'll lift your mood a bit. The sugar rush sends endorphins in your blood."

"Why do you have a stack of sweets in your car?"

"Well, the large box is for St. Anne's. This one's for me, but your need is greater than mine."

I check her face for any signs that she's pulling my leg, but either she's a stellar actress, or she's serious.

I take one cupcake, wondering how many more ways she can surprise me. Summer Bennett is different from the people usually surrounding me. Different in the best kind of way. Honest, not afraid to call me out on my shit, or to own up to her quirks. She has an inner warmth I haven't encountered in people in years.

"This is really good," I exclaim through the first mouthful.

"I know." Her longing tone is delightful.

"Don't worry, I'm only eating just this one. I'll leave you the rest."

She shakes her head, smoothly bringing the car into motion. "No, no. They're yours. I eat too many anyway. My scale will be thankful if I skip the cupcakes today."

"Forget that. You're beautiful, Summer."

She peeks at me, quickly returning her attention to the road. The pale skin on her neck turns a delicious shade of pink as she clears her throat.

"Thank you." She shifts in her seat, drumming her fingers on the wheel. Part of my job as an actor is to analyze body language. And right now, Summer's body language tells me she's not used to receiving compliments, which is a shame.

I close the lid on the small box, leaving the two remaining cupcakes untouched, then place the box in the back.

"I insist—" she starts, but I cut her off.

"I won't eat all your cupcakes, Summer."

"You're bossy."

"I was actually aiming to be courteous."

She grins. "Some shit actor you are, then. I knew it! They're plastering you on every poster only for your pretty face and to-die-for body."

"To-die-for body? That's a lot of appreciation from someone who doesn't want my autograph." I burst out laughing, feeling more at ease than I've felt in weeks. More alive, too.

Chapter Three

Summer

Out of the corner of my eye, I sneak a glance at him. I can't help myself. *Alexander Westbrook is in my car.* I estimate the distance between us to be about one foot. I can practically smell his cologne, and it's just as sexy as every other part of him. Oh, us mere mortals always hope stars aren't as beautiful as they appear on screen.

Nope, I can say with absolute certainty that he's even more gorgeous in real life. His green eyes really *are* that green, and deep and striking. His short, black hair is shinier than any hair in a shampoo commercial. And all that training for his superhero role paid off big-time. He's pure muscle everywhere.

He's more approachable and laid-back than I expected. Aside from the engagement ring freak-out, he's friendly enough. I wanted to reach out and comfort him, but man, did that backfire. Serves me right for poking my nose where it doesn't belong. I may feel like I know him because I've seen him on screen for years, but he's a stranger. A sinfully sexy stranger. When he told me I'm beautiful, my knees wobbled a bit. Thank God I was sitting down.

I tell him more about St. Anne's on the drive,

and half an hour later, I pull the car to a stop in the small parking lot in front of the establishment.

"I'll get the cupcakes," Alex offers.

"Thanks."

He easily carries the box in one hand, and after locking the car, I lead him through the small front gate onto the property. Juniper trees line the cobblestone pathway leading to the main building. I love their smell.

There are six houses on the perimeter. As far as group homes go, St. Anne's is one of the best. Each house has a supervisor, and there are no more than three kids in each bedroom. This isn't intended to be a permanent residence for the children, only a place to stay until they receive a place in foster care. But that can take years, so this is the only home some of them know.

The door of the largest house and the institute center swings open and Shawna, the director, waves at us.

"Mr. Westbrook, so pleased to meet you. Thank you for making time to visit us," she says, almost breathlessly. "I'm Shawna Delaware."

"Nice to meet you, Shawna."

Alex flashes her a winning smile. I recognize it from magazines and his movies. I can't quite pinpoint why, but it feels different than the way he smiled at me when we were alone. That smile seemed warmer, this one more studied. It's almost too perfect—the way it shows both his dimples and turns his expression into one of pure seduction. I like the real one better.

The kids are psyched when we enter the common room. All of them have gathered here, perched on couches or on the floor. The youngest ones are even dressed in Alex's superhero costume. It seems to me they start talking all at once, but Alex's experience with crowds shines through. He has no problem hopping from question to question, flicking his attention from one kid to the other.

"And when you jumped, you were like whoosh. I thought for sure you'd died," one of the seven-year-old boys says. "Was it hard to jump?"

"Not nearly as hard as it looked."

The boy's eyes light up. "Really? I wanted to try, but Ms. Shawna caught me."

Alex laughs, but I detect a hint of concern in his voice when he answers. "Best not to try it. It took me some training with the stunt master on set to be able to do it without hurting myself."

"Whoa, you do your own stunts?" one of the older girls asks.

"Yeah. Most of them, anyway."

A chorus of awestruck "cool" follows.

"Did you always know you want to be an actor?" the girl who asked him about the stunts continues.

Alex hesitates, then says, "Yes and no. Growing up, I wasn't very good at school, or at sports, or at anything in particular."

The crowd goes quiet, as everyone—myself included—hangs onto his every word.

"Then one day we had a filming crew at school. They were looking for a kid to include in a toothpaste commercial. Reading those two lines of the script was the first thing that ever came naturally to me."

His confession feels raw and real. I appreciate his honesty with the kids. It takes a lot of strength of character to admit your flaws, or own up to your failures.

For the next two hours, Alex talks to the kids and shows them a few stunts. They're utterly charmed. Maybe that charisma he exudes on screen, that inexplicable pull he casts at all times, comes from an inner place of openness and honesty. Shawna hops in and out of the room, checking in periodically.

After showing off yet another stunt, Alex heads straight toward me. I'm standing next to the drinks table at the end of the room.

"Need something to drink." His voice is so hoarse, his throat must be dry as dust. He's talked nonstop since arriving. But hot damn, that hoarseness is seven kinds of sexy, making me wonder what his bedroom voice sounds like.

"What's good? Not water, I need something thicker. Anything with honey?"

"The lemonade," I say automatically, hoping my voice sounds even. Alex nods, pouring himself a drink, then downing it with large gulps. Even the movement of his throat as the liquid travels down is sexy. He sets the glass down with a plunk.

"What's your stance on headstands?" he asks.

"Huh?"

"I need to show them how to do a headstand. I'd like for you to volunteer."

"No, I don't think so. I'm wearing a dress, and I really like my neck intact."

"Your dress is tight, it won't move much. And it's not dangerous. All you have to do is plant your palms firmly on the ground, I'll do the rest—hold your ankles, sustain your waist. The kids want to see it, but I don't want to demonstrate it with one of them. They tend to get overexcited and stop paying attention to the instructions. Don't want them to get hurt."

He pins me with those gorgeous green eyes of his. They look a little brighter in real life. Well, when he puts it like that, how can I say no? And true, my dress is tight.

"Do you promise I won't break my neck?"

He tilts his head forward and winks. "Of course, Summer."

My tongue sticks to the roof of my mouth as I nod, before wordlessly following him to the center of the room.

"Summer here has volunteered to help me with the headstand."

The next few minutes are not pleasant. I pull my hair into a bun using the elastic band that one of the girls gives me, then plant my palms firmly on the ground. Alex asks me to kick my feet up, which I do, and then he cuffs my ankles, lifting my legs up until

I'm a perfect vertical line. He holds me so securely that I don't even have to rest much of my weight on my palms, but it's still not comfortable to be upside down, to feel the blood rush to my head. After a few seconds though, I become accustomed to this new sensation. Which is when I become acutely aware of his hands on me. He's now cuffing both ankles in one hand, and the contact burns me, a delicious, sensual burn. Alexander Westbrook is touching my bare skin. And yes, I'm aware that I'm referring to him by using his full first name *and* his last name, but I feel like the situation requires it.

With his free hand, he points to my calf, explaining something about which muscles have to be activated to maintain a headstand without any help.

When he brushes his fingertips along my right calf, my entire skin breaks out in goose bumps. Not only on my legs, but also on my arms and chest. The kids are far enough away that they can't see this detail, but I'm 100 percent sure Alex sees them. When he places my feet back on the ground, helping me up, I avert my gaze, embarrassed. How can my body react so strongly to such a simple touch? Well, he *is* Alexander Westbrook.

"You're an excellent assistant, Summer." He pats my arm, which is when the second wave of goose bumps erupts all over me. *Holy Pop-Tarts and cupcakes*! I risk a glance at him and find him flicking his gaze from my lips to where he's touching my arm.

"You're a good teacher. I didn't feel unsafe at

all."

After the performance, I take refuge near the drinks table again, watching him. Over the next hour, our gazes cross repeatedly, and he holds mine with merciless intensity. I'm the one who breaks eye contact every time.

It's late in the evening by the time we bid the kids goodbye.

"That was great," I comment as we make our way to the car.

"They looked like they were having fun. How is St. Anne's financed? Public money?"

"Nah, all private donations."

He nods. "Can you send me their information? I want to make a donation. I'll add the ring to it too."

"Great idea. Turning that into something positive."

"Uh-uh."

"You don't want to talk about it, I get it. I won't prod, I promise."

"Amy and I can't talk about it, other than the obligatory 'we grew apart.' Literally. Our contract forbids it."

"Wow, that must suck. Talking is one of my top coping mechanisms. Just putting it out there, but whatever you say tonight won't get out. Just in case you want to get something off your chest."

He's silent for a beat and looks away. "She fell in love with someone else. The way she says it, she didn't start anything with him until after she broke up with me, but I flew to LA two days after our breakup conversation, and there he was already."

"Ouch. I'm sorry."

"The good part? I finally had no strings keeping me in LA. I wanted to move near my sister and my nephew for a long time."

"And now you have. You had fun tonight, right? I thought I saw a real smile back there, so it wasn't all an act."

He grins. "You made your opinion clear on my acting skills on the way here. But yeah, I did have fun."

"Okay, just to clear the air, I do think you're one of the best actors around. I was just teasing you."

He stops in his tracks, cocks a brow, expression solemn. "One of the best? Not the best?"

Shrugging one shoulder, I come to a stop too. "Sorry to bruise your ego, but no one can top Humphrey Bogart for me. Been a sucker for him ever since I saw *Casablanca*. Favorite movie of all time."

His faux-solemn expression morphs into an ear-to-ear smile. "Well, if that's my competition, my ego's safe."

I startle as cold drops land on my skin, making me shiver. The early June evening was pleasant enough that I didn't take my coat from the car.

I instinctively run my hands up and down my arms.

"It's raining. Come on, let's go to the car. You're already shivering," Alex says.

Without warning, he lays an arm around my shoulders, tucking me into him, presumably so I can absorb his body heat. *Oh boy.* Any red-blooded woman would take advantage of this. Right? Right? No, just me? Well, then.

I'll be dropping Alex home in half an hour, and then I probably will never see him again in person. A little lusting never hurt anyone. And because I'm an opportunist, I scoot even closer, taking thorough advantage of his generous offer.

He only lets go of me when we reach the car, and the second we part, cold grips me. The raindrops become larger, pour faster as we climb inside the car.

"Aah, just in the nick of time," I exclaim, gunning the engine and cranking on the heating in the seats, rubbing my palms together to warm up. Next to me, Alex doesn't seem to feel even a whisper of cold.

As I pull in front of his house a while later, a pang of regret grips me that the night is coming to an end.

"Well, here we are," I announce unnecessarily.

"Do you want to come in for a drink?"

I lick my lips, pondering his question. Part of me screams *Yes, Yes, Yes.*

Not just because he's Alex freaking Westbrook. In fact, I'd like to know more about the man behind the actor. I like what I see so far. But another part of me urges me to be cautious. Clearly, he's shaken after his engagement with Amy exploded in his face. Men are known to do silly things when they're shaken. Such as seducing impressionable women like myself.

"Not a good idea. I have to wake up at five tomorrow, and it's almost midnight."

He flashes me his winning smile, staring at me intently.

"Don't you dare use your smolder on me," I warn.

"My what?"

I tilt my head to one side. "Don't pretend you don't know. Google 'Alex's Smolder.' You'll find a million pictures of you looking just like this to the camera, *and* a Tumblr page."

Alex chuckles. "Okay, I admit. I know about it. My PR team actually started the Tumblr page."

"I am crushed. You start your own hype?"

He wiggles his brows. "Hey, they need the raw material to actually base that hype on."

"I bet those eyes and smile make you think you can get away with a lot of things."

"What exactly do you think I'm trying to get away with, Summer?"

He drops his gaze to my lips. God, the way he says my name and looks at me has my panties in a twist.

"I have to wake up at five," I repeat. "Not even your smolder is a match for my alarm clock."

"I guess I have to work on it, then."

"I guess so."

"Well, I'll leave you to your beauty sleep. But I'd like to see you again. I had a lot of fun tonight."

My heart beats faster, and a thin sheet of sweat covers my palms. Did he just friend zone me? But he looked at my lips before.... Why am I so bad at reading signals even after a decade of dating?

Despite the confusing signals, I do want to see him again. He seems like a nice guy. A nice, incredibly handsome man. Deadly combo, really. "You have my number. Use it."

"I will."

He leans into me, kissing my cheek. His lips are soft on my skin, his breath hot. His cologne is so deliciously manly, it sends my senses into a tailspin. I nearly melt from the sheer masculinity pouring off him.

With one last smile and smoldering look, he climbs out of my car, walking off into the night.

Chapter Four

Alex

"You're a grill master." Sophie leans back in her seat, chewing on the steak.

"That's pretty much the only thing I've mastered in the kitchen."

I take another steak off the grill, placing it on her husband, Neil's plate.

"Drew, dinner's ready," Sophie calls out to her son. He's too focused on the fish swimming around in my koi pond for dinner.

"Let's just save him something for later," Neil comments after several more futile attempts to convince Drew to join us at the table. That little guy is one hell of a stubborn seven-year-old. When the last steak is done, I join my sister and her husband at the table, raising my glass of wine.

"To Sophie, who found me the best house in San Francisco."

She really outdid herself. We're sitting on the deck spawning from my living room outside, surrounded by a landscaped patio. The wall of evergreens protects us from any curious eyes. It also obscures the view, but from the second floor of the house I can look out onto the ocean. I have a view of

Alcatraz on one side of the house, and the Oakland Bay Bridge and Coit Tower on another side.

They clink their glasses to mine.

"To you, brother, for finally getting rid of Amy."

Neil shoots her a warning look, but Sophie shrugs. "What? Drew's out of earshot, and someone has to say it."

My sister gives me a sympathetic smile. She never liked Amy much and had no qualms saying so.

"To a fresh start," I say, before taking a sip of wine. Drew and I had a blast today, fishing. At the end of our trip, I invited my sister and her husband over for dinner.

"What's the plan right now?" Sophie asks.

"I don't have any filming scheduled. I'm reading scripts for some indie movies in the downtime until the promo tours begin."

I have two premieres coming up. First, *Bree Shannon Finds Love #2*, a romantic comedy, and then the last installment in the superhero franchise. The promo for that one starts earlier though.

"Any idea when the spin-off will be green-lighted?" Neil asks.

"We're close to signing the deal."

"Hats off for wanting to do another franchise," he continues.

"They're fun."

I've been doing franchises for ten years. My big break came when I was cast as the lead in a dystopian trilogy at nineteen. It was a worldwide phenomenon, and I'll never deny it, it put me on the A-list. Filming that took five years, and then I started on the current franchise, which revolves around an ensemble of superheroes. Getting a spin-off for my own character is the big ticket to cementing my status, making sure my career won't fade into oblivion.

Most actors start turning up their noses at roles that made them famous, but I'm not one of them. I know I wouldn't be where I am without it. And yeah, it's grueling work, but I like playing the same character in multiple installments. It allows me to peel back layers, delve deeper. The spin-off will focus more on character development than flashy action scenes, which is right up my alley.

"I've talked to Mom and Dad, by the way," Sophie says. "Sent them a few more house descriptions to look at, but they're on the expensive side."

"Money is not a problem."

Our parents have been thinking about moving to San Francisco for a while to be closer to Sophie, but since housing here is exorbitant, I'm subsidizing the cost.

"You're spoiling them too much." Sophie presses her lips together, shaking her head. "And they're not making much of an effort in return."

Our parents haven't adjusted to my fame too well. I can't blame them, though. They've had paps pestering them, and on the one occasion they've visited me in LA, paps broke into my home. Gave them both a scare. Ever since, they've refused to visit me in LA and weren't keen on me flying over to Portland either. Over the last couple of years, I was lucky if I saw them twice a year. Whenever I broached the subject, they insisted they felt unsafe when I was around. Here's to hoping things will change now, even though they're more hesitant to move since I'm living here too.

"They're our parents, Soph. They're going to get used to all of this eventually. It'll be nice for all of us to be in the same city again."

This is exactly what lazy evenings should be for. Spending time with the family. After we finish all the food, Sophie says they'd better go, because Drew gets cranky if he stays up too long after his bedtime.

"Go out," she says, kissing my cheek goodbye. "Don't stay cooped up here all the time. This isn't LA. You won't have paps following your every move."

"I do go out. I went fishing with Drew today." I open her car door. She lowers herself in it.

"Smartass. I know that. I meant go out with people your own age."

"Don't you worry about me." I shut the door, and a second later, the car lurches forward.

I head back inside the house and slump on the couch. An image of Summer pops up in my mind, sitting in the same spot, her skirt moving up when she crossed her legs. I have the image of her sweet, perky body bubbling with laughter branded in my memory. I also remember the way her skin reacted to my touch, how flustered she got when I complimented her and when I touched her while she helped me with the stunt. I won't lie. I was tempted to touch her again, just to see her delicious reaction: the goose bumps, the blush.

I'm used to women reacting this way to me even if I'm not flirting. They see the on-screen character when they look at me and react accordingly. But I think Summer saw *me* last night, not any of the characters I've played. It was so easy to talk to her, to open up. I glance at my phone until I give in to the temptation of calling her.

"Hey! What are you up to?" I greet when she picks up.

"Alex?"

"Why so surprised? You told me to use your number."

"I know. Didn't expect you to do it… so soon."

Something in her tone is off. "Anything wrong?"

"No, just a sleepy Friday evening."

I pick up on the underlying sadness right away. "You sound down."

"Why would you think that?"

"Acting school 101. Conveying feelings through tone of voice. Just putting it out there, but whatever you say on the phone… stays on the phone." It's a wordplay on what she told me yesterday, and it earns me a tiny laugh.

"No biggie, just got a brush-off from a guy I

went out with last week. He texted me, and I quote: 'Please delete my number. No interest in repeating last week. Not my type.' I mean, wow."

"Summer, it's his loss. It's not a reflection on you."

"Actually, it might be. Not the first time this happened. At some point, I have to admit, it's not everyone else... it's me. I'm a lousy date, and I don't even know why."

"You're not a lousy date."

She chuckles. "You wouldn't know. You didn't actually go on a date with me."

"No, but I had a lot of fun yesterday. You're a fun person. A sweet woman."

"You sound like my brothers right now."

Except I'm not thinking about her in a brotherly way at all, damn it. I feel protective of her in an almost possessive manner, which is insane.

"But talking to you just gave me an idea. I'll watch *Casablanca* tonight. It'll be a good distraction," she says.

"I have a better offer. Let's go out. It's Friday evening, a goddamn shame for both of us to stay cooped in."

Sophie is right. This isn't LA. I have to be careful, but the chances of a pap showing up are slim, especially since my move here isn't common knowledge. Yet.

"I—okay. Where do you want to go?"

"Don't know the city too well. You pick a location. Just someplace that doesn't attract too much attention. Dim lighting is a plus."

"Uh-huh, I'll see what I can do, Jack the Ripper."

"I'd rather not be recognized."

"I know. Wait, I just had an idea. Did you ever take a tour of San Francisco at night?"

"I never took any tour of San Francisco, except checking out houses with my sister."

"What? That's such a shame. I'll give you a tour. Just let me think up an itinerary. Hmm… it's dark already, which rules out a couple of sights. Let's keep to the waterfront. Can you meet me at the Ferry Building? Then we can pass by the Embarcadero, end up at Pier 39. How does that sound?"

I'd say yes to any suggestion. Anything to spend some time with her tonight. I have no idea where the need to see her is coming from, but I don't want to stop and analyze it. I want to run with it.

"Meet you in an hour at the Ferry Building?" I suggest.

"One hour? Geez, some of us need more time to get ready. We don't all wake up pretty, like you."

"You're beautiful just the way you are, Summer. But if you need more time…," I offer.

"See you at the Ferry Building in ninety minutes?"

"Done."

Chapter Five

Alex

Ninety minutes later, I pull my baseball cap lower in the front as I pay the cabbie, who doesn't recognize me. Maybe I should kick the paranoia to the curb. As I step out of the car, I see Summer in front of the Ferry Building, wearing jeans and a red jacket, waving at me excitedly.

"I'm sorry about all the fog. It's inescapable near the water in the evening," she says.

"I'll take it over the smog in LA every day."

"Hmm... you don't like LA much, do you?"

"It's suffocating if you're in the movie business. How about you?"

"I like it. I have cousins there. I love visiting them." She points at my cap. "Lose that. I know it's the universal star trick, but it'll just attract attention. The sun has set, what's the cap protecting you from, moonlight?"

She has a point, but wearing a cap whenever I'm in public has become a habit. I feel exposed as I take it off.

"I'll keep it for you," she offers, opening her purse. I drop the cap inside. "Besides, I have an idea. If someone recognizes you, just say you're your own stunt double."

"What?"

She tugs at her lower lip with her thumb and forefinger. I barely swallow the urge to lick that lip, taste it for myself.

"Well, you do a lot of stunts. And I know you said you do many on your own, but people don't know that. They'll assume you have a stunt double, and those always have to resemble the actors, right?"

"That's never occurred to me," I say, surprised not only by her creativity but by the simple fact that she worried enough on my behalf to think up a story.

She draws her eyebrows together in concentration. "Or we could say you've applied to be your own double. No idea if it'll work, but it's worth giving it a shot."

"Definitely."

"Ready for the tour?" she asks in a serious voice. "You've got your own personal guide too, Mr. Superhero."

I'm used to people seeing my on-screen persona in real life, and it doesn't bother me… usually.

"I'd rather be just Alex tonight. With you."

Her eyes widen a little, but she nods, and I know she understands what I need. The night air is cool and misty, perfect for a walk. Five minutes into this, I realize it will take us the entire night to pass the three objectives on our list. Summer walks at a snail's pace.

"Hey, slow down. Where are you hurrying to?" she asks.

"Nowhere. This is... my pace."

She scrunches her nose, narrowing her eyes as if she's making a *plan*.

"Right. When's the last time you went out and about for no reason at all?"

I search my memory. "I went fishing with my nephew today. Before that... I don't remember. Maybe three years ago?"

She claps her hands. "You're out of practice. Step one to enjoying a walk: move sloooow."

"What's step two?"

"I haven't thought so far in advance. We'll see. Just enjoy the city. It's your city now too. Feel it a bit." She spreads her arms around her, closing her eyes and inhaling deeply. The urge to kiss her hits me squarely in the chest.

She slips into guide mode next, and she's excellent at it. I admit, I'm only half listening. I'm *consumed* by her. It's been a while since I've seen someone lose themselves in an activity so completely, live it so fully. She peeks at me from time to time, once even pointing her finger sternly.

"I can tell you're not listening. Don't be an ass. I'll quiz you at the end."

"What's my punishment if I fail the quiz? You'll make me write lines, sit in a corner?"

"You wish. I'm much more inventive," she retorts with cheek. "And cruel."

Even though the air is crisp for mid-June, as

we walk along the shore, I start feeling warm. So does Summer, because we push down the zipper of our jackets at the same time. She's wearing a dark blue sweater under it, with a diamond cutout over her chest. Only the top of her cleavage shows, but it's enough to spark my imagination, to make me wonder how she tastes there, how she'd react if I licked between her breasts, teased her nipples.

"Tell me about your job," I say. "How did you get into the art world?"

"I've always had an artistic streak. In my first years of college, I tried my hand at acting, but it wasn't really my thing. Then I started painting."

"You still paint?"

"Just as a hobby, for my friends and family. I wanted to do it full-time when I started out, but it's a bit of a lonely job, and as you can see, I talk. A lot. I'm a sociable person. I need to meet new people. Then I worked at a museum in Rome for a few years. They had a program for young artists, and I also had to do guide groups on the side. I liked it a lot, so now it's part of my job at the gallery."

Enthusiasm pours off her in waves, and I can definitely not imagine her cooped up alone, painting all day.

"We're almost at PIER 39, that's why it's getting so crowded," she informs me. "It's even worse during the day."

"I'm sorry," says a redhead with a southern twang, coming to a stop in front of us. "I have to ask. You're Alex Westbrook, aren't you?"

A few heads turn in our direction.

"I thought it looked like him," someone whispers.

Before I can even open my mouth, Summer laughs, turning to me.

"Oh, honey, I told you they'd say that. You really, really should apply for that job again."

I bring my hand to Summer's back, pulling her into me. "I applied to be his double, been racking up rejections into two digits by now, but I'm not giving up."

"Oh." The redhead's disappointment is clear.

"But he looks just like him, doesn't he?" Summer continues. "He can even imitate that smile Westbrook's famous for. With the dimples. He practices in the mirror every day."

The redhead steps back, shaking her head, pity in her eyes. The few who had stopped in their tracks to watch us go on their merry way. Summer is a genius. I could kiss her.

"Right," she whispers, once the redhead is far enough away, "I changed my mind. Going to PIER 39 was a stupid idea. It's crawling with people. Let's go to one of the other piers. How about Pier 7? We'll find a lot of fishermen looking for crabs."

"Lead the way."

Twenty minutes later, we reach the pier. I don't know about fishermen, but couples mill around on the wooden floor, sitting on benches, leaning against the black iron railing or against the lampposts casting a dim glow.

"Is this San Francisco's official kissing spot?" I ask when we come to a stop on a deserted stretch of the railing. The air is salty and fresh.

"It is quite romantic, don't you think? With the lampposts and the fog."

She turns her head to look at me. I don't even remember leaning in, but I'm so close, our noses are almost touching. I feel the reaction of her body as she becomes aware of how close we are. She straightens a little, brushing against my chest. Her lips part, her gaze dropping to my mouth for a second. *This moment here… Jesus.* We might have been playing a charade for the others earlier, but this feels so real. The underlying warmth in her glance, the simple fact that she was putting herself out there on my behalf. Her pretty, pink mouth beckons to me. Without thinking, I close the distance between us, capturing her lips.

She sighs, a sweet, perfect little sound, and then parts her lips in invitation. I slip my tongue inside, feverishly coaxing hers into a wild tangle. I feel her melt against me, her little body pressing into me. I slip my hand a few inches under her shirt, needing to feel her skin, to touch her. Kissing her lights a fuse inside me. Her reaction to me is intoxicating. She makes a small sound of pleasure at the back of her throat. I cup the back of her head, pressing her closer to me, fisting her hair in my fingers. I kiss her until we're both out of breath.

Summer steps back the next instant, her mouth pink and swollen, breathing hard.

"Wow," she whispers. "You can *kiss*."

"Summer—" I begin, but she cuts me off.

"Oh no. I know that tone of voice. I have a feeling a variation of the 'it's not you, it's me' speech is coming my way, and it's not necessary. It was a spur of the moment thing, I get it. I mean, look at this place. It's made for kissing."

She's still smiling, and there's no resentment in her voice.

"I want to explain anyway."

"Really, don't. I know what's going on, and I'm not interested in being your rebound."

"A rebound?" I ask blankly. "I didn't kiss you because I'm on a rebound."

Vulnerability flits over her features, and fuck if I don't want to kiss that away.

She backs away from me, gnawing at her lip. "I hate to break it to you, but you might not know you're on the rebound. Doesn't mean you're weak or anything, but it's a pretty normal reaction after a relationship implodes."

I eye this little spitfire closely, weighing the pros and cons of being 100 percent honest with her. The con is the usual—the risk of the media finding out. But with Summer, that never seems like a real risk. I feel more at ease around her than anyone else. And she deserves to know. I'd hate for her to think I took advantage of her. I look around us to make sure no one is within earshot, but everyone else is far enough away.

"I'm going to tell you something few people

in Hollywood know. We broke up four months ago, but it only slipped to the press last month. We thought we could keep it quiet until the premiere."

"Why did you want to keep it quiet?"

"My relationship with Amy started as a fake love story for the media. The studio executives explained that a supposed romance between us would be a golden ticket for the box office. We agreed to it because it seemed harmless, and we were almost done shooting. We'd only have to keep up the charade until the premiere. But the movie was so successful that the studio wanted a sequel. We were asked to keep faking. At some point, we fell for each other. The fake romance became a real one. The engagement was not a PR thing; it was real. But it all fell apart four months ago. She's with that guy…. Anyway, per our contract, until after the premiere, Amy and I can't be seen dating other people. But I'm not on a rebound. I want that to be clear."

Summer's mouth hangs open as she leans back a little.

"Wow, I don't know what to say. This sounds… straight out of a movie, if I'm honest."

"That's Hollywood for you. Lesson learned. I'll never agree to something like this again. As soon as the premiere is over, I can forget this happened. Anyway, I wanted you to know."

She tilts her head to one side, asking, "Why *did* you kiss me?"

"I couldn't not kiss you. I couldn't not taste you."

Her tongue darts out, wetting her lower lip. Then she tears her gaze away from mine. "I can see now why your PR team started the *Smolder* Tumblr page. Did they also come up with the Twitter handle @SuperSmolder?"

"Nah, the fans came up with it on their own."

"Hmm... I don't believe a word of it. Once you admit to PR sins, there's no going back."

I love that she has no problem handing me my ass.

"For someone who doesn't want my autograph, you're immersed in the fandom."

"I looked it up purely in the name of research."

"Exactly when did you think that research might be useful?"

"I'm not a fortune-teller. Hence why it's helpful to have such info handy. I've cut my teeth by using these tactics on my siblings, so I know what I'm talking about."

We burst out laughing, and laugh until the tension between us dissipates.

"You're close to your family, I take it?" I ask.

"Close doesn't even cover it. My sisters are my best friends."

"And your brother?"

"S. Plural. You only met Daniel?"

"Yes."

"Well, I'm one of nine kids. They're all married, and most have children, which means I have plenty of nieces and nephews to spoil. Anyway, I have two sisters and six brothers. They're great. A tad overprotective sometimes when it comes to my dating life, but don't worry, you're safe. Won't tell them about the kiss."

"Or what, they'd come bang down my door?" I challenge.

"I wouldn't put it past them."

The thought of Summer dating another guy irks me to no end. Jesus, I have to stop. One kiss doesn't give me any right over her.

"We should go. It's getting late," she comments. "There will be cabs at the end of the pier, I think."

A few minutes later, we reach the street. There are cabs driving in every direction. I hail one for her. I don't want our outing to end, even though I now fully realize that venturing out into the city with Summer was reckless. I'd feared paps showing up, but it slipped my mind that anyone with a camera can snap a picture. Summer's idea for me to pass off as a wannabe double was genius, but even so, I've been pushing my luck.

The studio would skewer me if I started dating someone new. I hate that they own me so thoroughly that they have a say in my personal life. But when you're young and stupid, you sign contracts without considering the long-term too much.

I could invite Summer over to my house, but after the kiss, I don't want to make her uncomfortable. Even though I want to listen to her talk about her family, or her job, or St. Anne's... or anything at all. I want to spend more time with her, but the smart thing is to do the exact opposite. Summer is too sweet and lovely to deserve being swept in my Hollywood drama.

So instead of inviting her to join me for a drink, I open the door to the back seat of the cab for her.

"Oh, before I forget...." She rummages in her purse, handing me the cap back.

"Thanks. I'll walk around a bit more."

I tilt my head down to kiss her cheek, just as she shifts to climb inside, and my lips land near her earlobe. I kiss her there, then trace my mouth to where a regular kiss should land. She lets out a sound so delicious, I barely keep myself from pinning her against the car and capturing her mouth.

Summer kisses my cheek too, a peck so quick I barely feel it. She avoids my gaze as she lowers herself into the back seat, and I close her door.

As I head toward the ferry building, I catch myself almost jogging, and slow down, smiling, Summer's voice popping into my mind. *Step one to enjoying a walk: move sloooow.*

I laugh, measuring my steps, wondering if Summer would approve of the pace.

Chapter Six

Summer

I crumple the sheet of paper, tossing it in the pile of discarded, scrunched sheets in the middle of my living room. In the winter, I toss them directly into the brick fireplace.

Rainy Sundays like today are perfect for painting, but my creative juices aren't cooperating. Possibly because I have other things on my mind. I read a disturbing article this morning. The ongoing Amy-Alex narrative took a nasty turn. Now the tabloids want to paint him as a cheater, and I hope to God our kiss on Friday didn't have anything to do with it.

I'm about to start with a blank sheet when my phone buzzes. Glancing at it, I see St. Anne's on the screen and immediately answer.

"Hey, Shawna. What's up?" I stand, rolling my shoulders and swinging my hips from one side to the other. I've been kneeling in front of my coffee table, bending over it long enough for my body to stiffen.

"Hey, Summer! How's everything going? Busy bee as usual?"

"You know me."

"Listen, I wanted to talk to you about the camp."

I'm helping her organize a camp for the kids at Lake Tahoe. It starts right after the kids finish the school year.

"It's a huge favor. They loved having Alex here. Loved it. Do you think he'd be open to stopping by the camp at Lake Tahoe and showing the kids some more stunt tricks? Or maybe even short acting classes?"

"I don't know his schedule, and the lake is hours away." I rub the stiff side of my neck, my wheels spinning.

"He's welcome to stay at the resort with us, of course, but I imagine he's too busy for that."

"I imagine that too."

"But will you ask him?"

"Seems like a lot to ask. I don't want to put him in an uncomfortable position."

"How close are you to him?"

What a loaded question after that amazeballs kiss. I'm still reeling from it, two days later.

"Not very close, but I'll talk to him."

"Thank you, Summer. You're… I can't tell you how grateful I am for everything you're doing."

"Oh stop, Shawna. You're making me blush. Or are you just buttering me up so I don't give up until I get some sort of promise out of Alex?"

"Shucks, I'm that transparent, huh?"

"Just a tiny bit. I'll talk to him and let you know what he says."

"Thanks, Summer."

After clicking off, I decide to try Alex right away. He doesn't answer his phone, though, so I return to my painting process, facing the blank sheet again. An idea strikes me, and I sketch two crossing, undulating lines in pencil. My phone buzzes before I manage to start the third line. Alex.

Clearing my throat, I pick up.

"Hey! Sorry, was on the treadmill when you called."

"No problem. Thanks for calling back. I just spoke with Shawna, from St. Anne's, and we have a huge favor to ask."

"I'm listening."

"We're organizing this camp for the kids at Lake Tahoe. They're going to have Spanish lessons in the morning and all sorts of activities in the afternoon. For example, I'm going to teach painting. And we were wondering if you could stop by and teach them some more stunts and tricks, maybe an acting class."

"When is this exactly?"

"Starts Monday in one week, lasts for two weeks."

"Which days are you driving up there?"

"Oh, I'm staying there."

"For the entire two weeks?"

"Yes. It'll be a vacation for me too."

"Okay, wait, I'm checking my calendar now. My manager marks all my appointments on it...."

I sit cross-legged on my floor, absentmindedly

tracing my thumb on the green and golden woolen carpet.

"Right, I need to fly out to LA for one day, but other than that, I'm free."

"Wow! I wasn't expecting that. Don't you have two premieres coming up?"

"I do, but things only kick up hard in the month leading up to it, and the premiere month itself."

"So, on which days do you want to drive to the lake? Or I can arrange a driver for you."

"I could stay there for the duration of the camp, think up an acting workshop."

"Are you sure? I mean, it's awfully nice of you, but that's a big-time commitment."

"Two weeks isn't such a long time. I'm currently reading scripts. I can do that there too. Besides, my sister and her family just left on a month-long trip to Europe, so I don't have much going on here."

I've helped Daniel organize a few events for his famous clients, and I know that people with Alex's pockets and status can *always* have something going on if they want to. And usually, they opt for something much flashier than volunteering, especially if they don't use it for PR purposes. The desire to peel back more layers and find out what lies under that gorgeous smile slams into me. *I could do that in two weeks*, a naughty voice pipes up at the back of my minds. Hot-white energy strums through my body at the thought. *Bad, bad thought.* I hug my knees to my chest, resting my chin on the right kneecap.

"I'll do some research on the best hotels in the area and send you some options," I say.

"Where are you staying?"

"In the resort where the camp's taking place."

"Any reason I can't stay there too?"

"It's not a five-star hotel."

"I don't mind. Besides, I'd be lonely, living separately from everyone else. If it's good enough for you, it's good enough for me."

That bad thought circles back. All because of a kiss, which I should really forget. We kissed, we talked, we moved on.

"Okay, got it. I'll set everything up. The kids are going to be very happy."

"So am I. Ah, before I forget. I have the same request again. No PR, no pics."

"That goes without saying, at least to the extent I can influence it. We'll ask the workers at the resort to respect your privacy, but you know that doesn't always work out."

"I know. But hey, I'll have you with me, my savior."

That makes me laugh. "Hardly, but I'll do what I can." I tap my fingers on the floor, wondering if I should bring up that article I read. If I were Alex, I'd avoid reading the press like the plague. But maybe this is something he needs to be alerted to. "Listen, I read an article today—"

"The one calling me a cheater?" The humor all but evaporated from his voice, which now has an edge I don't like.

"Sorry to bring it up. I was just wondering if it had anything to do with… Friday."

"No, that's just speculation. If there was a pic of us kissing, it would've already made the rounds, and the studio would be at my throat."

I startle as an unpleasant smell coming from the kitchen reaches my nostrils, then spring to my feet.

"Crap, I forgot I had a pizza in the oven."

I pray to all the gods the smoke detectors don't go off as I open the door to the oven and smoke whirls out. My pizza is burnt to the crisp.

"Shit, there goes my dinner," I mutter.

"You make your own pizza?"

"Not usually. I order from my favorite Italian restaurant, Vicente's, but they're closed on Sunday. It's the best pizza!"

"I have a hard time believing that."

"Oh, you better believe it, mister. I lived in Rome, and Vicente's is better than anything I ate even in Italy."

I pull out the pizza and poke at it to see if something is salvageable.

"I think I can eat some of the vegetables on it," I mutter to myself. "The pepperoni is only half burnt. And the artichokes aren't entirely black."

"That's a lousy dinner."

"Ugh, I know. Maybe I'll just order something else later. I'm not even that hungry. But I have to clean the kitchen now, or my entire living room will stink. I'll e-mail you all the details about the camp later, okay?"

"Perfect. Take care, Summer."

Cleaning up takes longer than I hoped. The mozzarella overflowed on the metal tray. My right arm aches, but at least the damn thing is close to squeaky clean. I straighten up when my bell rings. Maybe one of my siblings decided on an impromptu visit? It's not uncommon in my family, even though we usually call or message as a heads-up.

Swinging the door open, Carlo, one of Vicente's delivery guys greets me. "Evening, Ms. Bennett. I have your pizza here."

Stunned, I take the box he hands me. "I… err, didn't order. And you're closed today."

Carlo smiles knowingly. "Special delivery."

"Okay," I say slowly, "let me get my wallet."

"All paid for. Enjoy your evening, Ms. Bennett."

He takes off before I can ask for more details. After shutting the door, I grab a roll of napkins from the kitchen and head to my living room. Sitting on the floor, I open the box. My favorite pizza to boot. A smile plays on my lips. I don't want to get ahead of myself, but I suspect who the sender was. But how? Why?

As if on cue, an incoming message pops on my phone with a photo of a pizza that is identical to mine.

Alex: You're right. It's the best damn

pizza.

Summer: How did you make this happen?

Alex: There are advantages to being a star.

Biting into a slice of pizza, I succumb to the pleasure of the flavorful mix. Knowing we're sharing dinner, even from a distance, fills me with warmth.

Summer: Thanks.

Alex: I'm a useful friend to keep around. It's not all about helping me pretend I'm someone else, I promise.

Summer: Can I give you a list of my favorite restaurants, friend?

Feeling feisty, I type another message.

Summer: Can you have food delivered from other cities too?

Alex: You'll be surprised at what I can do.

Sighing, I shove the last bite of the slice in my mouth. I know I'm being ridiculous, but a man hasn't made me feel this special in a long time, maybe ever. I'm starting to like this friend-zone thing.

Summer: I'll send you the details about the camp as soon as I finish my pizza.

Alex: Take your time.

After I finish eating, I open my laptop, cramming all the information about the camp into one e-mail, trying very hard not to think about Alex's kiss-worthy lips and bite-worthy biceps. And definitely not thinking about that squeeze-worthy ass.

Chapter Seven

Summer

There are several perks of being the youngest in my family. Growing up, everyone had their place in the family hierarchy. Sebastian, Logan, and Pippa were the responsible ones, always looking after all of us. Alice was next in line, and I swear she was born kicking ass. My family didn't come from money, and until the oldest trio set up Bennett Enterprises, we were scraping by. I don't remember those times much, because I was a kid, but my parents made sure we youngsters didn't become spoiled brats. Guess who was the official whip cracker, bossing us into doing tasks around the house? Alice.

Christopher and Max, the first pair of twins were the official family pranksters, playing the identical twin card every chance they got. Daniel and Blake, the second pair of twins, tried to emulate Christopher and Max, but since they couldn't dethrone the pranksters, they became troublemakers. And then there was little old me, poking my nose in everyone's business and generally being spoiled by everyone.

I can now return the favor by spoiling my nieces and nephews. I have an entire brood to throw birthday parties for. In another life, I'd be an event planner. I love organizing events: birthday parties, bachelorette parties, weddings. It's my thing. I'm good at it—sometimes I go overboard, but hey, no one's perfect.

And one could say I did go overboard for Audrey's birthday party, if the number of balloons hanging from the ceiling of my brother Sebastian's living room is an indication. The theme is *Frozen*, so we have mini Olafs everywhere.

"You've really gone overboard," Sebastian says, sliding an arm around my shoulders.

I elbow his ribs lightly. "I think you mean to say, '*You're the best sister in the world, and you've outdone yourself. What would I do without you*?' But you have to say it like you believe it."

He chuckles and kisses my forehead. "I'm so lucky you can read between the lines. Thanks for organizing all this."

"How are you?" I inquire. A few months ago, he and his wife welcomed twins, a boy and a girl. They have their hands full with them in addition to Audrey and their son Will, so they gave me free rein with the organization.

"Okay."

I sigh. Of course he'd say that. Getting my brother to admit the truth usually requires sneaky interrogation skills and emotional blackmail. But I have an inkling I'll wear him down faster today, what with the mayhem surrounding us.

I tilt my head. "How are you really? Okay

doesn't count. I need a full sentence. If you're feeling generous, you can even dish out sentence*s,* plural. I promise to reduce the nagging accordingly."

"I'm tired. Both Ava and I are tired, but that doesn't mean we're not okay. We're learning that we should have valued sleep more when we had just Will and Audrey. I'm still trying to sell Ava on having a permanent nanny."

Right now, they have someone helping them through the day, but I can see what he means. Raising four kids while they both work? As I watch the general commotion in the room, then focus on my sister Pippa walking toward us, my wheels are spinning.

I hold up a finger. "I have an idea. I can organize a spa day at home with the girls, and we can talk her into it. We can be very persuasive."

"And very, very full of yourself. Why do you think you can convince my wife when I can't?"

Pippa joins us, indulging in a turkey sandwich. Between bites, she says, "Because talking to girlfriends is different. Sometimes admitting to your man that you can't do it all on your own makes you feel like you're not enough."

I nod sagely. "What she said."

"But we're together in this," Sebastian argues.

"Trust me." As an afterthought, Pippa adds. "Plus, we have skills you lack, brother."

"Yep, listen to Pippa. She's wise."

Sebastian pulls me closer to him and hooks his other arm around Pippa's waist. "Well, if you manage to convince her, I'll take you two out to dinner."

Oh, my brother is a jokester. "Now, see, I feel like we should get more out of this than a dinner."

"Well, whatever the two of you come up with, I'll be glad to indulge. Just make sure my wife relaxes that day and has a good time."

"We will," Pippa promises. As my brother heads to the bunch of kids grouped in the center of the room, I wonder for the millionth time if he's actually human. He runs a billion-dollar corporation, finds time to woo his wife, and raise four little souls. I'm still going with a radioactive spider bite. Possibly vampire. Though I need a good reason for why he can walk in the sun.

"Can we schedule the girls' day after I return from Lake Tahoe?" I ask Pippa.

"Sure. How did Olivia react to you taking off for two weeks?"

"Not happy, but nothing she can do about it. I have a lot of accrued vacation time." I shrug, heading to the buffet with my sister on my heels.

"Plus, that place is up and running mostly because of you."

"That too." I don't like to toot my own horn, but I kick ass at the gallery.

"Just saying, but you should think about opening your own again. You have far more experience than the first time around. And being your own boss has its perks," she says as I load my plate with a second serving of cake.

After graduation, I felt on top of the world. I wanted to open my own gallery. My three oldest siblings, Sebastian, Logan, and Pippa, founded a jewelry company years ago, and it was wildly successful. They gave each member of the family shares in Bennett Enterprises, regardless if we were working for them or not, so I had money to fund the dream. The gallery didn't bring enough revenue to even pay the fixed costs. Sebastian and Logan insisted I didn't have to close it. After all, I could use the money from Bennett Enterprises to cover the costs. But I manned up and closed it. I didn't want to be that person who lived off her siblings' work.

My sister Alice and my brothers Blake and Daniel are their own bosses. Neither of them work at Bennett Enterprises. Alice and Blake co-own restaurants and bars, and Daniel runs an adventure center.

Of course, they built their businesses on a cutthroat business plan. I approached the gallery with a dreamy enthusiasm, overlooking some serious flaws in the plan. I know what Pippa is saying, but this is not the moment to start making plans.

"This is a birthday party. No work talk. Come on, let's find Alice and plot Ava's downfall."

We find our sister Alice on the L-shaped couch we've dragged into a corner of the room to open up the space for the party. Pippa and I barely plop our asses on the soft cushions when Daniel walks up to us.

"I've been meaning to ask, how did it go with

Alex?" he inquires.

"Okay. The kids loved him. He was very sweet with them, patient."

"He's going to go to St. Anne's again?"

I shrug. "Maybe. He's joining the Lake Tahoe camp."

On my right, Alice stills. On my left, Pippa leans back.

"Wow. That's one A-lister with a lot of free time," Daniel says.

I shrug again. "He's not filming anything now, and he's got some time until he starts the promo tours."

"Let me know if you need anything," Daniel offers, shoving his hands in his pockets and returning to the party. Meanwhile, my sisters' gazes are skewering me.

Alice speaks first. "You know, Pippa, I have the feeling our baby sister has been holding out on us."

"I agree. Something doesn't add up. She's been mentioning Alex in every sentence today."

"That's not true," I say indignantly. "Only every other sentence."

Alice shakes her head. "But she's failed to mention that she'll spend the next two weeks with him."

"That's not true either. He's spending time at the camp. I'm spending time at the camp. But we're not spending it together."

Pippa grins. "She's rambling."

"Oh God. Stop talking about me in the third person."

Alice steals a bit of my cake, shoving it in her mouth. "Of course, as soon as you tell us everything. That kiss made a lasting impression, huh?"

I called them right away after getting home on Friday and spilled everything.

"You didn't meet him. He's even more charming than on screen. You'd have the hots for him too."

Alice feigns shock. "No, I'm married."

"So am I," Pippa reminds me.

"I still can't believe you made out with one of the hottest men in the world," Alice says.

Pippa gives me a probing look. "You'll be careful, right? You'll be spending two weeks with him, and… I just don't want you to get hurt. We all know you're an incurable romantic."

I point a finger at her. "Whose fault is that? You got me on the whole happily-ever-after train." Yep, I'm one of those creatures feared by men worldwide, the kind who has dreamed about her wedding since she was a little girl. I knew the type of dress I wanted ever since I skimmed my first bridal magazine. "Besides, you're projecting way too much. It was just a kiss because the surrounding was super romantic."

It was a delicious kiss. It held so much intent and sinful promises that my toes still curl thinking about it. But the thought that someone of Alex's caliber has given it half as much thought as I did is ridiculous. He's lip-locked with some of the most gorgeous beauties who've graced the red carpet, Amy notwithstanding.

Alice wiggles her eyebrows. "A kiss with *the* Alex Westbrook."

It dawns on me that Pippa's quiet. Pippa—like me—is never quiet unless she's cooking up something. I'm almost afraid of what's going to come out of her mouth next.

"How was it?" Pippa asks in a low, conspiratorial whisper. "Worth repeating?"

Yep, I was 100 percent right to be afraid, because now she brought forth the one thought I've been fighting to bury in the back of my mind.

"You two are a bad influence. You're my older sisters. You're supposed to talk sense into me."

Alice cocks a brow, giving my cake longing looks. Unfortunately, there is nowhere for me to shift it so that it's out of her reach. I'm flanked on both sides. Alice is the known food thief in our family, and I have no intention of sharing my cake.

"Sometimes a little fun is just what the doctor ordered," Alice muses.

"Right, that's it. I'm officially downgrading you from my trusted advisers to untrustworthy, corrupt influencers," I announce.

Pippa flashes me a grin. "What would you do without us, though?"

Actually, I know exactly what I'd do, because I was on my own in Rome. I loved the city, the food, and working at the museum, but I missed my family so much; it was like a physical ache I carried around with me. Then, after I returned, Alice moved to London for a while, but that was a bit easier to bear because at least I was close to the rest of my family. But I'm so happy that she and her husband moved back to San Francisco. I love it when the three of us are together, plotting and laughing, and plotting some more. I wish they hadn't fed the little devil on my shoulder, the one that spawns unruly, wicked thoughts of more kissing, but now that they have, well… bring it on.

Chapter Eight

Alex

Next Monday, I hop in my new car at 9:00 a.m., armed with coffee for the three-hour drive to Lake Tahoe. When I make it past the city limits, my manager, Preston, calls me. I put him on loudspeaker.

"Hey, Preston."

"Already at Lake Tahoe?"

"On my way."

"And you're sure you don't want to alert TMZ? Other outlets will pick up the story. It'll be great for your image. This is gold for the public, especially since the media is now running away with the story that your cheating caused the breakup."

"No, I don't want press." Spending time with those kids at St. Anne felt like the best thing I'd done in a long time. It's easy to forget movies aren't all about box office and awards, that at the front and center, it's really about entertaining people. Away from the camera, I can lower my guard and interact with them rather than act for them, and that's what they need. To see the human side of the superhero on screen. I don't want to bring the press into this, turn it into a PR circus where it'll be all about the best angle, the widest and fakest smile.

"Fine, have it your way. I don't need to remind you to keep a low profile where women are concerned."

"No, you don't."

"Well, thought I'd do it anyway. Just talked to the studio this morning, and they reminded *me* to remind *you* that, per your contract, you can't be seen dating other women until the premiere. I'm going to take this a step further and advise you not to be seen with women in public at all. The tabloids will spin it into something it's not. I know this isn't an ideal situation. But there are only a few months until the premiere. Then you'll be a free agent. Until then, just make sure you don't fall into bed with a resort employee or something. You know better than to get involved with anyone outside the industry. I've got to go, some advertising contracts just came in. Keep in touch. Let me know if you change your mind about the reporters."

"I won't."

His comment about not dating anyone outside the acting scene nags at me long after the line goes static. In my early days in Hollywood, I naively thought I could strive for the A-list and keep my old life. I had a rude wake-up call when the relationship with my high school girlfriend fell apart. I tried dating someone outside the industry one more time, two years later, but that didn't work out either. I started to understand why actors usually date actors. People in the industry know how things work, the sacrifices required. The long time spent apart on different sets, the lack of privacy, having most of your time planned out months in advance. It isn't fair to ask any woman to put up with that if she doesn't have to anyway for her own career.

When I arrive at the resort, there is no bus in the parking lot, so I assume the kids haven't arrived yet. Summer said the entire St. Anne's group will travel in a school bus. The four-star resort has a quaint, fisherman's village air to it. The main building houses the reception, the restaurant, and the conference rooms where some of the kids' classes will take place. The rooms are grouped in small bungalows across the property, spilling onto the waterfront.

"If there is anything more I can do, Mr. Westbrook, please let me know." The receptionist smiles, her eyes traveling up and down my body. "You can call the reception anytime. I can give you my personal number too."

"That won't be necessary," I say coolly, grabbing the key she slides me across the counter. She looks a little insulted at the brush-off, but I've learned it's best to cut off these things at the pass.

Following the signs on the property, I roll my suitcase on the path snaking between the trees, right until the perfectly manicured green lawn spills onto the waterfront. My bungalow is only a stone's throw away from the water, and a solid walk from the other bungalows.

As I approach, I hear two female voices.

"I am not allowed to let anyone inside," the unknown voice says. "I received specific instructions."

"I know," Summer says with exasperation. "I gave those instructions. I didn't mean myself."

Rounding the corner, the two come into view. A redhead wearing the same uniform as the receptionist stands in front of the door, arms crossed. I can only see Summer's back, but damn what a sight. She's wearing a white, short dress. My mouth waters as I take in the shape of her ass and the swell of her hips. She's not tall, but in this dress, her legs look endless.

"I'm telling you, I know him. And I'm not leaving until you let me in." Summer plants her hands on her hips, channeling all that fierceness inside her. This woman is a well of passion. I had a taste of that the night I kissed her, but I know I just tapped the surface. An image of her wrapping her legs around my waist flashes in my mind, but I push it away, forcing my feet up the stairs leading to the porch of the bungalow. The redhead's eyes widen. Summer turns her head and sighs in obvious relief.

"You're here, thank God. Maybe she'll believe you if you say that I'm not a crazy groupie."

I offer more than words. I rest my arm on Summer's shoulders, pulling her into my side. Damn, she feels like she belongs here. She melts into me, clearly feeling just as at ease. It's as if our bodies are already familiar with each other.

"Summer is a dear friend. Always welcome to my bungalow."

"My apologies, Mr. Westbrook, Ms. Bennett. I thought I didn't... I'll just leave now." Stuttering, she says goodbye and takes off. Summer sighs but doesn't pull away from me.

"Thank you. That show went on for ten minutes. I was running out of steam."

"Looked to me like you had plenty of steam left."

I dip my gaze, inspecting the front too. The dress isn't very low cut, so I can just see the tops of her breasts, but it's enough to stir my fantasy again. When Summer clears her throat, I snap my gaze up. She cocks a brow, but her tongue darts out, wetting her lower lip. Then she steps out from under my arm, as if just now realizing we were entangled in a half embrace. She plucks her purse from the bench under the window.

Unlocking the door, I push it open.

"Color me impressed, this place is huge."

"Well, it's their best room." Summer steps in behind me, glancing around. "It's the only bungalow with just one room, and I thought you'd appreciate the lack of neighbors. All others have between two and five rooms."

"I do appreciate the privacy. Very thoughtful of you. Thanks."

She smiles, twisting a strand of hair between her fingers. "Anyway, I told them to instruct the staff not to let strangers in your room under any pretext—

you know, in case any real groupies or stalkers show up. I figured that might happen, what with your face appearing in most tabloids."

"It's not out of the realm of possibility. I can't wait for that premiere to be over. The press attention is getting out of control."

"Well, as you can see, my plan backfired quickly."

"Why were *you* trying to get in my room?"

"Guess." She tilts her head, smiling. Her sass eggs me on. I step closer until I can smell her perfume. A delicious floral combo that makes me want to lick each morsel of her skin. I'd start with her mouth, make my way down her neck, then lower to her breasts.

Almost unconsciously, I dip my gaze to her cleavage, and *fuck me*. Her nipples press against the fabric of her dress. I imagine they're hard as pebbles, begging for a lick.

Summer clears her throat again, opening her purse and taking out a small brochure before I have a chance to join in on her guessing game, as if she's afraid of my answer. Good. She should be.

"I printed out the schedule of the lessons. I know we all have it electronically, but it's nice to have it printed out."

"It is! I'm a big fan of print. I read all my scripts printed out."

"Aww, you tree killer."

I point to the schedule she places on the table. "Pot, kettle. Thank you for getting me this bungalow.

And for placing rules to keep unwanted guests out. You seem to have experience with this kind of things."

"My family has had a fair share of run-ins with the press. Bennett Enterprises has brought us a lot of attention."

I believe that considering half of Hollywood wears their jewelry, and there have been enough articles written about the company.

"I'll leave you to settle in. The others will arrive in a few hours," she says.

"I don't need to settle in. Do you want to grab lunch?"

She pats her stomach, quirking her lips. "Okay. D'you want to go to the main restaurant? It'll be full of people, though. For the rest of the meals, I've asked them to set us all up in a separate room at the back of the restaurant. We're a large enough group to warrant the effort. But since it's just the two of us now… we could order room service. Eat it here on the deck?

Ooh, or we could spread a towel right in front of the water."

"Room service it is." I don't want the attention in the restaurant, and I want Summer to myself for a while longer.

Ten minutes later, we're sitting on the grass, a towel spread out in front of us. I ordered a burger and fries from the menu, Summer a burrito with avocado dip.

"Why are you in charge of the schedule?" I ask.

"I organized the camp. Thought the kids could do with a change of scenery."

"Who's paying for the gig?" I paid my own room, but a two-weeks stay in a four-star resort for so many people amounts to a pretty sum.

"I am. I mean, the money I donate isn't mine technically. Sebastian gave all of us siblings shares in Bennett Enterprises. But I don't need the money, so...."

She shrugs, but I'll be damned if I'll let her downplay it. This is incredible. *She* is incredible.

"I haven't seen you on the list of donors," I say.

"Like you, I don't want to make a fuss out of it."

Ah, a woman after my own heart. In Hollywood circles, donations are mostly a form of PR. I shift closer to her, touching her arm, resting my hand on her shoulder. Summer expels a sharp breath, her skin breaking out in goose bumps where I touch her. Her reaction to me is intoxicating. But when our gazes lock, I know that this thing between us runs deeper. I feel wired to her, and I don't want to break this connection, even if it would be the smart thing to do. I can't pull Summer into my messy life.

I move even closer to her until our hips are touching. We're half turned to one another, and I cup one of her cheeks, tilting her head up.

"You're doing a very good thing, Summer. Be

proud of it."

"I am."

Nodding, she looks away, stretching her legs, kicking off her sandals. "I think I'll book myself a foot massage."

She has a ring on her left middle toe, and it looks sexy as fuck. I eye her ankles, remembering how she reacted when I held them during our stunt exercise at St. Anne's.

I make a move to grab one foot to give her a head start on that massage, but Summer shifts at the same time, and I grip her thigh instead. My cock stirs in my boxers. Summer lets out a low sound, almost like a moan. She snaps her gaze from the point of contact up to my lips. It takes a superhuman effort not to move my hand further under her dress, to touch and explore her smooth skin. Even though it's the last thing I want, I pry my fingers away.

Summer's cheeks turn pink. "Well, I have to go prepare a few things until the group arrives. Thank you for lunch."

She makes a motion to push herself up. I'm quicker, rising to my feet, then taking her hand and pulling her up too. "You're welcome."

"What stunts are you planning to show the kids? Are they safe?"

"Of course they are. You'll see."

"I like to be prepared," she challenges. Ah, there it is. I like when she uses her fire on my behalf, but I like it even more when it's directed at me. I lean in until our lips are just a whisper apart and push a strand of her hair behind her ear. Her light brown waves are silky and soft, and now I want to thread my fingers through them, grip them, guide her head down my body. *Jesus.* I step back so she's out of my reach.

"I think you like being surprised more, Summer."

"Stars. They think they know better than the rest of us." She rolls her eyes, but her voice is breathy.

"I have fourteen days to lure out your adventurous side, Summer. Don't challenge me."

"Why not? Because you don't like challenges?"

"Because I win them."

She laughs, shaking her head. "See you around, Alex."

"Yeah."

She definitely will see me around. A lot.

Chapter Nine

Summer

My heart skitters like mad while I bid Alex goodbye. I head straight to my bungalow, holding my sandals in one hand, walking barefoot on the pathway. My skin's still hot where he touched me, as if he left an imprint on me. Now, if there would be a way for me to find out what he's planning to show the kids. But where to begin my snooping? I have a long history of snooping around. Goes with the territory of being the family's baby, I suppose. I was always in everyone's business and got away with it too. One of my first memories is of emotionally blackmailing my siblings into not getting mad at me by making puppy dog eyes and giving them sloppy kisses on their cheeks.

I take in my bungalow wistfully. It's two rows away from the waterfront. If I strategically place my lounge chair on the porch, I can spot the water, but it's nothing compared to Alex's view. Maybe I should change tactics, and instead of snooping on his teaching plans, I should put my snooping skills to better use, such as persuading him to more lunches out there so I can enjoy the view… and his company. I loved sitting there, talking to him. I felt like he was *listening* to me, really paying attention.

When I brought up the tabloids, there was no mistaking the shadow that fell over him.

I wanted to soothe him, but I had no idea how. Usually, I wish I had magic powers so I can turn all baked goods calorie-free, but if I had magic powers right now, I'd use them to make him forget his life is splashed over the tabloids.

Unfortunately, I don't have any magical powers. But what I lack in supernatural abilities, I make up for in persuasion and determination. So before heading to the reception to welcome the group, I stop by the resort's shop, inspecting the stand with magazines. As I expected, half the shelf space is dedicated to gossip magazines, and half of those have Alex and Amy's saga splashed on the cover.

"Hi, may I help you?" the vendor, a pretty blonde, asks.

"Yes. Here's the thing, you probably heard Alex Westbrook is a guest at the resort."

She nods excitedly. "Yes."

"You understand how uncomfortable it would be for him to see guests reading this." I point to the magazine whose covers he graces.

"Oh!" Her smile drops. "I can't do anything about it."

"Here's a suggestion: what if you forget to place an order for them for the next two weeks? It's always the same publications that run these stories."

She shakes her head, and I feel a vein

twitching in my temple.

"Can't. The orders are placed automatically. And even so, the store owner would throw a fit. They're our bestselling products right now. People come in asking for them."

I rub the back of my neck, attempting to dissipate the tension gathering there. Why do people enjoy so much reading about other's misery?

"I'll make you a deal. I will buy all those magazines. When you get the delivery, sort out all publications featuring Alex and Amy, and bring them straight to my room."

I used this exact tactic once before, after Pippa filed for divorce from the asshole that was her first husband. Alice and I took her to a spa retreat. I went to the hotel's shop to buy sunscreen, and I saw my sister's name in a gossip magazine. I bought every single copy.

The blonde stares at me. "We get about fifty copies of each. That's a lot of—"

"Doesn't matter. I'll pay up front if you want. Just bring them straight to my room. If anyone asks—your boss or the resort customers—just say they sold out. Start by giving me all the copies you have right now."

She shifts her weight from one foot to the other, glancing at the stack of magazines before nodding. "I suppose it's fair game. You're buying them, after all."

"Great. Can you take them to my room? I need to be at the reception."

"Sure thing. I'll just put a sign on the door that I'll be back in ten minutes."

"Thank you."

After paying, I leave the shop with a pep in my step. The hotel guests could always go out and buy magazines, but the resort is all-inclusive, so most people don't have a reason to go outside. I'm banking on their laziness trumping their thirst for scandal.

***

Over the next two days, I keep a close eye on the guests' reading material, but Alex's name or face doesn't stare back at me from any cover. So far, it seems my bet is paying off. Word spreads that he's in the resort though, and he signs so many autographs that I'm surprised his arm doesn't fall off.

The camp schedule is a little frantic for the kids, what with the Spanish lessons in the morning and all the activities in the afternoon. I, on the other hand, am a woman of leisure. I teach painting for a few hours. Other than that, I fill my time with lying in the sun… and spying on Alex's classes. It was completely unintentional on day one. I was sitting in the sun when the sound of his voice caught my attention. He brought the youngest group to the corner of the waterfront I've asked the hotel to reserve exclusively for our group.

Midway through his demonstration of a stunt, which included some fight moves and throwing himself on the grass, he took his shirt off. All that taut skin on display made me break out in a sweat… and also swear, because I wasn't close enough to see him properly.

I solve this issue the next day, placing my sunbed strategically closer to their practice spot. I turn my sunbed at a perfect angle. One could easily assume I chose the angle to see the sunset better. I also have a book with me, and I can peek from behind it without it being too obvious. Even though the end of June at Lake Tahoe isn't exactly hot, I'm still determined to soak in as much sun as possible. The view is absolutely gorgeous. Perfect blue water surrounded by mountain peaks and a clear sky. If I could marry Lake Tahoe, I would.

When Alex arrives, with the kids in tow, I sit up a little higher in my sunbed. A few short minutes later, he pauses his stunt performance and takes off his shirt again.

Holy Pop-Tarts and cupcakes. I've seen him shirtless on magazine covers and in his movies, but nothing beats seeing him live. All those lean, defined muscles. I don't know where to look first. His chiseled abs or those fan-tab-ulous biceps. This would be an excellent moment for him to ask for my assistance. I don't even care what I'd have to do. Plus points if it involves skin-on-skin contact.

How would those strong arms feel around me? Pulling me to him, so I could feel every inch of that incredible chest. The longer I look, the more surreal his body seems. I mean, I knew he had a rigorous training regimen for his superhero role, but I assumed he laid it off in his free time. Evidently not.

"Summer, do you have anything to drink? I just finished my water bottle," Alex calls.

His voice snaps me out of my daydream. Good God, did he see me looking? Even though I'm wearing sunglasses, I lower my gaze to the grass, willing my thoughts to scramble in their place.

"Ice-cold lemonade."

He strides toward me, and while he downs a gulp, my phone, which lies face up next to my thigh on the sunbed, lights up… with a notification from SoulDates, the infamous dating app. I scramble to hide it, but only manage to draw Alex's attention to the phone.

"You're on SoulDates?" he asks incredulously.

"A work colleague signed me up. Swore it can't get worse than my dating history, and she had a point. I sure have enough bad experiences: mommy's boy, daddy's boy, the cheater, the egomaniac, the one who doesn't want a relationship, the one who does want a relationship, but then bolts because I require too much attention. The list goes on."

He sets the glass on the small table next to my sunbed, lowering himself on his haunches. His jaw ticks, like what I said makes him mad, but he doesn't say anything. I slip right into crazy-defensive mode.

"Don't judge me."

"I'm not judging."

"Oh yeah? Then what's that clenched jaw

about, huh? And the narrowed eyes?"

"I'm worried about you. I don't want you to get hurt. You really think you'll find…" He seems to be weighing his words carefully. Meanwhile, I'm melting a bit at the idea of being important enough to him that he worries about me. "You really think SoulDates is the way to go?"

I deflate. "No. I only let her install it because she was nagging. I was thinking about deleting it."

"You do that."

"Would you sleep better if I did?" I grin, suddenly feeling like prodding is in order. Why exactly does he care? How *much* does he care?

"Yeah, I would."

"Okay… Mr. Bizarrely Protective." Fiddling with my phone, I delete the app, then show him my screen. "Now, go back to kicking ass. You're really good with those fake takedowns."

"I'm good at a lot of things." His gaze drops to my mouth before snapping back up.

"We're still talking about stunts?" I challenge.

"What else?"

He winks, his face breaking into that smile I love so much. A few drops of sweat trickle down that gorgeous chest. He's *so* lickable. I catch myself drawing my tongue over my lower lip. My nipples have perked up. When our gazes cross, I hold up my book, signaling I want to get back to it.

Mercifully, he rises to his feet and turns his attention to the kids again, this time giving me a view of his back. He's wearing jeans, which I find a singularly terrible choice of clothes. I mean, we're at the lake, the sun is shining. Couldn't he grace some shorts?

With a sigh, I snap my focus on the book. Tempting as it is to keep glancing at Alex, I don't want to give off the wrong vibe. I've always had a penchant for choosing the wrong men, but an actor whose contract dictates his love life and who was engaged would be an exceptionally huge mistake. But looking never hurt. Why not indulge in the muscle-fest taking place right in front of me? Lowering my book just a smidge, I discover I'm excellent at juggling two activities: reading and Alex-gazing.

As the day goes on, I catch him looking at me almost as often as he catches me looking at him. *Oh man.* There are only so many times I can pass off his winks as eye twitches, or his blatant perusal as lazy eye syndrome. Whether he *wants* to flirt, that's another story. All signs point to no. When I catch him in the act, he glances the other way.

But then he goes and does it again as if he can't help himself, which makes it even hotter.

Chapter Ten

Summer

Two days later, I wake up too late, and I run to the breakfast room as if something's chasing me. Our group has its own open buffet in the separate room where we have all our meals, but muffins are popular.

If I don't make it to breakfast in time, there won't be any left. To my utter disappointment, I was right.

"Summer, come here!" Alex motions me to join him at his table, which is empty otherwise. Claudia, one of the Spanish teachers, and the three other supervisors usually sitting with us are already gone, the kids too.

I grab some ham, tomatoes, and bread before heading to the table.

"Here, look what I saved you." He points to the plate in front of him, which contains two muffins.

"For me?" I ask unnecessarily, thrilled to the tips of my toes.

"Yeah."

"How did you know?"

"First day, you gave Claudia the stink eye

when she asked if she could have one of your muffins, since you had two and there were none left. And yesterday, you told Billie he had to wash his hands because he'd been patting a stray cat. Then you took the last muffin."

"That was for his own good," I protest. "He'd already had five."

"Liar! You did it because you wanted the muffin for yourself. Admit it."

Setting my elbows on the table, I drop my face in my hands and whisper, "Okay, I admit it. I know it was selfish, but I just really needed that one bite."

Kicking his leg playfully under the table, I attack the muffin. The cherry and chocolate flavor melts on my tongue. Parts of me melt too as I realize how much attention he's been paying to me. Maybe it's silly to put so much stock in such a little thing, but it makes me feel cared for. Important.

"I'm going out on the water with a Jet Ski in about an hour, want to join me?" he asks.

"Thanks, but no. I don't like being too far from shore. I don't like deep water."

"Why? You can't swim?"

"Oh, I do swim. But I nearly drowned when I was little, and every time I don't feel the bottom of the sea or the pool, I panic."

"That blows. But sometimes pushing against a fear pays off. I wouldn't let anything happen to you."

His expression is warm and reassuring, and I believe him. It's astonishing how much I trust him.

I'm sharing things with him I usually only talk about to my family, and I fear I've started down a slippery path. Along with trust, I tend to give my heart.

I weigh the pros and cons of taking him up on his offer. I always did want to fight this irrational panic, but I feel a tingling in my neck, like spiders crawling up my throat, at the thought of being surrounded by all that bottomless water. Nope, can't do it. Not even for the possibility of skin-on-skin contact—in my imagination, life vests or wetsuits don't exist, and I'd snuggle up right behind him, my breasts pressing against his back, my arms circling his middle, fingers tracing the hard ridges of his abdomen before gripping him for support.

"I know, but... maybe another time. Oh, by the way, we're organizing a bonfire tonight." Having finished my muffin, I rub my hands together in excitement. "I'm dying for s'mores. I can roast marshmallows like nobody's business. I even have my specialty."

"Oh?"

"Wait and see. It's delicious."

He swallows, a playful glint in his eyes. "I bet."

Holy Pop-Tarts and cupcakes. Is he flirting? Even if he is... I'm handling it.

"I bet everything you make is delicious."

Still handling it. That slippery path feels like a steep glide. But stop just because I'm going down in flames? Not my style.

"Do you even like marshmallows?" I inquire.

"I'll love yours."

Folks, Alex Westbrook is flirting with me. It's official, and I can't lie to myself. I'm not handling it anymore. I'm a little hot and very, very bothered. We finish eating in companionable silence, and after breakfast, I use the quiet morning hours to finish a painting for my mom. I prop my canvas on my bungalow's deck, placing it so I can glance at the water over it.

My hand moves of its own accord, across the canvas, stroke after stroke. Now, that's what I call having a stroke of inspiration. Those muffins have the most peculiar effect on me this morning.

***

"Summer, this is perfect. Wow. You're so good at this!" Elise exclaims later that evening. At seventeen, she's one of the oldest girls at St. Anne's. She asked me if I could braid her hair after the painting lesson finished. Braggart that I am, I showed her pictures of my nieces during the break, and she pointed out how beautifully their hair was braided.

"Thanks. My sisters kick ass at this, but I had plenty of practice on my nieces."

She smooths her palm over the braid, her shoulders hunching a little. "It must be nice to be so close to your family."

I press my lips together, nodding. Whenever I'm with the kids at St. Anne's, I'm reminded not to take my family for granted. "Come on, let's go get started on roasting those s'mores," I say.

Turns out that a bonfire is a dangerous idea when a fourth of the kids running around are under ten, which seems to be the cutoff age for finding the idea of sticking your fingers into an open flame interesting. I also chug down non-alcoholic daiquiris like it's nobody's business, thirsty from all the effort.

"No, Bobby, I'll give you the marshmallows as soon as they're roasted." I fend off six-year-old Bobby for the third time. Holy bejesus. I thought I had plenty of practice fending off kids from suicidal missions since I regularly babysit my nieces and nephews, but I'm in over my head. We're six adults, supervising thirty kids, but I can only take a breather once everyone under the age of fourteen goes to bed.

When I'm done roasting, I take refuge on one of the rattan sofas. Well, it looks more like an apple than a sofa. It's shaped like a globe, and I appreciate the rattan walls for shielding me from view. I love being with these kids, but I need a ten minute time-out. None of the kids discover my hiding spot, but Alex does.

"You're right. Your marshmallows are delicious," he says with a grin.

"Would you believe I didn't even have one?"

"I know, I was watching you. You were in over your head, roasting for the kids flocking around you while trying to keep them out of the fire."

"I was. But so were you. Why d'you have so much energy? I feel like I've just swam a mile and my arms will fall off." Not to mention my head is spinning a little.

"I've had worse in training."

"I'm dying for a marshmallow, but I have no energy to move." I pout, massaging my temple.

"Stay where you are. I'll feed both of us."

He walks to the fire, roasting a stick of marshmallows. When he glances at me, winking, I become aware of the sweaty hair clinging to the back of my neck. In fact, my entire body seems to be covered with a thin sheet of cold sweat. I shiver a little but have no desire to go near the fire again.

"Are you cold?" Alex asks upon returning, watching me rub my arms with my palms.

"A little. I got all sweaty roasting, and now my skin's clammy."

Before I realize what he's doing, he climbs in the rattan globe, sitting right behind me, stretching his legs alongside mine, his inner thighs touching my outer thighs, his chest touching my back. A sizzle replaces the shiver, and I keep my hands in my lap, unsure what else to do with them. I'm wearing a knee-length cotton skirt and a neon-pink top with puff sleeves, but for some reason feel as exposed as if I were naked.

"What are you doing?" I ask.

"Warming you up and feeding you."

He takes one marshmallow off the stick, holding it in front of my mouth. I bite into it without hesitation, sighing in delight at the delicious flavor. I lean my head back a little, resting it on his chest. I make the mistake of closing my eyes. When I blink them open again, the stars are spinning in front of my eyes. What the hell? Out of the corner of my eye, I see Alex shove the half-eaten marshmallow in his mouth. Oh God, this feels so intimate. Sitting here, sharing marshmallows. His body is cocooning around mine as if he's determined I should never ever feel cold.

I can feel his breath on my jaw and the crook between my jawbone and my neck as he leans to pick another marshmallow off the stick. Shit, his hands seem to shake before my eyes. When he brings the marshmallow in front of my face, I have to grip his wrist to stop myself from seeing double. I bite off half of it, then go back for the rest, my tongue swiping the pad of his finger in the process.

"Summer." I feel a low groan reverberate in his chest. As if through a haze, I feel the fingers of his other hand digging into my thigh. His chest feels so good against my back. So hard and good. I want to lick every crevice in it, drag my tongue over all those muscles. Looking down, I realize I've been shamelessly feeling up his thighs.

Whoops. Where on earth are my inhibitions?

"Baby, how much did you drink?" he asks softly in my ear. Panic rises in my throat.

"What do you mean? The daiquiris were non-alcoholic." But even as I say the words, I know it can't be true.

"No, the mojitos were non-alcoholic. The waiter didn't tell you?"

"Oh God, I don't know. He might have, but I was so busy with the roasting, I wasn't paying attention. I heard him say non-alcoholic and assumed it referred to both. I didn't feel the alcohol."

"You're not supposed to in a good daiquiri."

"I had about four, or six." And now the effect is slamming into me. "Alex, do you think you could help me to my room? I don't want anyone to realize I'm drunk… and I don't trust my legs."

Or my hands… or any part of my body. My licking his finger and feeling up his thighs very well prove I'm not to be trusted tonight.

"Sure. Do you want me to carry you?" he offers.

Yes, oh God, what an epic chance to feel all those muscles, all that hardness. I could rest my head in the crook of his neck, lick him there, just to check if he tastes as good as he smells.

Whoa, shit! I need to pull myself together. A couple of neurons still seem to function outside the alcohol haze. They'd better keep me from embarrassing myself.

"No, just keep an arm around my waist… in case I lose my balance or something."

"Okay. Up we go, on the count of three. One, two… three."

Chapter Eleven

Alex

I draw on fifteen years of acting skills and my popularity with the group to make this look like we're just going for a walk. I walk with her along the shore, thinking the fresh air will do her good.

"Oh, this is better," she says, "so much better." A few steps later, she untangles herself from my grip, running right into the water.

"Summer, no, come back."

Grinning, she launches herself into a series of backstrokes laps. Does she even know she's fully clothed?

"Summer!" Cursing, I enter the water. This is dangerous for her, and the fact that she doesn't realize it tells me exactly how drunk she is. I chase her through the water for a good few minutes, pulling her up straight against me when I find her.

"Summer, we need to get out of the water. It's a dangerous place to be when you're drunk."

She purses her pretty lips, looking up at me with wide, innocent eyes. "I thought it might wake me up."

She's the happy-drunk type, which is a relief. It's much more difficult to look after a drunk who's crying their heart out.

"It won't. Come on, you're all wet."

"So are you."

Yeah, but I'm not the one who'll need help changing into dry clothes.

"Come on, baby, let's get you in your room."

Before she can escape again, I hook an arm around her waist, the other under her knees, lifting her up in my arms.

"Mmm, this is nice." She rests her head on my chest, and I'm already on shore when I realize she's undoing my shirt buttons.

"Summer, stop that."

I look down to her at the same time she looks up, and the heat in her expression sends a jolt straight below my belt. I'm not just toast, I'm skewered. Instinctively, I look around. Even if someone were to snap a pic of us, there wouldn't be much to see. The waterfront is dark, the only light source is the bonfire in the distance.

"Skin-on-skin contact will help us warm up," she purrs. I cross the resort with quick strides, but she's quicker, undoing all the buttons until I reach her room.

"I need your keycard," I say. She stops in the act of reaching for my belt.

"It's in my front pocket. Unless I lost it in the water."

I put her back down and reach into her pocket because she's too busy figuring out how to undo my belt. Fucking hell, I need to get her to bed and get out of here!

"Here it is."

I swipe the card, push open the door and guide Summer inside. She sways dangerously, and I grip her waist from behind, steadying her. She sags against me, her butt pressing against my cock, which is semihard already. "Summer, you need to change into some dry clothes. I'll bring your clothes. What do you sleep in?"

She grinds her ass a little, whispering, "I sleep naked."

Fuck, fuck, fuck. My semi turns into a raging hard-on. I have to get out of here, right now. Summer's too far gone to know what she's doing, but I'm not. But if I leave before she changes, there's a good chance she'll fall asleep in her wet clothes, and she'll be sick tomorrow.

"I'll bring you a robe. You need to dry off before climbing into your bed."

I button up my shirt on the way to her bathroom. The robe hangs on the back of the door.

"Ouch, ouch, ouch!"

I hurry back, finding her beside her bed, trying to take off her shirt. Her arms are raised, her head bent at a weird angle, everything entangled in her shirt. All blood pours south when I realize she's buck naked from the waist down. Her skirt and panties are lying in the center of the room. Her ass is perfect, small and perky.

And when she turns around, gasping, "Alex, I forgot you're here," my brain turns blank.

Her pussy is waxed clean, except for a thin strip on the center. The need to bury my head between her legs and kiss her until she explodes on my tongue slams into me. I pull on every ounce of self-control, raising my gaze to the entangled mess of limbs and fabric. Crossing the room, I hold the robe in one hand and disentangle her with the other, throwing the shirt on the floor. She's not wearing a bra, and her breasts are even more enticing than her ass, just as small and perky. I cover her with the robe, rubbing my palms up and down her arms to dry her off. Her eyes are heavy with lust but unfocused from the alcohol. I need to remember this. That she'd never do this if she were sober. But now I have the image of her sweet naked body imprinted in my mind.

"I feel a bit cold."

A hot shower would help, but I don't trust her not to break her neck, and I don't trust myself to help her shower.

"You'll warm up as soon as you're under the covers. I promise."

"Aren't you cold? You're still wearing all these wet clothes. And you buttoned your shirt back. Oh, you threw away all my hard work."

I laugh because she sounds genuinely disappointed. I push away her fumbling hands when she starts working on the buttons again. Damn woman, why does she have to be so persistent?

"Climb in your bed, Summer. Come on."

Sighing, she does that... without letting go of

me. I lose my balance, barreling on top of her. My erection slams against her thigh.

She giggles, cupping my dick over the denim. "Mmm, is this for me? All for me?"

I try breathing in to regain control, but her smell invades my senses. The delicate perfume of her skin… mixed with the scent of her arousal. She's wet for me. It takes everything I have not to lower my hand between us, work her clit, slide my fingers inside her. I wouldn't stop there. I couldn't.

"Don't tempt me like this, sweet girl. You're drunk."

Another giggle. "Shh, I know."

Levering myself on one arm, I lower the other between us, pushing her hand away from my dick. Big mistake. She uses my momentary distraction to plant kisses on my neck, and the tenderness in her gesture nearly shatters my resolve. I want to let this woman kiss me like that all over, and I want it more than I've wanted anything else.

Even though the studio would ruin me, even though I don't want any Hollywood drama to touch Summer, I want her. I fist the sheet to keep myself from fisting her hair and pulling her into a kiss.

"Summer, stop." She kisses my jawline, moving further down. When she lifts her hips, grinding against me, I nearly explode. "Please, stop."

"Why?" she asks in a small voice, prying her lips away. I immediately pin her hands to the bed above her head, shifting my ankles so they're on top of hers, immobilizing her. Every muscle in my body is wound tight. My control hangs on a very, very thin thread.

"Why are you shaking?" she whispers.

"Because you're tempting the hell out of me, but you're drunk, sweet girl." I kiss her cheek, her temple. "I won't take advantage of you. Not gonna join that list you have of assholes."

She stills. "You really listen."

I pull back, watching her straight in the eyes. We didn't turn on any lights, but the moon is bright, and there's enough light for me to see that even through the haze of alcohol, she understands what I'm saying.

"Will you let go of my hands and ankles now?" she whispers.

"If you promise to behave."

She frowns. "Fine, I promise I'll behave."

I let go of her ankles first, then her wrists, then move down from the bed. Afterward, she shoves a pillow under her head, crouching on one side, bringing her knees to her chest.

"Thanks, Alex."

The robe slides sideways, and I catch a glimpse of that perfect round ass before

pulling the cover over her, tucking it under her chin. She closes her eyes, and I sit on the edge of the bed until her breathing slows down and I know she's asleep.

Then I back up, intending to leave when two stacks of magazines on the windowsill catch my attention. My face is on them. Why would she have a stack of them here? All still wrapped in plastic foil, unopened. I look closer on the small stamp on the plastic and recognize the name of the resort shop. I passed by it yesterday and today, checking the rack of magazines. I was so relieved they didn't have anything about me. I couldn't believe my luck when I didn't see a single person holding a magazine with my face on it. Smiling, I look at the huddled figure under the covers. I wasn't being lucky. Summer was looking out for me.

Pulse racing, I walk back to her, pushing down, down, down the impulse of taking her in my arms, telling her how much this means to me. So I just kiss her soft hair, then let myself out.

Chapter Twelve

Summer

"I'm going to die," I mutter for the millionth time.

"No, you're not." Claudia pushes a glass of water toward me. "You just have a hangover. You need to hydrate."

"I need to get out of here. The smell of food makes me sick."

"You should eat something," she urges. We were the last to arrive for breakfast.

"I'm so sorry. I didn't mean to drink last night."

"Summer, you don't need to apologize. You were just having fun. And you've earned your daiquiris after roasting marshmallows for ninety minutes." She looks at me curiously, then adds in a whisper, "Between you and I, did something happen with Alex?"

My heart leaps into my throat, where my stomach has been for the past few minutes as well.

"Nope, he just helped me to my room." I pulled on all my courage to come to breakfast, because I thought he'd be here and I planned on apologizing for last night. Unfortunately, I'm not one of those whose memory becomes unreliable when faced with alcohol. I remember pretty much everything, and I owe him a big-ass apology. Now I just have to find my courage again and go track him down.

"Sorry, I need fresh air. See you later, Claudia."

When I step outside the building, I inhale deeply. The fresh air tugs at my memory. Me sprinting in the water, then Alex carrying me out of it... while I was unbuttoning his shirt. Another flash of memory, of him helping me out of my soaking shirt, but nothing else. Tingles creep up my spine, not the good kind of tingles either. Drawing in a deep breath, I put on the proverbial big girl pants and head out to find him.

I head straight to his bungalow, but after a few insistent knocks at the door, I recognize defeat. Where could he be this early? I know for a fact he's not teaching the kids until later. I survey the waterfront and narrow my eyes at a jogging figure in the distance. Yum, I'd recognize that muscular frame anywhere, the outline of his arms. I sit on the porch steps, admiring the view. I might as well squeeze in some gratuitous staring before I apologize.

I only take my eyes off him when he's close enough to see me looking.

"Morning!" He comes to a halt in front of me, panting, sweat dripping in rivulets over on his face and neck. He's wearing a tank, which is a damn shame. Why isn't he one of those guys who runs shirtless? "How is your head?"

"I've had better days."

"I bet."

"Listen, about last night. I'm sorry about everything."

"You have nothing to worry about."

I can't believe I forgot he was in my room and dropped my panties and skirt. My cheeks burn.

"I don't usually—"

Alex crouches in front of me, his eyes kind and warm. "Hey, I told you, you have nothing to worry about."

"How can you say that?"

"I'm an actor. I've filmed plenty of scenes involving naked women. It's no big deal."

Thump, thump, thump! That's my pride crumbling. Then again, my body is nothing to write home about, especially not when compared to a Hollywood beauty.

I paste a smile on my face and rise to my feet.

"Well, thank you for being so easygoing about it."

"You're still embarrassed."

I shrug one shoulder. "Well, I don't have your vast experience with naked people, so...."

He steps close enough for me to smell him, and it turns my knees mushy. When he places a hand on my waist, his touch lights me up instantly. "If I strip naked, would that level the playing field?"

"Hate to break it to you, buddy, but remember those scenes where you take off your shirt? And that one where you flashed your butt? I've already seen it all." Personally, I didn't understand the point of that scene, unless it was to make every woman in the audience swoon. On second thought, that probably was the whole idea. And I can confirm it worked like a charm. I was one of those in the audience, swooning and sighing like it was my job.

"Not up close, not in person," he says.

There's about an inch of distance between us, but his body radiates so much heat, it obliterates the safety of the small distance. The only positive part of him being so close and my gaze being cast downward is that he can't see me ogling his glorious bicep. I can perv at him in peace. Apparently, perving makes use of all my neurons, because I'm scrambling for an answer. A sassy reply. I need a sassy reply. *Come on, brain, be of some use here.*

"What's the stripping offer include? If it's just the shirt, don't bother."

"Way to make me feel cheap, Summer. And it's a full body offer."

"You're going all out, huh?" I mumble.

"Only for you."

He brings his hand to my cheek, tilting my head up until our gazes cross. He's grinning. My face is on fire. His presence is all-consuming, I swear. It sucks up the air and all my willpower. My saving grace is my shame. Alex might be all blasé about the incident, but I'm still mortified.

"Very generous, but I'll have to pass. Not sure it would help my mortification."

I take one step back, and then another.

"Are you flying out to LA this evening?" I ask, remembering he's got a panel scheduled tomorrow.

"Nah, tomorrow morning at four o'clock."

"Aww, that sounds like hell."

He shrugs. "When I'm filming, I wake up at four most days, no big deal. I just have to go to bed early."

"No bonfires planned tonight, so you'll get plenty of sleep."

"Wasn't the bonfire that kept me up late yesterday."

"Oh, what was it then?" I have a sinking feeling that I'm digging myself into a hole, but what the heck?

"Someone's shenanigans."

"Silly someone. Threatening your beauty sleep." I laugh nervously. "Well, I'm going. I need to finish a painting for my mom."

He nods, pointing to his soaked clothes. "I'm going to shower."

"I'll leave you to it."

Swirling on my heels, I head in the direction of my bungalow.

"If you change your mind about the stripping offer, you know where I live," Alex calls after me, and I nearly trip over my own feet. *Hot damn.*

Once I'm inside my bungalow, Alice calls. I pick up right away.

"Hey!" she greets. Pippa's voice comes

through as well. "Hey, baby sis. How's camp?"

"Lovely."

"Listen, we were thinking about having that home-spa thingy Thursday evening the week you come back, at Ava and Sebastian's house," Alice informs me.

"Sure, that sounds great," I reply.

"We're going to pool together our nail polishes, masks, the whole Shangri-la," Pippa continues.

"I'll scour my beauty cabinet and bring everything I find." I slump on my bed, already making a mental inventory. "Just so I'm up-to-date, do we have another master goal except for convincing Ava?"

"Nah, that's all," Alice confirms.

Ava is one stubborn woman, but no one else could go toe-to-toe with Sebastian. But between us girls, we'll tackle her. I know we will. When we put our minds to it, there isn't anything we can't do.

"So beyond lovely, what can you tell us about the camp?" Pippa continues.

Crap. Of course, she wouldn't be satisfied with a one-word answer. I know I wouldn't.

I clear my throat. "Kids really like the lessons and the lake."

"Yeah, I'm picking up secrecy vibes," Pippa exclaims. Yikes. I know my strengths and weaknesses.

Talking my brothers into doing my bidding? I'm your girl, hands down.

Keeping something from Pippa or Mom? No can do. I do plan on telling them, but no way am I owning up to last night's faux pas over the phone.

"Girls, stop cornering me. I know these tactics. Besides, I need to go to a class." Yep, when it comes to this, only evasive maneuvers help postpone the inevitable.

"Don't think you're off the hook," Alice calls.

"Oh, I wouldn't dream of it. Talk to you later."

They bid me goodbye in unison, and after the line goes static, I finally start working on my painting. I settle on the deck outside, placing the canvas in a strategic spot—plenty of sunlight and a direct view of the water. The latter doesn't help with the painting per se, but watching Alex pass through my field of vision from time to time sure helps with bursts of inspiration. Once or twice he catches me looking, and the smile he flashes me is enough to make me wonder exactly how serious he is about that offer to strip. Or if I should take him up on it.

Chapter Thirteen

Alex

Preston picks me up from LAX the next morning. Most managers wouldn't bother, but he's more hands-on than others in the industry, and I appreciate it. It saves us both time because we can use the drive to discuss the schedule and any other open issues.

"Everything's running on time. The rest of the cast is already there. The panel will be one hour, maximum ninety minutes. Then you'll have an autograph session."

"How long?"

"Maximum one hour. Depends on the crowd. If they get too aggressive, we might pull you all out sooner."

"Got it."

"You're in a good mood. Lake Tahoe suits you."

I don't correct his assumption. Technically, it's true, even though I've got a spitfire of a woman to thank for my good mood. It felt strange eating breakfast alone this morning and knowing I won't see her at all today.

When we reach the panel venue, we take the

back entrance because there is already a crowd in the front, and I don't want to be mobbed this early in the morning. I love pleasing the fans, but autographs will have to wait for later. Early on, I thought the actors who walked around with security and avoided autographs unless there was a metal fence between them and fans were snobs. But at the premiere of my first big-budget movie, a fan ripped my shirt and the crowd tugged at me from every direction, until I thought they'd tear me apart limb from limb.

"Good to see you, man!" Jake greets me. He's one of the fellow superheroes in the franchise. Even though this one will premiere after *Bree Shannon Finds Love #2*, my romantic comedy with Amy, the prerelease events start earlier.

"Thanks. Where have you been?" I ask him. We wrapped shooting on this almost seven months ago, and while I do keep in touch with my costars, we don't update each other regularly.

"Everywhere. Living the big life. South of France, Italy, LA. Chicks everywhere love superheroes. You should enjoy the status too, now that you're finally off the hook."

The other guys in the room cheer Jake on, while Lena, one of the two female superheroes in the franchise universe, rolls her eyes, muttering something that sounds like "Men."

No one in this room knows about my contract clause with the studio, but even if I weren't bound by it, the life Jake's describing wouldn't be for me. Bedding women whose names I wouldn't even remember the next day never held much of an appeal for me. Most actors don't care that those women are throwing themselves at them only because of their fame, but I do. I actually like getting to know a woman before having sex with her.

My thoughts immediately flick to Summer and how perfect her body felt in my arms two nights ago. I've only been gone a few hours, and I already wish I was back.

The crowd cheers when we enter the panel room. The long table is set on an elevated island at the back of the room, and a red cordon separates the crowd from the island. There are two bouncers at every corner of the room. If something goes awry, they can sustain the crowd just long enough to call for reinforcements.

I sit between Jake and Lena, and as the other six take their seats, we all tap the mics in front of us, checking if they work. They always do, but the familiar gesture breaks the ice and settles some of the nerves. I've done this over twenty times by now, but live, recorded Q&A sessions with the fans always make me nervous. I admire singers and theater actors. I would never be able to slip into a role knowing a crowd is watching my every move.

The panel starts like any other, with easy questions about our characters, even though there's a melancholic air because this is the last movie in the franchise, and this is the last first panel so to speak. Of course, if I get my own spin-off, I'll be doing this for a long time, even if the rest of the guys won't be here with me.

"Alex, there are rumors you'll join the action series Werner Ellman is producing. Anything you can tell us about that?"

"Sorry, that's just a rumor. No truth to it."

I did read that script, but action movies come too close to superhero movies where acting range is required. I don't want to be pigeonholed.

"How about the rumor that you were cheating on Amy with every woman in sight?" a question comes from the crowd. I stiffen, narrowing my eyes, trying to discern who asked. The topic of Amy should not be an issue today. She has nothing to do with this franchise. The fandom for the romantic comedies profiled as being different than the ones for my superhero movies.

"No questions about their personal lives, please," the moderator says. Lena and I exchange a look.

"If he's got nothing to hide, why doesn't he answer? No one likes cheaters," another voice peeps up.

And then a third. "Yeah, you think fans will line up to spend money on a cheating bastard?"

The crowd buzzes, an angry buzz that makes everyone at the table stand a little straighter. I nod at the moderator, leaning into my mic.

"I have nothing to hide. Amy and I said this before. We broke up because we grew apart. Working sixteen hours a day on different continents can do that to people." My face is a mask of cool calm, even though the fakeness of the situation weighs on me.

I hadn't thought that this rumor escalated so much, so fast.

"That's bullshit. All you people say that when you can't keep it in your pants. Don't feed us lines."

"You'd better not show up with a skank in one month and try to shove down our throats how you just met her. We're not stupid."

"Folks, let's focus on the movie," the moderator tries.

"Yeah, I'm offended no one asked about my regimen to gain the extra ten pounds of muscles," Jake says with his usual humor. "None of you ladies noticed them on the posters?"

He wins back the crowd... for about ten minutes, and then they circle back to Amy and me. It's like a goddamn ping-pong match. The ball's in the movie domain for half the time, my personal affairs the other half. We skip the autograph session because there's a real risk someone's going to rip my head off.

When they lead us backstage, Preston is fuming. Jake, Lena, and my other costars throw me glances that range from murderous to sympathetic.

"What in the ever-loving fuck was that?" Jake asks, downing a soda.

"A fiasco," Calvin, one of my other costars, supplies helpfully. "Alex, man, you need to get this shit under control, or we might as well cancel all the panels."

Lena brushes her hands through her red hair, frowning. "I didn't know there was such a huge fan crossover."

"Me neither," I admit. "But this is just one panel, one crowd."

The group exchange glances.

Jake points his bottle of soda at me. "Yeah, man. But these are supposed to be our biggest fans. Not everyone gets tickets to these panels. If our biggest fans turn against you…."

I drag my hands down my face, leaning against a wall. "I'm sorry, guys. I wasn't anticipating this. I figured this type of question would pop up at most when Amy and I will appear together for promos."

Cynthia, our other female costar, shrugs. "You two were Hollywood's golden couple. You were the fairy tale come true. Rich, beautiful, eternally in love. Now the fairy tale exploded in their face, and they want to blame it on someone."

Jake throws his hands in the air. "Who cares why they're doing this? The point is, it's messing with our panels."

The conversation goes on and on, until Preston steps in and says it's time for me to go back to LAX. By his grim expression, I expect more bad news. He starts dishing it out the moment we're inside the car.

"Got a call from Newman. He went berserk."

Newman is the director of the studio.

"You're trending on Twitter. And the comments section in the Facebook live transmission was all about you and Amy. He's got a lot riding on you. He's concerned about people boycotting *Bree Shannon Finds Love #2*."

"He's a drama queen," I say flatly. "People don't boycott movies because the costars broke up."

"Sometimes they do. Especially if they think the male lead is a cheating bastard."

I sink lower into the leather seat of the car. Few things can damage an actor's career almost to the point of no return: drug scandals, violence, and cheating.

"We need to calm Newman down, at least long enough to greenlight the spin-off," Preston says.

"I have no ideas right now."

"I'll talk this through with our PR team."

"How did this get out of hand so badly?" I ask.

It's more of a rhetorical question at this point. Exhaustion creeps into my bones, and I barely pay attention to what Preston says on the way to the airport. I guzzle down soda, trying to keep a headache at bay. I'm dehydrated as hell.

Thank God, Preston arranged for a private jet today. The press would have been all over me after the panel fiasco, and I have no energy to keep lying through my teeth. I love my job, but the PR aspect of it drives me insane.

I can't wait to be back at the resort. I wonder

if Summer will still be awake.

Chapter Fourteen

Alex

Hours later, I climb the steps to my beach bungalow. When I enter my room, a basket on the windowsill catches my attention. There is a bottle of red wine in it and a note.

After the day you've had, I figured this would help.
Summer

I laugh out loud, the first real laughter for today. I forgot the entire thing was streamed live and that she said she'd be watching. Pulling the phone out of my front pocket, I dial her number. It's not that late.

When she picks up, I can practically feel some of the tension bleed away from between my shoulder blades.

"Hey! You're back?"

"Just walked into my room, found your basket. You give me too much credit. I can't drink an entire bottle on my own. Can I come over to your room? We could sit on your porch. Drink and talk. Or just talk."

"Umm, I'm already in bed."

I sleep naked, she told me that night. Is she naked now? The thought sends a shot straight to my groin.

"And I have neighbors. My porch is not safe. Do you want me to come to your bungalow?"

"Yes, come here, Summer."

"Okay. I'll get dressed, and I'll be there in ten minutes."

Fuck, she *is* naked. After hanging up, I head straight to the shower, trying and failing to chase the memory of her naked body, of that deliciously trimmed pussy out of my mind. I rub soap everywhere, toying with the idea of rubbing one off, but there is not enough time until she gets here.

I barely have time to put clothes on before I hear a knock at the door.

"Come in."

She steps inside, looking like a little angel in her short white dress, with a black ribbon around at the center of her waist. I walk straight to her, but instead of kissing her cheek, I wrap my arms around her waist, burying my head in her neck.

"I take it that was much worse in real life than the video," she says softly, lacing an arm around my neck.

"Yeah. I'm so glad you came."

She shivers lightly, and I pull back, already missing her scent, the softness of her skin.

"Do you want to order some food too?" she asks.

"I ate on the plane."

She scrunches her nose. "I never eat on planes. Makes me queasy at landing. Shall we take the wine on the porch?" she asks.

"Sure."

She grabs the bottle. I take the glasses from the minibar and the small package I bought at the airport. She goes straight to the round sofa lounge, climbing on it.

"When I returned, I was half hoping to see you here."

She gives me a small smile. "I thought about it, but figured you wouldn't want to see a soul tonight. That you'd need your space to recharge."

I climb next to her, sitting so close that our arms touch. "I wouldn't want to see anyone except you."

She searches my eyes, frowning as if trying to decipher something, then holds up the glasses. I uncork the bottle, pour us each wine.

"Do you want to talk about today?" she asks as we lean back on the couch.

"Not tonight. I like that this place is drama-free. Thank you for making that happen."

She widens her eyes, then groans. "You saw the magazines."

"Yeah. I wanted to thank you yesterday but thought bringing the evening up would just make you uncomfortable again. But thank you."

"You're welcome." She takes a small sip of wine, sinking lower on the couch.

"What's wrong?"

"Just residual embarrassment for that night. I'll get over it. Eventually."

I turn to her, framing her jaw with my hand, leaning in. "Summer, we've been over this."

A small sound escapes her, somewhere between a chuckle and a choke. "You probably forgot all about it already."

The gentleman thing would be to tell her I did. But I don't have the energy to act any longer tonight, and I don't want to act around her. I want to be honest, and something in her body language tips me off that she needs that honesty.

"I don't think I'll ever forget it. The sight of your beautiful body is branded in my brain."

Her mouth pops open. "But… you said it wasn't a big deal, that you'd seen plenty of actresses—"

"I was trying to put you at ease." By the looks of it, I did just the opposite. "You have no idea how hard it was to keep my control, Summer. I wanted you so badly."

She sucks in a breath. "You did?"

"I still do."

She parts her lips, her eyes widening with surprise. I bring a hand to her face, caressing her cheek, resting my thumb at the corner of her mouth.

Her skin is so smooth, it spurs a need deep inside me, to touch more of her. To taste her. Would she taste as sweet as I remember? Have I idealized the kiss, the memory growing sweeter, more real the more time we spent together, the more I learned about her?

"I've missed you today," I confess.

"You did?"

"Yeah."

"So did I. I arrived late at breakfast, and no one saved me muffins."

"I brought you something." I pull the small package out of my pocket and take out the necklace with a little key pendant. "I saw it at LAX. It made me think of you."

"I love it."

"Let me put it on."

She turns around, baring her neck to me. I clasp the necklace, lingering with my fingers at the back of her neck. She lets out a little sigh. I trace the contour of her shoulder, needing to touch more of her. Summer tightens her grip on one of the couch cushions.

I move closer until my chest almost touches her back, rubbing my thumb gently in the crook of her neck and shoulder. When she tilts her head slightly to the other side, giving me access, I don't hesitate. I lower my mouth, pressing kisses to her skin.

"Alex!"

The vibration in her voice is the sexiest sound. I bring one hand to her waist, spin her around, then capture her mouth with mine.

She parts her lips, granting me access, entwining her tongue with mine as soon as I request it. I deepen the kiss, moving my hand from her waist to her thigh, bunching up her dress. I want to feel her skin, taste it, because she tastes even better than I remember, and I want to explore all of her.

"Alex," she whispers again when I trail my mouth down her neck. "One night. Just this one night."

I hold her close, breathing her in. "Just this one night," I agree. I know the smartest thing would be no night at all, especially after the accusations thrown at me today. But we've both gone past that point. I want this woman. I need her. Working her dress up, I groan when the fabric finally gives way to skin. It's so smooth and inviting….

"Let's go inside," I say on a growl.

"Don't stop touching me."

"Once we're inside, I won't stop touching you, tasting you. I won't stop until I make you cry my name, Summer. I'll make you come so hard that you won't forget this night anytime soon. You won't forget me."

Rising from the couch, I pull Summer to her feet. Hands intertwined, I lead her inside. The second I close the door, I press her against it, kissing her, touching her. I only pause enough to pull her dress over her head. Lust shoots through my veins at the sight of her in underwear.

"You're so beautiful. Unclasp your bra, Summer."

She looks like something out of a sinful dream, standing there, legs slightly apart, reaching behind with one hand, obeying me. She makes a move to hook one thumb in her panties next, but I stop her.

"No. I'll do that."

Summer swallows hard, then leans against the door, her hands at her side. I love the challenge in her eyes and the silent invitation to do anything I want to her.

I suck in one nipple, then pull back, circling the wet skin until the peak is a tight bud. With the other hand, I push her panties down. I only push them until they're halfway down her thighs before I lose my composure. I trace the fine line of hair from her pubic bone, going down, down, down until the pad of my finger touches her clit. She presses her back into the door, snapping her eyes closed.

"Look at me, Summer. I want you to look at me." Her breath is already labored as I draw small circles around her clit. When she blinks her eyes open, they're full of lust. I want to watch her every reaction, but I want to kiss her more. I need to be closer to her, want the intimacy of a kiss, and by the sweet sound she makes when I capture her mouth, the way she laces both arms around my neck, so does she.

I kiss and stroke her until her legs are quivering and she's so wet that my fingers are slipping down her folds. I want a taste of her desire, but her hold around my neck is tight, and I don't want to break away. It feels too good to be in the circle of her arms. I don't want to pull away... not even after this night ends.

When I sense that she's close to the edge, I slip two fingers inside her, pressing the heel of my palm against her clit. She climaxes the next second, and I eat up the delicious, primal sound she makes, nearly exploding in my jeans. Then I pull slightly away, just enough to look at her, all flushed and out of breath.

She came before I even finished taking her panties off.

As if reading my mind, she glances down at her panties, still around her thighs, then hooks a thumb on one side. But then she stills, as if not knowing if she should pull them up or push them down. I hook a thumb on the other side, and she lets go, giving me free rein. I push them down, and as she steps out of them, I can't help myself. I swipe my tongue along her entrance. She buckles forward, nearly collapsing over me. I catch her arms and pull myself up until I'm facing her.

"You can't do that without any warning. I'm too sensitive," she whispers, poking my chest. Then she starts unbuttoning my shirt. I kiss her cheek and move to her ear.

"Here's your warning, Summer: I'm not going to give you a break. I'll push more and more. You're going to love it, I promise."

The trust in her eyes does me in. We're a tangle of limbs, but I feel like we're entwined on a deeper level like she's part of me already.

"I want you in my bed, beautiful. Now."

***

Summer

I feel exposed, walking naked through his bungalow. I feel him right behind me, except for a brief moment when he steps sideways. I don't look back, but the sound of foil on foil tells me he's fetching a condom. When we reach the bed, I sit on the edge and finish undoing his shirt, then lick down the bare skin, tracing the fine dents of his muscles.

I haven't had a one-night stand before, but I'm pretty sure you're not supposed to feel as vulnerable and open as I do. Alex won't own just my body tonight. He'll own my soul too.

We get rid of the rest of his clothes together, and then I follow the dusting of hair starting under his navel with my fingers, until I reach the base of his cock. I pump my hand twice before letting him go, and he bends, hooking an arm around my waist, hoisting me right in the center of the bed. He's so strong, and his arms feel *so* good around me. He kisses me with so much heat that my legs shake. But there is tenderness in his kiss too, like I matter to him just as much as he matters to me. He kisses and touches every inch of my skin, and I do the same with his body. Eyes pinched shut, I feel the mattress shift, Alex moving away, then hear foiled being ripped. By the time I open my eyes, he's moving on top of me. He's sheathed himself already.

He positions his tip at my entrance, and as he slides inside, inch by delicious inch, he laces our fingers together. He brings his mouth to mine, our tongues twirling together while our bodies move together, perfectly in sync.

I don't know if every sensation is magnified because my body is still strung together from the orgasm, or because he's making love to me as if I'm his lifeline, the single most important thing in his life. I cherish every second of it, memorize every detail: the scent of his skin, the sounds he makes, and all the emotions he stirs inside me.

When I feel him widen inside me, I flex my inner muscles, wanting to squeeze him good, to make this as delicious as he's made it for me.

He goes over the edge, taking me with him. Letting go of my fingers, he cradles me in his arms until my pulse regains a somewhat normal rhythm. Then he moves away, taking care of the condom quickly before returning to my side. He holds me to him until I fall asleep.

Chapter Fifteen

Summer

Tap, tap, tap.

The sound jolts me awake. I blink, frowning at the unfamiliar bed and room. Then I see Alex, lying on his belly, deep asleep.

Oh no, no, no. I broke the golden rule of one-night-stands. *Thou shall not fall asleep in the other's bed.* Granted, the man wore me out last night. But that's no excuse for my breaking the one-night stand code. As silently as possible, I climb out of bed and go about finding my clothes. My cheeks burn as I find them tossed around the room. *Please, don't let him wake up before I'm gone.*

Though I haven't had any one-night stands before him, twice I mistook weeks of dating and one night in bed as a relationship, but they informed me of my naivety before the sheets cooled.

But Alex and I agreed on the same thing last night. How embarrassing!

I take one last look at him before heading to the foyer. God, he looks so deliciously lickable, with his entire back and half his ass on display. He holds the pillow tightly under his head, and I remember those arms holding me just as tight last night, as if he didn't want to let me go.

Tap, tap, tap.

"Alex, are you in here?" I freeze in my steps, halfway through the foyer. The sounds that woke me up were knocks at his front door.

"Mr. Westbrook?" the voice asks even louder. It belongs to one of the younger boys in the group. Well, now I've done it. How the hell am I supposed to get out? There is a large window I could escape through at the back of the bungalow, but my two experiences with window climbing as a kid made a lasting impression on me, considering I twisted my ankle both times, and knocked out a front tooth the first time.

I refuse to risk maiming myself during my walk of shame. Which leaves me… nowhere.

I swallow when Alex appears in the foyer, already wearing jeans and a fresh shirt, his eyes small with sleep.

"Why are you hiding in the foyer?" he asks. *Ayayayay*. I realize I was holding onto the hope that maybe he'd want last night to be more than a one-time occurrence. Which is more than a little foolish.

"There's someone outside… and I don't know how to get out."

"Oh yeah. That's Bobby. I promised him I'd sit at his table at breakfast today. Seems he thought it safest to get me." He motions with his head toward the door. "Let's go."

"Umm… he might get the wrong idea if he sees me here."

"Okay, then I'll go with him, and you can stay here and close up. Give me the card at breakfast." He checks his smartphone. "We don't have that much time left."

"I'll skip breakfast today. I need time in the morning to make myself presentable."

"What are you talking about? You look perfect."

That brings a smile to my lips, and my heart might just have skipped a beat, though I'd deny it to my last breath.

"My hair is out of control."

He twirls a strand between two fingers. "Like its owner. You're a wild thing, Summer. After last night, I won't be able to look at you the same way."

I feel my cheeks burn. "Don't leave Bobby waiting. Go. I'll find you later and give you the card."

"I'll bring you muffins."

***

After Alex leaves, I wait for five minutes before skipping out the door. My gaze darts around as I head to my bungalow. Is it still called the walk of shame if no one sees you? Well… no one you know. Plenty of the hotel residents pass me by, and I pat my hair in a fruitless attempt. My stomach growls, protesting the lack of food. Excitement wires me up as I remember Alex promised to find me some muffins, but then I force myself to think about something else, because I'm still running a little high on last night's shenanigans, and my brain cells are not fully awake yet. That's a recipe for drawing the wrong conclusions. I'm a pro at misinterpreting men's intentions for more.

After freshening up, I stuff my notes for today's classes in my beach bag and head outside. I'm only teaching in the afternoon, but I like reviewing my notes every morning. Typically, I keep mulling over them at the back of my mind for the rest of the day and come up with new examples or a better way to explain a technique.

My feet carry me to the stretch of water near Alex's bungalow almost by themselves. When I spot him sitting on a sunbed, phone pressed to his ear, I get cold feet at the potential for awkwardness. I wish there was a handbook with instructions for a one-night stand with a man you know and are stuck with for another week. A man you like very much. I reason that since we've set free all that pent-up sexual tension, I might not get all... tingly around him anymore.

Yeah, that's just wishful thinking. The closer I get to him, the signs become more poignant. He's with his back to me, but I warm all over at seeing those corded muscles, the strong arms.

When I notice the plate with three muffins next to him, butterflies roam in my stomach.

God, help me. Butterflies have no business here. Putting his phone down, he runs a frustrated hand through his hair, then turns around, a corner of his mouth twisting up when he sees me.

"Look what I got you." He points at the plate.

"How did you manage to get three when you got there so late?"

"By employing my irresistible charm and talent."

I drop my bag on the sand, sitting at the other end of the sunbed. "Fess up. Does that include distraction or stealing?"

"Negative. I went directly to the kitchen and asked for a new batch."

"Oh, wow."

I bite into a muffin, taking him in. He runs his hand through his hair again, frustration etched onto his features.

"Sooo, who was that on the phone?"

He hesitates. "Amy. She called about the fiasco yesterday. Her manager and PR team are going berserk."

"Why? You're painted as the bad guy."

"Yeah, but this will impact the box office turnout for our movie."

"Wow, really?"

"When you use the costars' real-life relationship as a main selling point, yes."

I move on to the second muffin, pondering just how screwed up it must be for your professional life to be so entangled with your personal life. A question burns on my lips, but it's not my place to ask, damn it.

"Summer?"

"Yeah."

"What is it that you want to ask me?"

I startle, squeezing the muffin so tight that my fingers sink into it. Am I that transparent?

"I... doesn't matter."

He eyes the half-mashed muffin in my hand. "This is the first time I've talked to her in a month. I don't have romantic feelings for her anymore. If I'm honest, things between us were rocky long before we broke up. Does that answer any... potential questions?"

I swear to God, my heart just sprouted wings, and it's about to take off from my chest.

"Wow. Yeah, you could say that."

I cross and uncross my legs, then cross them again, trying to finish eating the smashed mushed-up muffin as elegantly as possible.

Alex scoots closer until he's right in my face. "I don't want you to regret last night."

"Last night was spectacular. No place for regrets."

I have the strangest feeling that Alex senses I'm having trouble separating physical sizzle from emotional connection.

"Tell me you gave her a piece of your mind about sending you that ring like that," I say.

"I did. She apologized, said she didn't know how to handle it."

"How will you manage the situation from yesterday?"

"My manager and PR team will talk to the studio, and then they'll draw up a plan."

"Isn't it weird, having other people decide so much for you?"

He laces his fingers on top of his head, looking out on the water. "It's a relief most of the time. When I'm filming a project or promoting a movie, I don't even have time to deal with stuff like that. I know it's not neurosurgery or something, it's not like what I do is vital. But I love my job. I love entertaining people."

"Hey, I'm with you on this. I think arts are important. They feed the mind."

"I like not having to decide on all the PR stuff. Anyway, the damage in this case was done years ago when I agreed to let the studio use my private life as a marketing tool. The studio will have the final say on how to handle this. They put a lot of money in both movies."

"My head is spinning."

"Mine too, trust me."

I foresee many unpleasant days ahead of him. He needs some serious distraction, but all I come up with are sinfully sexy activities. Nope, not going there again, not even mentally. I'm happy we're still on a friendly basis, that the awkwardness didn't overshadow that. But even as I mull those thoughts over, I fear I can't just be Alex's friend.

"I'm going back out on a Jet Ski later today. What do you say? Time to take on that fear of deep water head-on?"

"Maybe."

"What will it take to convince you to join

me?" he asks.

"Aww, come on, you know my weakness. Muffins."

He licks his lower lip, his eyes raking over my body. "I'd say I discovered a few more things that make you weak."

Wait a minute... are sexy innuendos on the table? What kind of double-edged sword are these one-night-stand rules? How am I supposed to do this without letting on how much I want him again? *Wait*, does it mean he wants me again? I don't want to let myself think that. It's a fool's hope, given the drama surrounding his love life. And maybe one night was enough for him. Why the teasing, then?

"Not the ones that make me weakest," I reply. There. See what he does with *that*.

"Are you challenging me?"

"Something wrong with that?"

"You're delicious."

His eyes flash, and I wonder if he's remembering that moment when I nearly toppled onto his face. Heat rises to my cheeks, so I turn to look out on the water, feeling like my entire face—even the roots of my hairs—are going to catch fire. I'm not even going to address the situation between my legs. I've passed the stage of fire there. It's a billowing inferno.

I focus on the lake and the prospect of taking it on. And being on a Jet Ski isn't the same thing as being in the water. I'll be guessing how deep it is, but I won't experience that dreadful feeling of not being able to touch the floor.

"I won't let anything happen to you. Go out on the water with me."

I startle because I hadn't realized Alex had shifted right behind me. He rests a hand on my waist, warm and reassuring. If anyone else asked me, the answer would be a firm no. But Alex has seen me in some quite vulnerable moments already, and I can't help but trust him. And really, this fear of mine is ridiculous.

"Okay. I'll go."

***

"Why aren't you wearing a life vest?" I ask later as a hotel employee helps us onto a Jet Ski. Alex goes first, sitting in front.

"Because I feel hot as it is. I'll cook in it."

So will I, probably, but no way in hell am I going out without one. I'm wearing a wetsuit too, even though I don't plan to actually touch the water, but you never know. Several brave souls are swimming bare-skinned, but I'd need the water to be at least twenty degrees warmer for that.

I look like a little robot with the neon orange vest reaching all the way to my ass and the black wetsuit. I sit behind Alex, eyeing the water like the fiend it is.

"Hold onto me," Alex instructs, which I do, wrapping my arms around his middle, my palms flat on his stomach. Yum.

This will be a Jet Ski ride with benefits. I get to feel him up and call it holding on to him. He stirs the motor to life, and I yelp as he propels us forward, scooting even closer to him until I'm pressed tight against his back.

"If you want me to stop or turn around, just say so, okay?" he shouts over the sound of the engine and the water splashing around us.

"Okay," I yell back.

"But try to relax a bit and enjoy the view." I try to ease my grip on him and look around us instead of hiding my face in his back. That's not the point of this outing. If I was going to be a coward, I could have stayed on shore.

After a few more minutes of cowering, I finally sit up straight, holding my hands on the sides of his waist only. Feeling brave, I even push myself back a little on the seat, so I can move freely, turn on one side, then the other. My heart rate slows down gradually, as I immerse myself in the glorious sight. Endless blue sky, endless blue water and beautiful mountains surrounding us. Gosh, the water's beautiful. I spot one or two multicolored fish swimming leisurely around. Leaning a bit on the right side, I try to make out if one of them is indeed neon green, or if it's a light trick.

WHAM. SPLASH.

Chapter Sixteen

Alex

It takes me a few seconds to realize that the breeze suddenly hitting my back means Summer isn't on the Jet Ski to block it anymore. I turn my head wildly around, but I can't see her in the water. Fuck, where's my girl?

I press the brake, but through sheer residual propelling force, the Jet Ski covers a few more feet before stopping. The second it comes to a halt, I scan the water all around. A knot lodges in my throat when I see a pair of flailing arms almost half a mile away. Jesus, how did I drop her?

Chewing the inside of my cheek, I speed in her direction, stopping when I'm just one foot away and dive right into the water.

"Summer!" I catch one of her hands, stopping her wild flailing, pulling her into my arms.

"I can't touch the floor. I can't touch it," she says feverishly between sobs. Her entire body is shaking, tears streaming down her face.

"Summer, you have a life vest on, and you can swim anyway. And you have me."

She doesn't seem to hear a word. She keeps trying to sink deeper, and it takes me a few seconds to realize she keeps hoping she'll reach the bottom. Jesus, how do I show her she's safe?

Keeping myself afloat just by paddling with my feet, I cup her face in both hands.

"Summer, look at me."

She braces her hands on my wrists, her eyes, large and wild, and so damn scared it cuts right through me. "The water is deep here, but you have nothing to worry about. I can't touch the floor either, but it's easy to keep afloat. And you have a life vest. You couldn't drown if you tried."

She grips my wrists so tightly that my skin hurts, but I wouldn't care if she stopped my entire circulation.

"H-how deep do you think the water is?" she whispers. Well, shit. I don't know exactly, but I have to make her focus on something else.

"Let's get you on that Jet Ski, sweetness. Hold on to one of my arms."

She releases one of my wrists slowly, then quickly grabs the other with both hands.

"That's perfect. You're doing great. Just look at me while I get you on the Jet Ski. Personally, I don't know why you'd look anywhere else anyway. I'm by far the sexiest thing around."

She gives me a small smile, but fear still lingers on her features. She doesn't break eye contact once. She's putting all her trust in me, and I won't let her down. When we reach the Jet Ski, I lift her onto it first.

"Do you want to drive? It's really easy, and

you'll feel in control."

She shakes her head. "You drive. I trust you."

I propel myself out of the water and slide in front of her. She immediately wraps her arms around me, holding me so tightly I barely breathe.

"Feel me up all you want, sweetness. I'm here for you to take advantage of."

She chuckles but doesn't loosen her grip. I lurch forward.

Several of the older kids are lined up the shore as we approach. Aren't they supposed to be in their Spanish class? Maybe it's already time for their first break.

"Summer, what happened?" one of the girls asks as the two of us come out of the water.

Another is bouncing up and down the balls of her feet. "Are you okay?"

We were close enough to shore that Summer's wild arm flailing didn't go unnoticed. She's still shaking.

But she straightens up, gazes at the bunch of scared kids, and smiles. "Just being silly. Fell off the Jet Ski, but nothing happened. I'm okay." Her voice is remarkably steady given that she's still shaking. "I just need a hot shower, and I'll be as good as new."

Several kids seem unconvinced. Summer smiles at them. "I'm okay. Don't think you can use me as an excuse to weasel out of the class. When's your break over?"

"Five minutes ago," one admits.

"What? Off you go! Come on."

They leave, walking slowly and glancing over their shoulders. Summer keeps smiling until they're out of sight. Then she seems to fold into herself.

Wordlessly she walks past the sunbed where we sat before the ride and picks up her beach bag, then starts in the general direction of her bungalow. I walk right beside her, and since she doesn't say anything, I gather that she needs me by her side as much as I need to make sure she's all right.

A few guests look at us on the way, and the thought any of them might snap a picture crosses my mind. But what if they did? There's nothing to see. Just two friends walking together.

When we reach her bungalow, I take the card out of her shaky hands and unlock the front door.

"Thank you, Alex."

Her voice falters on my name. As much as I admired that she pulled on every ounce of her self-control to reassure the kids, I like that she doesn't feel the need to play brave for me.

"I'll wait for you to shower, okay?"

"I promise I won't have a panic attack in the tub. I was so silly." She shrugs, smiling in a self-deprecating way as we go inside. I'm not having any of it.

"You were scared, Summer. You have nothing to be ashamed of. Everyone has irrational fears."

"What are yours?"

"Tiny elevators and finding worms in fruit."

She gives me a small laugh.

"Hey, these aren't even my worst ones. Go ahead and shower, I'll wait here."

Later, when she comes out, hair dry, a towel wrapped around her, covering her from her chest down to her knees, she walks straight into my open arms. I hold her tightly, inhaling the smell of her shampoo.

"Alex?" she whispers.

"Hmm?"

"Can you stay with me? Just for a little while?"

"Yes." I wrap her even tighter in my arms. "I'll stay. But I need to shower too, or I'll mess up your room."

"I suppose you should."

I never showered as fast in my life. Wrapping a towel around my waist, I head back to her. She's already curled in her bed on one side, sheet up to her chin. I slide right next to her and notice she's wearing shorts and a loose tank top. The swell of one of her nipples is showing. Lust loops through me. I barely resist teasing her about going to bed naked. This isn't why she asked me to stay. She hugs her pillow, falling asleep almost instantly. A while later, so do I.

I wake up with a hard-on. Summer is turned with her back to me, her ass pressing straight against my erection. I have one arm around her waist, my hand wedged between her side and the mattress, as if trying to keep her from moving away from me. Carefully, I attempt to take my hand out.

"You're awake?" she whispers.

"Yes. How long have you been awake?"

"A while, but I didn't want to move in case you woke up too. And, umm… I think your towel slipped off." She sounds as if she's fighting a giggle.

I check under the cover, and the towel sure had sure slipped off. I groan. "You can add that to my list of fears. Having a raging hard-on at the wrong time."

"You're in bed with a seminaked woman. Don't be too hard on yourself." This time she does giggle. I take that as a sign that she's over the deep-water incident.

"What time is it?"

"We were only asleep for an hour." She points to the digital clock display in the right-hand corner of the TV. Then she turns around, and I get a glimpse of her nipple again. All blood pulls south.

I focus on her eyes, which are trained on me. I caress the side of her face, and she leans into my touch, kissing the heel of my palm. The contact zings me.

"Summer, I want you."

She giggles again, but the sound is breathier. "The sword under the cover gave that away."

"I know we said one night, but I can't keep that promise." I swallow, searching for the right words. "I know my life comes with an XL-sized bag of complications… even though it doesn't feel like it when I'm here, with you."

"Is that because I make a fool of myself every

chance I get?" She bats her eyelashes, grinning. "Or because I still haven't asked you for an autograph?"

"Nah, the way you moan my name when I'm inside you won me over."

She gasps mockingly. "You did not just say that."

"You're unlike anyone else I ever met, Summer. You're everything I didn't know I wanted."

Her lips part, a mix of tenderness and surprise etched on her beautiful face.

"So let's forget about the complications while we're in here," she whispers. "Let's just be Alex and Summer for the next week."

I'd take anything she wants to give me. Given the messy state of my affairs, I don't have more to offer beyond this week anyway. But this attachment I feel for her will only grow if we spend more time together. The smart thing to do would be to pull back altogether, but all I want is to give her more.

I kiss her, desire sweeping through every cell in my body. I lick her lower lip, tugging it between my teeth before moving lower, kissing her neck. I roll her onto her back, needing to feel her under me.

Her eyes wide and searching, she holds onto my shoulders tightly, shimmying under me until we're touching at so many contact points that I don't know where she ends and I begin, but still, she pulls me closer. I cradle her to me, needing that closeness too.

Having a carte blanche for one night is one thing, but this... this is different, deeper. She opens up, cradling my erection between her thighs, and I instinctively know what she needs. I'm going to give it to her in spades. I rub my hard-on against her center, the thin cotton of her shorts the only thing between us.

She gasps, fisting the sheet with one hand, my hair with the other. Kissing every inch of skin within reach, I rub back and forth, feeling her arousal dampening the fabric.

"Summer, do you have condoms?"

"No," she says, shaking her head, her hips arching up when I move downward, pulling her shorts. The sight of her swollen, glistening flesh beckons to me. "But I need you to touch me."

"Oh, I will. I can make you feel good without being inside you, sweetness."

I drag the tip of my tongue up one fold, almost near the clit, but not quite, watching as she pinches her eyes shut in anticipation. I suck on her clit once before descending, licking her entrance, going even lower. She straightens one of her bent legs with a start, her back arching.

"Alex! Oh, Alex!"

I love seeing her open up to me like this. When she's so close to a climax that I feel the muscles in her thighs and ass clench together, I pull back, kissing up her belly, bunching the tank top higher and higher, gobbling up every inch of skin I reveal. After yanking the top over her head, I capture her lips with mine. I could kiss her for hours, just kiss her. I can't get enough of her sweet mouth.

Lowering one hand between us, I play with her clit. She fists my cock at the base, pumping all the way up, pressing the heel of her palm on the tip.

"Summer, that's so good."

Tension pulls at the base of my spine with every stroke. Summer comes undone beneath me, writhing and moaning. I can tell when every wave of pleasure spreads through her, because she squeezes harder, moves her hand faster. I come seconds after she does and nearly collapse on top of her.

Chapter Seventeen

Summer

"You are a bad man! Look at the time," I exclaim once I'm dressed, and Alex has put on the only item of clothing he has in my room, his swim shorts. We were supposed to take a quick shower. Well, I suggested that. Alex had sexy plans, and he only shared them with me once I was already trapped between his hard body and the tiled wall.

"You could have said no," he says.

"Mmm… I'm not very good at telling you no."

"You do know I'll take advantage of that, don't you?"

"Oh, I hope you do."

He stalks toward me, intent written on his face. I point a finger at him.

"Not right now. You're going to make us miss lunch. And you still have to go change into clothes."

"I wish I could stay in here with you all day."

Sighing, I head to the small vanity table and start brushing my hair, avoiding looking at him in the mirror. "Far be it from me to want to bring reality into our little dream world, but we have to be careful, so no one can put two and two together about us."

"I'm sorry. My contract is very strict on that point."

"I know. Even if it wasn't, being seen with a woman wouldn't please your fans." I shudder, remembering the vitriol in his fans' voices during the panel.

Alex walks right behind me. Taking the brush out of my hands, he disentangles my hair with slow, gentle moves.

"You don't mind that we have to keep it secret?"

"I'd love it if we didn't have to, but it's not a big deal. And it's just for a few days anyway."

Alex's hand falters for a split second. *We're just for a few days*. My stomach sinks at the thought, but I square my shoulders, smiling at him in the mirror. So what if we'll go our separate ways in a week?

Is there a real risk I might fall for him? Yes, there is.

Will I let that hold me back? Most certainly not.

I foresee a need for a copious amount of sugar and sisterly love when I return to San Francisco, but I won't let that thought get in the way.

When he finishes brushing my hair, he peppers my shoulders with kisses, glancing at me hungrily in the mirror.

"No," I say firmly. "I want that lunch. Don't make me miss it."

He grins, his gaze raking up and down my body. "I promise I'll make it worth your while."

Right… how do you let a man down gently when telling him you rate food—especially when you're starving—above sexy times? I decide not to pussyfoot around.

"Sorry, mister, but your schmexy skills aren't reason enough for me to go hungry."

He abruptly straightens up, his eyes flashing. *Yikes.* Clearly, honesty is not always the best policy. In a second, he wraps his arms around my waist, trapping me against his chest. His naked chest.

He has an advantage over me right here—all that skin on display makes it hard to think of anything beyond how lickable he is. I become aware that we're moving toward the bed. I get all tingly at the prospect of more sexy time. A second later, I remember I had a *good* reason to say no. Then I remember my hands are free. I can use all this shameless display of hard chest against him. More for me to touch and taunt. I start my grand plan by splaying a palm on his chest. Then I have a stroke of genius, and I lick his nipple. That earns me a groan.

I lick the other nipple. Alex presses his hips against me, and I feel his erection wedged between us. Hmm… I'm not sure if I'm winning this.

He's losing composure with every passing second, but we're also moving in the direction of the bed. Did I mention I'm hot and bothered as hell?

"I mean it. I want to get my lunch," I warn.

"No, you don't. You want me. You tempt me, be prepared for the consequences."

He skims a large hand over my breast, as if to

prove a point. I bite my lip as my sensitive nipple grazes the fabric of the bra. I've got to give it to him. Point proven. Now, how to torment him in return? I shimmy my lower body, feeling his hard and hot length pulsing against me. I hear a growl low in his throat. His control hangs on a thin thread. Yep, time to cut that thread. He's at my mercy here. I'd feel like a powerful seductress if I wasn't at his mercy just as much.

His gaze is molten, his mouth hard as he pulls me into a kiss so hot and dirty, I might never recover. This man will climb into my heart and stay there. I know this with the certainty I know that my name is Summer Bennett. This doesn't keep me from giving in to him.

Oops, I guess I lost the battle. But if I'm honest, when it comes to feeling Alex's lips and hands all over my body, there's no losing, only winning.

***

Alex

"You're right. I should buy more, or my nieces and nephews will fight over them," Summer says almost a week later, scanning the racks with magnets. We've been in the resort's shop for thirty minutes and are having a blast buying souvenirs for our families.

I like that I can be myself around Summer,

that we can have fun doing even the simplest things. I often feel like an impostor in Hollywood, where liking extravagant parties and exorbitant clothing is a requirement to fit in. Summer doesn't look at me as if she's measuring my net value in everything I do or say.

"Okay, I'll buy one of each," she declares, nodding at the vendor. Once we're out of the shop, her phone pings. She pulls it out of her bag, her brow scrunching when she reads the lengthy e-mail.

"My boss. I pitched an idea about featuring young artists, but she's not a fan. It's important to nurture young talents. Having confidence in them boosts their own self-confidence."

"You're right. One of the reasons I like to give feedback to young actors. Come to think of it, why don't you have your own gallery? You have the funds to open it."

She smiles impishly. "It's my dream to open one. I'd display collections by established painters and classics in one part, and new talents in another. I'd also love to offer painting classes."

"That sounds like a plan. Why don't you do it?"

"I opened a gallery after I graduated college. It failed spectacularly. I was… naive. I was too focused on young talents, and that's not a draw with the masses. Never even came close to making a profit, so I closed up shop. Worked at several museums afterward, including abroad in Rome."

"You know what they say. Nothing is really a

failure, but a learning experience."

She waves her hand. "I don't mind calling things by their real name. Learning experience or not, failure is failure."

I take in her delicate frame. She might be small and fragile-looking, but Summer is made of a stronger clay than most people I know.

"You have more experience now," I reason.

"So my family keeps saying."

"I like your family already. So, what's holding you back?"

"Oh, courage, where art thou? I'm still looking for it. I'll let everyone know when I find it."

I'd like to be there when she does, hear her tell me all about it.

"I can take both our gift bags to my room," I tell her. She has a painting class now, and I have some free time.

"Thanks." She cranes her neck to the left, then the right. "My neck's stiff."

I lean in closer but still don't touch her, because we're in a public area of the resort.

"You need to relax. I can help with that."

"Hmm... yes, you're good at that," she says pensively.

"I'm amazing," I correct her. "*You* keep telling me that. And you seem to mean it 100 percent."

She rolls her eyes, blushing. She does say that, repeatedly... in bed. "Fine, you're amazing. Happy?"

I flash her a grin. "We're two hours away from of being alone, baby. I'll show you what makes us both happy then."

Summer sighs contentedly as she heads toward the conference room where her painting class is taking place. Damn, I don't want to let this woman go.

Chapter Eighteen

Alex

"Ten more. Go, go, go."

"You're enjoying this far too much," I reply between breaths.

Summer grins, dipping the spoon in the ice-cream box.

"I have to say, watching you do crunches while I eat ice cream just made my top ten guilty pleasures."

Since we have such limited time together, we steal every moment we can, including my daily training session. Because I don't need to beef up for a role right now, I exercise using my body weight only, so I'm doing the routine on the floor of my room. Summer sits cross-legged on one of the armchairs, flicking her eyes from my printed training plan in front of her to me.

One day. We just have one more day until the camp's over. How did this week go by so fast?

"One, and done!" She claps her hands. "Planks are next."

I laugh, laying back on my elbows. "Don't I deserve a break?"

"Nope. It says on the plan you're only

supposed to take a break after the planks. I'm doing a favor to women worldwide by not letting you off the hook. We need your lickable hotness to remain that way, gives us all something to drool over. I'm doing this purely on humanitarian grounds. Not because I like to see you sweat and make all kinds of delicious manly sounds."

The things coming out of this woman's mouth, I swear. I rise to my feet, stalking toward her.

"Oy, that's not a plank," she admonishes as I prop my palms on the armrest, caging her in.

"What are you going to do about it?"

"Keep on like this, and you're not getting goodbye sex."

My chest constricts. Fuck, I don't want to say goodbye. I kiss her hard and deep. Can she feel how much I don't want to let her go? Does she want this between us to go on as badly as I do? What if this one-week fling was enough for her? And if it wasn't?

It wouldn't be fair to her to ask her to put up with all the drama surrounding me.

"Mmm. How can I resist you when you kiss me like that?" she asks when I pull back. She licks on a spoonful of ice cream, which gives me an idea. I dip a finger in it. Summer blinks up at me, watching my lips. But I don't bring it to my mouth.

"Open your legs, Summer."

She gasps a little, but immediately shifts in the armchair, opening up, even bunching her dress to give me access.

I bring my hand straight between her legs,

push her thong to one side, and drag my finger up and down her entrance.

"Alex! Whoa, that's cold."

"I'll warm you right up, baby."

I kneel before her, spreading her legs even wider. She clutches the box in her hand, looking down as if she can't believe what I'm doing. I bunch her dress tightly against her and pull her ass a little further down the seat so she has a perfect view. I lick her clean, teasing her until her legs shake. Then I pull back.

"What are you doing?"

"Planks."

"Alexander Westbrook, get back here," she warns.

I grin, folding my arms over my chest. "Are you going to put your own pleasure above the interest of women worldwide? Not very humanitarian."

Narrowing her eyes, she covers herself and tucks her legs underneath her again. "On my count."

Planks are my least favorite part of the workout, but they're effective as hell.

"And, you've just broken your record!" she announces after an eternity.

Explains why my arms feel like they're about to explode. I lie on the floor, breathing raggedly for a few moments before pushing myself up.

"You're the best trainer I've ever had."

"Well, you just tell your trainer to ramble incessantly while you hold the plank to distract you."

"Won't work. Only ramble I'm interested in is yours."

"Maybe you should keep me, then."

She sucks in a breath, then casts her gaze away from me, shoving a huge spoon of ice cream in her mouth. My throat goes dry as I mull over her words. My heart rate, which had just begun to slow down after the workout, picks up speed again.

***

Summer

Now I've done it. I couldn't just keep my mouth shut, eat my ice cream and pretend like the fact that we're going our separate ways tomorrow doesn't make my heart weigh one hundred pounds.

When he sits on his haunches in front of me, I add embarrassment to that dead weight. I stubbornly focus on detaching a frozen bit of ice cream from the carton.

"Summer, look at me."

His voice is so soft, I want to sink into this chair until I disappear. I don't want his pity or a gentle reminder that we'd agreed on… well, on some vacation fun, I guess. I know all that, I'm just having a bit more trouble accepting it than I initially thought.

"Summer, do you mean that?" he asks, his hand now on my head, angling my face up. Gathering my strength, I'm about to wave my words away, but then I see his expression.

His eyes are wide and searching, like he's hoping I'll say yes. Or am I just reading into this what I want? Taking a deep breath, I decide to own up to it, even though it feels a bit like peeling one of those protective layers I've put over my heart.

"Yeah. Yes." I bite the inside of my cheek, then add quickly, "But I know what our deal was, so—"

"That doesn't matter. Let me think for a minute."

He bites his lower lip, furrowing his brow. I swear I can hear his mind spinning. Meanwhile, my heart leaps into my throat.

He moves from his haunches onto his knees. "My contract with the studio ends in three months. One and a half months after the premiere. We wouldn't have to hide. Can you... would you be willing to wait for me?"

"Three months? Yeah, it's not so long."

It *is* a long time, and God knows what can happen during so many months, but I'm not ready to let this man go. We could work it out.

He slides his hand into my hair, his fingertips pressing on my scalp as he draws me nearer to the edge of the armchair. I lower my feet onto the floor, parting my legs so he fits in between.

"That's not fair to you. Asking you to wait," he murmurs. "And it's not fair to ask you to hide with me either."

"Alex, what do you want?"

"You! Any way I can have you."

My limbs feel lighter, as if an invisible weight pressing down on them has shifted.

"But even after the whole studio mess is over, my life always has a dose of crazy. That's Hollywood: insane filming hours, travel. The paps always make up stuff. I won't be able to protect you from all that, as much as I want to."

"You don't need to protect me, Alex. I'm not a damsel or a kid."

He kisses my palm, then moves my hand to his cheek. "In my early years in Hollywood, I had relationships with a few women who weren't in the industry. It overwhelmed them."

"And I've dated men who acted like I was disposable. Like they could walk all over my feelings. Everyone has a history. You know what they say about kissing frogs. I'm tough." I shrug, smiling, even though I feel like jumping up and down, screaming my happiness to the four corners until my throat is raw. "And I don't want this to end."

He pulls me into a kiss, hooking an arm around my waist, pulling me out of the armchair. I topple him over, until he's sitting on the floor, and I'm in his lap. We're laughing, and kissing, and I feel like the luckiest woman. He sweeps me onto my back on the thick, plush carpet, lounging over me, kissing me deeper. God, I have never been kissed like this, not even by him. It feels more intimate than making love.

"I want to kiss you for hours," he murmurs,

swiping his tongue over my lower lip. "Just kiss you. It's the first time I can do this without counting down the time we have left."

Emotion wires up my entire body as I bring my mouth to his. We kiss until we're both shaking, and then move to the bed. After sheathing himself, he slides inside me, moving slow and deep until I come apart so hard I see stars behind my eyelids.

Although the temptation to remain in this room, wrapped in our cocoon, is high, we head out to the goodbye bonfire. Alex and I do our best to act as if we're simply friends—which we've done the past week too—but I think if anyone looks closely, they'll see the barely disguised joy on our faces. We end up not sleeping at all, watching the sunrise and heading straight to breakfast.

Alex pulls me to one side once we're out of the breakfast hall. "Preston, my manager, will be here soon because we're flying together to New York."

Alex is flying around the country for the next two weeks for more prerelease promo for the superhero movie.

"I'd like for you to meet him," he continues.

"You're telling him?"

"It's best if he knows. He can help. It'll be easier to manage all this secrecy if he knows. But if you're not comfortable with that—"

"No, it's okay. If you think it'll make things easier, I'll meet Preston."

***

Preston nearly cries when Alex explains everything to him.

"You've got to be kidding." He looks between the two of us, as if hoping someone will jump up and say April Fool's. Slumping down on the armchair in Alex's room, he pulls at his mustache, which is dark brown with a few silver streaks, like his hair. His crisp suit wrinkles as he crosses his arms over his chest.

"No offense, Summer, you seem like a nice person, but, Alex, this is the worst time for you to be with someone. Have you got any idea what the tabloids would do with this info? How the fans would react? The studio?"

"I have a pretty good idea, yeah," Alex says dryly. He's leaning against the wall, in arm's reach from me. I chose to sit on the bed, but standing would have been better. Preston's reaction is unnerving me.

"The success of these two movies is hinging on the public opinion, which at the moment is against you. Do you know what two box office bombs would do to your career? You don't have the luxury to play hide and seek."

Alex's jaw ticks. "Pull yourself together, Preston. It was one panel gone wrong, you said so yourself."

Preston is sweating in earnest now. "The studio did some polls. Your popularity is at an all-time low. If the three interviews next week don't go better, we're neck deep in shit."

My stomach constricts, fear gripping me on Alex's behalf. I'm also dreading that he might change his mind about us.

No, just because other men walked all over my feelings doesn't mean Alex will. It's not fair to hold him to those low expectations. As if sensing my apprehension, Alex takes my hand to his lips and kisses it.

"We'll be careful," I promise. "And I do have experience with the press. They've been stalking my family for years."

Preston narrows his eyes. "Summer Bennett... any relation with Sebastian Bennett of Bennett Enterprises?"

"I'm his sister."

Preston nods. "Okay, if that's really what both of you want, I'll share with you the security protocols."

"Security protocols?" Wow. That's something my family has never needed, even at the height of the media's interest in us.

"How to go unseen when you're together and the press shows up, or if you want to visit him while he's on the promo tour, a few tactics about avoiding fans—"

"Let's take this one step at a time," Alex says coolly. "Don't scare my girl away."

It's my turn to reassure him now. I squeeze his hand, rolling my shoulders. "I'm not scared. Just surprised. I didn't realize you had protocols. Please, tell me everything I need to know."

Preston levels me with his gaze. "The most important thing is you can't tell anyone until the month after the premiere."

"This doesn't include my family, right?"

"Yes, it does," says Preston, at the same time Alex says, "No."

Standing up, I pace the room. "Look, I won't tell anyone else, but I can't keep this from my family. I'm too close to them."

"How big is your family?" Preston inquires.

"Depends if you count only those related by blood or those who married into my family too, but you're looking at double digits anyway."

He drops his head in his hands. "You two are going to kill me."

"I trust them with my life. They wouldn't tell anyone," I reassure him.

Preston sighs, straightening up in the armchair. "The more people know, the more chances of a slipup."

"Preston, move on. She's telling her family. No negotiating."

Preston checks his watch. "We don't have time for a full debrief on protocols. I'll set up a phone call with you, Summer. Alex and I need to board that plane. He'll give me your contact data."

"Okay, sure."

Preston stands to his feet, looking expectantly at Alex.

"You go ahead, Preston. Wait for me at the

reception."

"Don't be late. You've got ten minutes tops."

"I won't be late," Alex says.

"It was nice meeting you, Summer. Sorry about the circumstances."

"Don't worry, Preston. We'll take care of our superstar."

Smiling, he shakes my hand firmly, but his shoulders hunch as he leaves the room.

"So, did that go as expected?" I ask Alex.

He chuckles. "More or less. He'll get used to it."

I lean my back against the wall, my fingers tapping the cool surface. "But—"

"I don't want to talk about Preston."

He brings both his hands to my face, his thumbs pressing the corners of my mouth.

"I'll miss you," he says.

"Maybe I'll miss you too."

"Maybe, huh?" He tugs my lower lip between his teeth, and a sharp impulse lights a fuse inside me. When he licks where he bit before, I fist his shirt.

"Maybe I need a reminder of what I should miss," I say breathlessly.

He pulls me into a kiss so hot, I barely fight the urge to dry hump him. With a groan, Alex pulls away, looking between us. Whoops, I've been pressing my hips against him. *Completely* unintentional, of course.

"Woman, do you want to drive me insane?"

"Hey, if I were naughty, I'd make you late for

that flight. I'm being very selfless right now."

He pinches my ass. "When I return to San Francisco, we'll work on that definition of selfless."

I grin, shuddering for effect. "I can't wait for the lessons, Master. Can I pick my rewards?"

"The way you're going, you're more likely to earn punishments. I promise you'll love them." He doesn't take his eyes off me, and sweet bejesus. Hot gaze and sinful words are an explosive combo.

"I think you're all talk and no play, Westbrook," I say coyly, touching his bicep languidly, so he knows I mean business. In response, he grips my hand, kissing the pads of my fingers. For anyone watching, this could seem like a sweet gesture. Except that he works in a flick of tongue.

"I'm not about playing at all. I'm all about winning. Anyway that ends up with you begging for me to be inside you is a win in my book."

Boom! That explosive combo did the job thoroughly. I'm so turned on I want to climb him. But I'm not *completely* selfish. I know he has a plane to catch.

"Don't be late for meeting Preston. I'll miss you, Alex. Good luck with the interviews. I'll keep my fingers crossed."

"Thanks. And tell me if Preston bugs you too much, or if you want to talk about the protocols. They're not as scary as they seem."

"It takes a lot to scare me, Alex. Don't worry."

He gives me one last kiss, more of a chaste

peck on the lips before leaving the room. Sighing, I run my hands up and down my arms, already feeling cold where he touched me before.

Chapter Nineteen

Summer

"And starting with this painting, we enter a new phase in Monet's career."

I glance around at the group of ten, trying to gauge if everyone's still with me. The audience is always a mixed bag. Some are at the gallery because they genuinely like art, some because their friends or significant others dragged them here. Others simply want to check off attractions on their lists.

As I lead the group through the remaining paintings, I pepper my explanations with random trivia from Monet's life, even add a few questionable but fun rumors, which earn me chuckles. It's the best way to entertain even the visitors who aren't art enthusiasts. We get a lot of tourists in July.

After the tour ends, I head straight to the small kitchen at the back, smoothing my hands down my skirt. God, I missed my high heels and pencil skirts and shirts. I feel like I have more purpose when I dress up.

I prepare myself a coffee at our Nespresso machine. After having slept in until eight for the past couple of weeks, waking up at six these last three days has been brutal. I also miss waking up with

Alex's arms around me. How can I miss him so much? Well... he does have the sexiest, strongest arms. Missing him is totally appropriate. And I'll see him in two weeks. *Oh boy*! I'm already showing signs of Alex-withdrawals.

"Summer, you're free. Good," Olivia says, stepping inside the small kitchen. "How did it go with Rupert Felton?"

"We're golden. He agreed to lend us the collection for two weeks."

Rupert Felton is eighty going on one hundred and could pass off as the Grinch. I met him while working in Rome, which is why Olivia asked me to reach out to him.

"I don't know how you do it." Olivia nods, picking a feather from her black sweater dress. I'm jealous of the dark green glossy belt at her waist and the matching shoes.

"Rupert isn't as grumpy as he seems. Especially when I treat him to the best steak with Gorgonzola sauce San Francisco has to offer."

She cocks a brow. Ha! I don't like that judgy look. Some would call my tactics underhanded. Unorthodox is a better word. Much more elegant. A convincing sales pitch takes people skills, which I have in spades. You cannot grow up with eight siblings and not have people skills.

"You're not planning any more extended leaves, I hope?"

"I had a lot of accrued time, Olivia. Still have some left."

In times like this, I can understand my siblings' desire to own their businesses. She purses her lips but doesn't add anything else as my colleague Diana joins us.

"Oh, coffee, how I need you," Diana says, hurrying to the Nespresso machine. Olivia backs out of the kitchen.

"Thank God you're back," Diana whispers, even though we're alone. "She was super cranky while you were gone. By the way, a reporter called earlier, asking for you."

"Oh?"

"She was asking if you and Alex Westbrook are close. She said something about you both being donors at an orphanage. I told her I know nothing about that."

I freeze in the act of placing my empty coffee cup in the dishwasher. "Right. Thanks for telling me."

She nudges me with her hip. "Anything you wanna share, Summer?"

Diana is very dear to me, but she's a terrible gossip. Plus, I agreed to only share this with my family.

"Nope, absolutely nothing. But I do need to go. I need to send some e-mails before my next tour."

I rush to my small office, pull up St. Anne's website and navigate to the donors' page. Crap, both Alex and I are on it, even though I explicitly asked for neither of us to be listed. *God damn, damn, damn it.*

I call Shawna right away. The words tumble out so fast from my mouth when she answers, I'll be surprised if she understood any of it.

"Oh, I'm so sorry, Summer. My assistant just updated the list of donors. I think she just checked the incoming funds without looking over the list of people who want to remain anonymous. I'll remove it right away. In fact, wait a second, I'll do it right now."

I bite my nails while I wait, wondering how many people have seen it already, and if that reporter will dig deeper.

"It's done. You're both removed. I'm really sorry about this," Shawna says.

"Thanks for doing this so fast," I reply, trying to keep my tone even, even though anger simmers inside me. It was a mistake, I know. But we can't afford any mistakes.

After clicking off, I still can't get the reporter out of my mind. If she does dig deeper, what will she find? We'd been careful at Lake Tahoe. We haven't kissed in public. The most she can find is that we've been there at the same time. But so was the entire staff of St. Anne's and the Spanish teachers.

Taking a few deep breaths, I tell myself I have no reason to panic. I also shoot Preston an e-mail, informing him about it. Letting him know about any contact with the media is part of the security protocols. He talked to me at length about them, then e-mailed me files upon files. I'm not sure how I'll remember everything, but I'll do my best.

Ugh, this day took a nosedive, and it's not even lunchtime. The silver lining? The spa evening at Sebastian's house with my sisters and Ava. Some girl time is just what the doctor ordered.

***

"I can't win against the three of you," Ava exclaims that evening, waving her hands around so the red acrylic on her fingernails dries faster. We've pooled all our beauty resources on the floor of her expansive living room, and we're so stocked up, we could open our own beauty store. We're sprawled on the L-shaped couch, Pippa in the corner, Alice at one end, Ava and me at the other.

I grin. "We know."

"But our nagging is in your best interest," Pippa informs her solemnly, even though it's hard to take her seriously when she has a mask the color of chocolate on her face. "Look, I'm a mom too, and I know how hard it is to balance work and family. Having someone helping you doesn't mean you kick ass any less, it means you'll have time to breathe."

Ava pouts. "You make too much sense. I can't believe Sebastian. Tossing me to the sharks like this. Fine, I promise I will seriously consider hiring a permanent nanny."

Alice pumps her fist in the air, perfectly summing up how I feel. Then she rubs her hands and points both forefingers at me. "Now, Summer, I believe you have something to share with us?"

I swear to God, everything just spills out of me. I only stop when my throat is dry and Pippa's mask start to peel off.

"Wow!" Pippa exclaims.

"But the secret part might be tricky," Alice says reasonably.

Ava, who just found out I knew Alex at all, looks at me open-mouthed. "He's too famous for that."

I shoot daggers with my eyes at them. "Don't ruin my buzz with practicality. I love living in my bubble. It's comfy. I can't believe I have to wait so long to see him. He'll be here in two Saturdays."

Alice tucks her legs under her, propping her elbow on the backrest. "Oh, that's the day Mom and Dad invited us to their pizza party. Are you bringing him?"

"I didn't ask him yet. But I plan to." My stomach clenches. It's been a while since I introduced anyone to my family. Mostly because whenever I brought that up, it resulted in my date running for the hills.

Alice grins. "I promise we won't be too obvious when we check out if he's as hot in real life. And we'll keep our brothers on a tight leash, so they don't grill him... too much."

Pippa bursts out laughing. "Alice, you're overestimating us. When have we been able to keep our brothers from going into alpha overprotective mode?"

Alice inspects her freshly polished nails in

response.

"I thought so," Pippa says. "Damn, this mask smells so much like chocolate that I'm hungry."

Ava rubs her stomach. "Anyone up for raiding my kitchen?"

"Nope, I try not to eat after 9:00 p.m.," I say seriously, though my mouth already waters, because Ava's fridge is always stocked up with goodies.

My eldest sister bats her eyelashes. "She has apple strudel with vanilla sauce."

Alice springs to her feet, already heading to the kitchen.

"Sold," I say wistfully. Who am I to say no to that, really? Besides, some vanilla courage might be just what I need to ask Alex about meeting my family when I talk to him in two hours.

"Oh, I've got whipped cream too," Ava announces.

"Now you're just actively sabotaging my healthy-eating plan," I admonish.

She shakes her head. "Everything we eat during girls' night doesn't matter."

Alice chuckles. "How did you figure that out?"

"Gossiping burns *a lot* of calories," Ava says seriously. Both my sisters laugh, but Ava's mention of gossip brings front and center thoughts of that reporter.

Chapter Twenty

Alex

I love photo shoots. Not because I enjoy having my photo taken, but because it doesn't require talking, answering questions… or fielding them.

"That's a wrap." The photographer holds her thumb and forefinger in a circle, smiling.

"Thanks, Rebecca."

"Always a pleasure working with you. You've killed it, Westbrook. I swear you look hotter every year. Readers will eat this up. Wanna go out for a drink?"

"No can do. Still have to get to a radio interview. Evening slot."

I scratch my jaw because they wanted a one-day beard for the shoot and my skin is itchy as hell.

"How long are you in town?" She plays with her hair, looking me up and down. She's been hitting on me ever since I arrived. We've known each other for years, but this is the first time she's come on to me.

"I've got every minute planned."

The guys in charge of lighting start dismantling the equipment, and we move out of the way.

"You seeing someone new?" she asks.

"No." The lie feels bitter on my tongue. For someone who slips into other people's skins for a living, this should come easy. But I don't like playing pretend in my real life. "But I'm laying low for a while."

"Your loss, big boy. D'you need a ride to the radio station?"

"Thanks, but my manager already arranged for one. Do you know where they put my jacket?"

"I'll bring it for you." With a wink, she takes off in the direction of the changing rooms.

The studio is a blur of activity even this late in the evening. They have four adjacent sets, and the other three are still in action, the hair and makeup team running between them for retouching. The air is thick with the smell of hairspray and nail polish. The constant buzz of voices is wearing me down.

Rebecca returns holding my jacket.

"Here you go, mister. And if you change your mind, let me know." When I don't answer, she adds, "Good luck with the interview."

After bidding goodbye to everyone on set who doesn't have their hands full, I step outside. My car, a black sedan, is already waiting in the front, but I don't climb in yet. I fill my lungs with fresh air. Well, fresh is relative considering the constant stream of cars, but it's better than the stale air inside. And I much prefer the air in Chicago in July than in New York. I flew in yesterday from New York, and the humidity was insane.

I step out of the way of a hurried teenager, who has his earbuds on and his eyes on the screen of his phone. That's a disaster waiting to happen. I barely form the thought when the guy veers left into a side street… and walks right into a water hydrant. Ouch.

Stifling my laughter, I climb inside the car. I take out my phone, and almost call Summer to tell her about the water hydrant incident before I remember she's with her sisters.

As a general rule of thumb, I dislike interviews, but radio interviews are the lesser of all evils. At least I don't have to work on my facial expression or body language. The host tonight, Jimmy Hendricks, is a laid-back guy. Whenever I'm here in Chicago, even if we don't have interviews planned, I go out with him for drinks. He's a major fan of the superhero franchise.

As such, he keeps the questions mostly character-related, which is a relief. I can talk about my character—motivations, hidden wishes, and aspirations etcetera—for hours. I put a lot of thought into my acting, trying to delve deeper than what the script offers.

Roles based on books are easier, because there's a lot of information to sink my teeth in, but I also love a challenge when it comes to bringing a character to life.

"Ladies and gentlemen, my job here is done," Jimmy says after an hour. "The floor belongs to you now. If you have questions for our superhero, just call us."

To me, he whispers, "We've got our first caller."

I nod, and he presses a button on his dashboard.

"Hello, Veronica. What's your question for Alex?"

"Hi, Alex! I'm a huge fan. I was wondering if you plan to do more of the Bree Shannon series?"

I clear my throat, not liking that the focus has shifted from the superhero series already. "There are no plans for a third movie, no. After you see the second one, you'll understand why. We've wrapped it up nicely, but I can't say more. Don't want to spoil anything."

"Thank you. But—"

"Just one question per listener, sorry, Veronica," Jimmy says apologetically before the line goes static. "Another caller," he says, and I nod.

"And, we have Mike next. Mike, what's your question for our superhero?" He winks at me, as if reassuring me he knows this is a promotional tour for the superhero series, not the romantic comedies. But we both know the listeners ask whatever they want to.

"Hi, Alex! My question to you is, did you ever break something while doing one of your stunts?"

I sit up straighter, lowering into the mic. "Twice. Once it was just my thumb, no problem, but another time it was a rib. That set back production by a week, and hurt like hell."

"Thanks. And I know it's just one question, but my wife will not let me sleep in our bed tonight if I don't ask her question too."

"We don't want you kicked out of bed, Mike. Go ahead," I say.

"She wants to know if the rumors you're dating someone new are true. And for the record, I'd never ask you that. She's making me."

I drink some more of the tea, silently cursing. Third question and we're already in private life territory.

"Not true at all, Mike. Just rumors."

"Thanks, man!"

After the line goes dead, Jimmy speaks into the mic.

"Folks, keep the questions related to his movies. What a man does in his free time isn't relevant."

But his warning has the exact opposite effect, and things get out of control over the next five phone calls.

We close the line to the public after someone calls just to say, "You're being paid big bucks to be an example for everyone. Can you honestly say you deserve all the fame if you're another Hollywood womanizing bastard?"

Jimmy rubs his hands over his face. "I'm sorry, man. I don't know what's gotten into them."

"Yeah, that's starting to become a pattern," I deadpan. I did two more panels with the superhero troupe this week, and they didn't go better than the first one.

"When they turn on you, they turn on you. Just give them no evidence to actually hold against you, and they'll get over it… eventually."

I politely thank him for the advice, then can't get out fast enough. I jump in the sedan again and cross the city to the hotel.

The second I enter my room, Preston calls me. I've been avoiding him, because he's been repeating things ad nauseum. How dating Summer right now is too risky, too whatever. He's been even more relentless ever since Summer told him about that reporter sniffing around.

"Hi, Preston," I say.

"Hey, listen up, I have a new script for you. A period drama. Filming wouldn't take long, and you could squeeze it in before the spin-off starts filming. Assuming we do get that greenlighted, of course."

"Send it over. A period drama would be an interesting change."

There's nothing like the rush of reading a script the first time, getting to know the character, and then figuring out the best way to bring it to life, to do it justice. This is why I do this, what the dream is all about for me.

"Great. I discussed some of the protocols with Summer today. She's surprisingly knowledgeable about reporters. I'm assuming all those years the press harassed the Bennett family served as exercise. But—"

"Preston, stop beating a dead horse. I know the timing isn't good, but this will blow over. Summer is important to me. I want to know if you're on my side on this."

"You know I am."

"Okay, good. Then make sure my girl is as comfortable as possible."

We talk about the script for a few minutes longer, and the second I finish the call, I dial Summer's number, a pleasant warmth coursing through me in anticipation of hearing her voice.

"Hello! Summer Bennett's phone. Who is this?" a male voice asks. I stop in the act of pouring myself a glass of water, the warmth from before turning to ice.

This can't be what I think. She wouldn't... would she? It's 11:00 p.m. in San Francisco. What male friend is she seeing this late? She said she was meeting her sisters....

"Who am I talking to?" I croak.

"Oh, give that here, you jerk, or I'm officially kicking you out of my favorite brothers' list," Summer's voice sounds somewhere in the background. Her brother. Just her brother.

"Hey, sorry for that," she says sweetly. "My brother Logan came to bring my sister some papers and then drove me home. Hang on, I'm entering my house now."

I lean against the railing of the small bar area, basking in the feeling of relief, and hating that I was so quick to be suspicious.

"Yeah, I'm in. Sorry, again. My brother saw my phone light up and decided to prank me."

"Why would he do that?"

"Possibly because I have a photo with a heart instead of a photo with you."

A heart. Only Summer would do that.

I chuckle. "Next to my name?"

"Well, see… I thought putting your name in might be a bad idea. What if it falls into the wrong hands? So, I just put a nickname."

Something in her voice alerts me that she doesn't want me to press the issue further, which is exactly what I do.

"What's the nickname?"

"Sexy Super Lover."

I burst out laughing, gripping the water bottle so tight that, if it were plastic, it would crumple.

"Summer, you make me laugh more than anyone else."

"I'll never hear the end of this, will I?"

"Not a chance." I walk over to the bed, kick off my shoes, and climb onto the mattress. "I can't wait until next Saturday."

"Me too. God, I wish I could see you sooner."

"I'll make love to you the entire day."

"About Saturday… I want to spend the day with you, but there's a family gathering at my parents' house, and I don't want to miss that. Would you mind coming too?"

"Sure. I want to meet them."

"Really?"

"Yeah. Do I need to wear a helmet? Your brother sounded pretty intense. Will I have any other fans except Daniel?"

"Full disclosure: not sure if Daniel will be your fan anymore once he knows we're dating. You might need full body armor, but I'll give you all the details on Saturday." She says this very fast, as if wanting to rip off the Band-Aid.

"We'll figure it out. Why are you so nervous?" I punch two cushions against the headboard so I can lean with my back comfortably.

"Just... thanks for saying yes."

I wish I could see her face right now, because my Summer is vulnerable, and I don't know how to soothe her over the phone.

"Did Preston tell you about the incident with the reporter?" she continues.

"Yes. And I don't want you to fret about it. Sniffing around is nothing new. They always do that."

"Oh, okay."

Fuck, I don't like the sound of that *okay*. Feels more as if she means, *"Really? That's screwed up."* Which it is, of course. I just got used to it because it's business as usual in Hollywood. I wonder, again, if pulling her into this kind of madness is the right thing to do. Yet, I don't want to imagine a day where I won't have phone calls from Summer to look forward to.

"Ooooh, I forgot to tell you. We have a large

group of tourists coming in tomorrow, and they requested to see some of my old paintings. They *specifically* asked for them."

"I thought you just painted for friends and family."

"Yes, now, but I have a gazillion from when I used to paint daily. They're spread between different galleries, but I managed to call in some favors and have a few sent here.

"I'm so proud of you, babe. Can you show me when I'm in town?"

"They're only here this week. I need to send them back to the gallery where they belong."

"Pity. How was the evening with the girls?"

"Better than an actual spa trip. I even used one of those fancy body scrubs that taste like fruit. I'm so lickable right now."

"You're always lickable."

"Alex, Alex! No need to charm the pants off me. I'm naked."

The thought that she's been taking off her clothes while talking to me drives me insane.

"I've been thinking… we should talk in the mornings too. I bet *that* will make your days much better. I tend to bring good luck, you know. Especially if I throw in some dirty talk."

Her voice all chirpy and unaffected, while my dick is straining in my pants.

"Ah, you're doing this on humanitarian grounds again? Sacrificing yourself, are you?"

"Of course. All in the name of bringing you

good luck. Do you want a sample of the dirty talk?"

"Are you sure you want to go down that road?" I ask.

"Uhh… that sounded scary. *Not*. Yes, yes… I do want to. I want to discover what's at the end of that road."

I don't miss a beat. "Happy ending. For both of us."

"Right…."

"Woman, are you doubting me?"

"Well, we've been talking every night, and so far, I got zilch in the dirty talk department. You'll forgive me for thinking you might not have any game on the phone?"

"I'll do better than forgiving you. I'll prove to you I've got game."

I laugh out loud at the silly sound she makes. This woman is everything, I swear. No matter how shitty the day goes, talking to her turns everything around. I'm so deep into this, I can barely believe it. What if this is all just some good fun for her? I push that thought away. She wants me to meet her family. Surely that's a sign that she's at least half as deep into this as I am.

Chapter Twenty-One

Summer

The next day starts with an unpleasant surprise. When I walk into the gallery, Diana points to a blonde at the far end of the room, inspecting a Monet.

"She's the reporter who called yesterday. Wants to talk to you," Diana whispers to me. My insides clench as Preston's list of protocols flashes in my mind. Steeling myself, I walk right over to her. I've got this. I'm not afraid of a reporter. I just have a deep dislike of them. They've been bugging my family forever. They started when Bennett Enterprises rose to fame, and even now they're digging for dirt every chance they have.

"Everyone's favorite," I say, stopping right next to her. Extending my hand, I add, "Summer Bennett. My colleague said you wish to speak with me."

She flashes me a botoxed smile, shaking my hand. "Tara Delaware. Nice to meet you. Sorry for barging in like this…."

I wave my hand as if dismissing her worry. "Nonsense. My colleague said you asked about St. Anne's yesterday. I've been hoping to get some publicity for the orphanage for a long time. You want to come up to my office? I can tell you more about what we do there."

The corners of her duck lips tug downward. Golden rules where reporters are concerned: throw them off their game. Overwhelm them with topics they don't care about, drown them with meaningless details.

"I've seen that Alex Westbrook donated there recently—" she begins.

"Ah, yes. That slipped out, I'm afraid. He wishes to remain anonymous. Pity, I'm sure his name would have brought more donations. So, what are you thinking about? Featured article?"

"Not sure the big bosses think it would have enough appeal for a featured article."

I can read through the lines. Of course, no one gives a damn about group homes or donations. She's fishing for a juicier story.

"How long have you known Alex Westbrook?" she asks.

I fake having to think about it, run a hand through my hair and frown, even though I know the exact date and time when I met him. "No idea, a few weeks, maybe? Saying I know him is pushing it, though. He donated, I donated. That's about it."

Tara doesn't believe me. Her mocking expression sends chills up my veins. I want to toss her out the gallery, tell her never to step inside it again, but I know the one way to ensure reporters harass you is to antagonize them. Boring them to tears is the best solution.

"I have time for a coffee until my first tour starts," I tell her. "Come up, I'll give you all the details about St. Anne's. How many kids there are, what they do with the donors' fund, and so on."

"No time today," she says quickly. "I just wanted to touch base."

Riiiight, that's why she made the trip here.

"Well, you let me know when you have some time," I insist. "And talk to your bosses about that feature. We really do need more publicity."

Her gaze darts to the door. *Perfect.*

"Sure, I'll… I'll let you know."

"It was nice meeting you, Tara."

We shake hands again, and I only become aware of how tight my body has been strung by tension when she steps out of the venue. I managed to throw her off… for now.

***

"Bring them in here. There's just enough space for all of them to fit in."

The delivery boys poke their heads inside the storage room, taking a look around.

"Right away, ma'am."

Overlooking the delivery of a new collection isn't my favorite thing to do on a Friday evening, but sometimes you've got to do what you've got to do. The storage room is behind a sliding panel, so it's not completely separated from the main display room on the ground floor. I pace the space, watching the guys bring in the first two paintings. I cringe, because they're each carrying one, and the paintings are too large for one person to securely carry them. Once they set them down, I say, "Please carry each painting between the two of you, even if it takes longer."

"Ma'am, we do this every day. We can each carry one with no problem."

Straightening up, I roll my shoulders. "I'm not risking an accident. Those are expensive paintings."

They roll their eyes but head outside without another comment. A buzzing sound coming from the other end of the room startles me. Oh, my phone.

I briskly walk over to my bag, which I've left at the closed welcome counter near the main entrance. Pulling out my phone, I fully expect to find a message from my boss. Wrong. It's from Alex, aka Super Sexy Lover.

Alex: Bossy looks hot on you.

I reread the text a few times. Wait, what?

Summer: Are you... at the gallery?

My heart begins to race while I wait for his answer. When he'd asked me earlier about my plans this evening, I thought he was just curious. Way to underestimate him.

Alex: Yes. Undo the top button of your shirt.

Holy Pop-Tarts. My mouth goes dry, my palms sweaty.

He must be upstairs. The gallery has an open floor plan. The ground floor opens up to the second level, except for a narrow corridor with an iron railing serving as a pathway between our offices.

I can't see much, because I turned off the lights upstairs. But if Alex's there, he's got a direct view of what's going on down here.

Summer: Where are you? You won't see anything if I undo the top button.

I'm wearing a high-collar blouse, which I tucked into my pencil skirt. I'd have to undo about three buttons before there's even a hint of a cleavage.

Alex: I know. But knowing you do what I say turns me on.

It turns me on too. I undo the top button just as the guys step inside with the second painting.

Alex: Good girl.

Thank heavens for the dim lighting, because my cheeks are burning. The burn spreads through my entire body when the next message arrives.

Alex: Take off your panties when you're alone and put them in your bag.

I look up again, but damn it I can't see anything. My heart's hammering now. I step behind the reception desk, waiting for the delivery guys to head back outside. Once I'm alone, I climb off my heels and reach under my skirt, pushing down first my pantyhose, then my thong. A shiver of awareness runs through me as I bunch them in my hand, stealthily hiding them in my bag. I swear my center pulses when my phone buzzes with an incoming message.

Alex: Which one's your office?

Summer: Third door from the top of the staircase.

Alex: I'll wait for you inside. Get rid of the guys as fast as you can.

I hold my breath as I listen to what's happening upstairs. When the unmistakable sound of a door opening and closing reaches me, I become slick between my legs. What is this man doing to me?

The next fifteen minutes are excruciating. The second the guys leave, I lock the back door and skid right upstairs, barging into my office.

"Alex?" I whisper after closing the door. It's dark, except for a patch of moonlight on my desk. Alex steps up from the darkest corner, smiling. I run right into his arms.

"What are you doing here? You were supposed to arrive next week."

"I missed you. I moved a few things around so I can spend the weekend with you."

He kisses me long and deep, making my toes curl.

"This is so romantic," I whisper. "And reckless. You shouldn't be here. I received an entire list with instructions from Preston, and he wouldn't approve. This is risky."

He covers my mouth again, whispering between kisses, "You're worth every risk. I needed to see you."

His lips trail down my neck, his fingers working furiously on the buttons of my shirt, until he yanks it away, leaving me in my bra. He will have me here. In my office. Lord help me, but I want this so badly, I'm barely holding back from jumping him. Taking my hand, he leads me to my desk.

"How did you get in here?"

"Sneaked in when you were with the delivery guys out at the truck."

"You could've just told me, you know."

"I wanted to surprise you, tease you a bit." He reaches under my skirt, bunching it up until his fingers touch the bare skin between my legs. I'm slick and his finger slides inside me with so much ease, I'm almost embarrassed.

"Get rid of your clothes, Summer. I want you completely naked."

A nervous laughter bubbles up my throat, but it turns into a moan as he slides in another finger, pressing the heel of his palm against my clit.

"I've never done anything like this in my office," I confess, yanking my shirt over my head, unclasping my bra. When it falls to the floor, Alex pulls his hand out, motioning to the chair behind my desk.

"Sit there."

I'm so turned on, I don't hesitate even for a split second. Specks of moonlight fall on my chair, and on me as I sit down, the black leather chilling me.

"Spread your legs for me, Summer."

As soon as I do, he kneels between them, licking up my left inner thigh, then my right one.

"Whenever you sit in this chair, I want you to

remember this." He licks further up on my inner thigh until he's at the apex, teasing my clit with the tip of his tongue. My hips slide further down of their own accord. I spread myself wider, shamelessly, crying out when he sucks my bundle of nerves between his lips.

"Oh, Alex."

"That's my girl. I have a condom in my back pocket," Alex whispers, kissing up my belly and my breasts until he reaches my mouth. I kiss him back with all I've got, my inner muscles clenching when he places an unopened condom on my thigh.

I work on his pants and underwear until his erection springs free. With trembling fingers, I rip the foil, sheathing him.

I feel his hands slip under my ass, lifting me up. Instinctively, I wrap my legs around his middle, my arms around his neck. His erection presses against the length of my seam. Alex walks with me until my back reaches a wall.

"You feel so good," he whispers as he lowers me onto him, stretching me until I think I might come just from the sensation of being so full. Pinning my ass against the wall, he slides in and out. This angle is killing me. His tip rubs a soft spot inside me, coaxing pleasure from deep within. There's just enough light in this corner to make out his features, but the semidarkness makes this all so much more intense. All my senses are wrapped up in him, and I love taking it all in: his hot breath sets my skin ablaze, his grunts and the sound of our bodies slapping against each other fill the room. Waves of pleasure string my nerve endings together, until I'm pulsing on his every thrust, squeezing him tightly when he cries out his release. Still holding me to the wall, one hand under my ass, he pinches one nipple with his other hand, then lowers it between us, dragging his thumb over my clit.

Pinching my eyes shut, I lean my forehead against his jaw. I brace my palms on his shoulders and press my heels against his ass. As if sensing my insecurity, he whispers, "Let go, baby. I'm holding you safe. Let go."

A shock of pleasure ripples from the base of my spine, making my entire back arch, and one of my legs go rigid.

Alex holds me close while I ride my climax, and even after, kissing me softly, as if feeling how much I need this sweetness and tenderness.

"Baby, I want to hold you longer, but I have to take care of the condom."

"Oh right! I completely forgot."

We clean ourselves up quickly with some wet wipes I keep in a drawer and then dress quickly.

"I can't believe this evening," I murmur after we're both dressed, watching his boyish grin.

"It's not over yet. I'm taking you on a date."

"Oh? But Preston—"

"We can play by the rules, and I can still take you on a date. Trust me."

"Let's go then."

"Wait, I need to take my jacket. I forgot

where I put it. Do you see it anywhere? It's black leather."

"Nah, too dark. Wait a second." I switch on the light and immediately spot the jacket on the floor right next to the door. As I pick it up, a crumpled piece of paper falls from one pocket, tumbling on the carpet.

Without thinking, I reach for it, freezing as I realize a phone number is scribbled on it, and a text. *Call me, handsome. I'll warm up your bed - R.*

"What's that?" Alex asks, shrugging into his jacket. His happy expression morphs into one of concern as he scans me. "Summer?"

"You'd tell me if you change your mind about us being a couple, right?" My voice shakes.

"What? Of course I haven't changed my mind."

I hold out the paper, trying to control the tremble in my hand. "Who... who is R?"

Alex casts his glance to the note, then takes it out of my hands.

"Summer, I have no idea why this was in my jacket. I don't know who..." He sighs. "Yeah, I do know. At least I think so. Rebecca, the photographer I had a session with on Thursday. She must have snuck it in when she brought me the jacket at the end of the shoot. I didn't call her. I didn't even know the number was there, but even if I did, I wouldn't have used it. You know that, right?"

Rooted to the spot, I fumble with my thumbs. "Why... why would she give you her number?"

He hesitates for a few seconds before answering. "She tried to flirt, but I didn't encourage it at all."

For some reason, my chest clenches, constricting my breath.

"If you want, we can call that number right now together, and you can ask her yourself."

"We don't have to do that. I believe you."

But my chest continues to clench, my throat closing up. What is wrong with me? I feel a freak-out coming on, and I'd like to at least know why I'm freaking out.

"Don't do that," Alex says, voice harsher than before. "Don't shut me out. I want to know. I don't want us to play games. If something bothers you, tell me. We'll talk it out."

I swipe my suddenly sweaty palms on my skirt. "I'm not shutting you out. I'm just… I'm freaking out, and I don't like being watched when I'm at it."

He frowns, his eyes searching my face. "Why are you freaking out?"

Cupping both my cheeks in his big, strong hands, he rubs little circles with his thumbs on my cheeks, and some of the tension melts away from my body.

"I think this is the first time I actually realize how many women want you." Wow. Wow. I'm slipping into full meltdown mode, and I don't know how to stop it. How can I not have realized this before? He's an international star and has more

Sexiest Man titles under his belt than I can count. "This happens a lot, doesn't it?"

"I'm not gonna lie, it does. But I usually throw out the notes right away. I just didn't see this one. For the record, I only called back a few times when I first started out. I haven't done that in years, and I don't plan to."

He draws me closer to him, tipping my head up, lowering one hand over my left boob. A split second later, I realize his intention isn't to fondle my boob but to feel the rhythm of my heart.

"I don't want your heart racing unless it's with happiness. Talk to me. What are you afraid of?"

I bite at the inside of my lower lip, feeling small and foolish as I admit, "That you'll feel lonely or bored at some point when you're away and give in to temptation."

"The same thing applies to you. When I'm away filming, you could get bored, want someone to warm your bed."

"No, no, I won't. My libido is on high alert only around you," I joke, but raw vulnerability shines in his eyes.

"Summer, whatever happens between us, promise you'll be upfront and honest about it."

"I promise."

"Then can you believe that I promise you the same?" Kissing my forehead, he pulls me into his arms, and I lose myself in his warmth and all that hard muscle. Believing someone's promise is more complicated than gifting them with yours, because when you chose to believe someone, you give them power over you. But cocooned like this, wrapped in Alex, I know we're kindred spirits—we don't make empty promises.

"Yes, I do, Alex. I do."

Tipping my head up, he kisses me, and I melt against him. God, I'm so happy he's back. My chest fills with little bubbles of joy as realization seeps in that he flew in just to spend time with me.

"Let's go, beautiful," he murmurs against my lips. "Our night is just starting."

"Umm… I'm quaking in my boots. Well, my peep-toes."

"Very well. You should."

"Was that a threat or a promise?" I should perhaps wait with the teasing until we're out of here, but I can't help myself. He has the most delicious replies, and each and every one of them either makes my toes curl or my lady parts tingle—sometimes both.

How he does it, no clue, but instead of studying the phenomenon, I intend to enjoy it. It's a much better use of my time.

He smiles. "I'll leave you guessing for now. One hint: you'll enjoy it either way."

Yup, everything is tingling: toes *and* lady parts.

When he takes my hand, leading me out of the room, a current of awareness sizzles through me. I don't think he means to, but he strips more and more of my defenses every time we're together. And the scary part? I want to let him. More than that, I want to do the same to this delicious man.

Chapter Twenty-Two

Alex

"Wait a second. I want to see your paintings before we leave," I tell her once we're on the ground floor. "They're still here, right?"

Her eyes widen. "Yes. You really want to see them? You don't have to humor me."

"I do want to see them. That's why I came directly to the gallery."

Taking my hand, she leads me to a separate room on the ground floor, smaller than the one in the front. She doesn't switch on the main lighting system, just the installations projecting above every individual painting.

"These are mine. I sold two to the group today."

I follow her gaze to the right wall. She paints nature, and she's amazing at it. They look real. I can almost feel myself standing on top of the mountain, on a field in Tuscany, out on the sea, in a rainforest. Her paintings have a lot of heart. Just like her. I wrap my arms around her from the back, kissing her neck, keeping my eyes on the wall.

"They're beautiful. Is the one with the

mountain still for sale?"

"Yeah, but—"

"I want to buy it."

"Alex, don't be silly. I'll gift it to you."

"But I want to buy it."

"You really want that hanging in your house?"

"I do. It's perfect."

"Okay. I'll pack it for you."

"Are we leaving with my car?" she asks after we step out in the cool evening air a few minutes later. "Or did you bring yours?"

"We'll take yours. One of my security guys dropped me off here."

She stares at me. "You have bodyguards?"

"Not always. But I thought it would be smart to have him secure the area before I showed my face around here after that reporter showed up."

She scrunches her face, nodding. "Smart thinking. My car's just around the corner."

I'm so proud of her for the way she dealt with that situation. I wish she didn't have to. The list of things I wish she didn't have to deal with keeps growing.

I also can't believe Rebecca. But I'll be damned if I ever let something like this happen again. That look on Summer's face, that crushing fear? I don't want to ever see it again. She doesn't deserve that. I'd realized something bad had happened the second she lunged for the note, because her whole body had gone rigid, and all my instincts were to crush whatever had caused that reaction. Turns out that was me. If need be, I'll double check my own pockets.

"Where are we going?" she asks once we're inside the car.

"First, we're going to make a pit stop by your house."

"Why?"

"You're going to need a change of clothes."

"For our date?"

"Nope, for tomorrow morning."

She folds her arms over her chest, cocking a brow. "Mr. Westbrook, don't you think you're assuming a bit much? What makes you think I'll spend the night with you?"

Closing the distance between us, I bring my lips a whisper away from hers. "I can still smell you on me, Summer."

"It's not polite to mention that."

"*That*'s a sensitive topic?"

"You're awfully infuriating right now."

"And you're awfully cute when you find me infuriating, so you'll forgive me if I do it on purpose."

But then it occurs to me that I might be assuming too much. We spent every free minute together in Lake Tahoe, but we were in vacation mode back there. I made plans without consulting her, just assuming she'd be over the moon with the idea of spending the weekend with me. What if we're not on the same page here? Am I rushing things?

After the engagement fiasco, I thought it would be a long while before I'd allow myself to get attached to a woman. But I hadn't met Summer when I thought that.

"Summer, you don't have to spend the weekend with me. It was a suggestion."

Every muscle in my limbs strings tight as I wait for her answer.

"You make all suggestions without a question mark?" she teases, and I feel the muscles in one leg loosening, then the other. "I'd love to spend the weekend with you."

The muscles in my arms relax too. I take one of her hands from the wheel and kiss it.

She pulls in front of her house a short while later.

"Wait here, I'll be quick. Are you sure I shouldn't change for our date?"

"Positive."

She nods, swiping her tongue over the bow of her upper lip. "Okay. Five minutes."

While I wait, it occurs to me I've never been in her house. I wonder what the inside is like, if I could tell it belongs to Summer just by being there. I bet I'd find signs of her everywhere. Post-its glued in random spots, with reminders and smileys scribbled on them. Paintings. Books.

Summer comes hurtling out of the house a few minutes later, a small backpack on her shoulder, which she throws in the back as soon as she climbs in. "Done! Now, what's this fancy place you're taking me to?"

Unease claws at my insides as she guns the engine, setting the car in motion.

"You'll see."

Twenty minutes later, I glance at her out of the corner of my eye as the double gate to my house opens, and we drive inside. I watch as realization dawns on her face and keep my fingers crossed for her not to be disappointed.

When she grins, I let out a breath of relief.

"You're a genius," she says wickedly. We step out of the car, and when she moves to take her backpack, I stop her, instead slinging it over my own shoulder. Then I open the front door for her and lead her straight to the patio in the back.

"Wow," she exclaims, stepping outside. "When did you do all this?"

She takes in the table for two, complete with tablecloth and candles, which I still have to light.

"Landed a couple of hours ago. I called a catering company for the food. I just set the table."

Summer smiles warmly. "This is so beautiful. Thank you."

I hold out the chair for her. "Take a seat. You're keeping your jacket, right?"

"Yeah." She sighs. "When I lived in Rome, I loved that you could eat outside almost always. Maybe not in winter, but here we don't even get real heat in mid-July."

As she sits, I plant a quick kiss on her neck.

"Any time you want to escape someplace hot, just say the word."

"Mmm, that's tempting."

"*You* are tempting. I'll take you anywhere you want, Summer."

After one last kiss, I move on to loading the food on plates.

"You really planned this," she says in wonder as we dig in.

"I told you there are advantages to dating a movie star. It's not all drama, I promise."

She touches my leg under the table, and I reach for her hand.

"It's all good, Alex. I'm sorry I freaked out."

"You have nothing to apologize for. If I found another's man number in your pocket, I wouldn't have reacted well."

She waves her other hand. "I don't believe that."

"I almost choked on jealousy when your brother answered your phone... before you told me he was your brother, obviously."

"Wow. I couldn't tell."

"I'm an actor, sweetheart."

Her eyes narrow. "I don't want you to act around me. I want to know what you're thinking. All the time."

That makes me pause. Acting is a self-preservation technique, but I know what Summer's asking for, and I can't resist her. "Okay."

Maybe her trust in me when finding that

number moved me more than I'm ready to admit, but I don't want to hold back with her, even if it might get me burned. I accept that risk. I want to take it.

"What was your favorite dish as a kid?" Summer asks, while we eat bread with the several spreads that came as appetizers.

"Donuts. Mom makes the best donuts. Sometimes we'd go out to this restaurant close to the Japanese Garden. Good times."

"Do you miss Portland?"

"Nah, just my parents. Sophie and I are still campaigning to convince them to move here."

"What's keeping them from doing that?"

"Ironically, I am."

"What do you mean?"

"I think they'd be happier if I had a regular nine-to-five job. All this media attention is too overwhelming for them. We had some incidents a few years ago with paparazzi, and they're still wary, so convincing them to move here is a work in progress."

"Well, until they do, you'll have a gazillion Bennetts smothering you."

"I thought I needed a helmet for meeting your family."

She holds up the forefingers of each hand. "First you will need a helmet. That's a rite of passage. Assuming they like you, if you'll want to keep them at bay, you're probably going to need a bat."

"Assuming?" I challenge.

"Don't worry, I'm talking you up." She grins, pointing at the food. "This will certainly earn you points."

After we finish the starters and main course, I come to the troubling realization that the catering company forgot our dessert. I check the fridge, then call them.

"It'll be here in half an hour," I tell Summer, who's inspecting my fridge like it's some diamond mine. Sophie stocked it for my return. Summer pauses only to glance over her shoulder and say, "No need. I'll make us a tiramisu. You've got all the ingredients, and it's easy to make."

I blink. "Summer, you don't have to do that—"

"I don't mind, I promise. Don't order anything."

I bring the phone back to my ear. "We won't need that dessert after all. Thank you for your services."

After clicking off, I watch Summer kick off her heels, battering eggs in a bowl.

"Why is your fridge so well stocked?" she asks.

"My sister took care of it. Sophie is dying to meet you."

"You told her about me?"

"Of course."

"I'd love to meet her. And by the way, sneaking up in my office was superhot, but I've got to admonish you. It was risky. I think Preston would have a mental breakdown if he found out. I've looked over that list of security measures he sent me… my mind is still spinning."

Walking up to her, I wrap my arms around her, flattening her back against my chest, resting my nose in the crook of her neck.

"After this whole premiere mess is over, I promise things will calm down a bit. And then I'll take you to the fanciest restaurants, on the fanciest dates."

She stills, covering my hands with hers, turning her head slightly. "Alex, I don't care if we go out, or we stay in. I just like spending time with you. I get it that things are a bit crazy now, and your life in general is more… colorful than most people's, but I can handle it."

I cradle her tighter in my arms, kissing her neck, barely believing how lucky I am that she's mine, and that she's taking all this in stride, like I'm worth all her effort. I've never felt more appreciated.

"I can't get enough of you. Now I just have to make sure you can't get enough of me either."

"And how do you plan to do that, mister?"

"I have some aces up my sleeves."

"Hmm… I'm torn between admitting you don't have to work that hard, and egging you on so you use all those aces. Whoops, I guess the cat is out of the bag."

I smile against her neck, watching her hands move rapidly on the counter.

"How can I help?" I ask, finally letting go.

"List your skills in the kitchen, and please don't pimp yourself."

"I'm very skilled at sneaking into kitchens and charming the personnel into doing whatever I want. The rest of my skill range expands from sandwiches to boiled eggs."

"Right." She eyes my hands thoughtfully. "But I bet I can count on you for brute force. How does whisking eggs sound? My arms are already hurting."

"Feel free to put me to the best use as you see fit."

She smiles, pushing her hair out of her face, smearing her forehead with yolk in the process. "Hate to be so blunt, but I think your best use… will not be in the kitchen. I'm optimistic about the bedroom though."

Stepping right in front of her, I wet my fingers under the sink, clean off the yolk smears on her forehead, then kiss those spots. Nothing's ever felt more real, more important than having Summer in my house, in my life. I lean in even closer, whispering in her ear.

"That's because you don't know yet what I can do to you on a kitchen counter."

Chapter Twenty-Three

Summer

On Sunday evening Alex flies out again, and I count down the days—if I'm honest the minutes too—until the weekend and I get to see him again. I keep an eye out for Tara over the next few days, but she doesn't show her face at the gallery or attempt to contact me.

Meanwhile, Olivia is working hard on earning the *Neurotic Boss of the Year* title, which is completely unwarranted. This is the gallery's most profitable year. By the looks of things, it will also be the year I sprout my first white hairs.

Midweek, my sisters surprise me by showing up at the gallery near closing time. They're both flashing their "we're up to shenanigans" expressions.

"We're here to whisk you away to a speedy spa session," Pippa explains. "We have instructions from a certain hot superhero to help you relax."

"Wow, when did he talk to you? How does he know I need to relax? I haven't complained about anything."

Pippa hooks an arm around mine, leaning in conspiratorially. "Any man worth his salt can pick these things up from the tone of voice, willingness to engage in sexy talk on the phone, and so on."

"I think he's trying to get under mine and Pippa's skin, so he's got some backup on Saturday." Alice gives me a thumbs-up. "It's totally working."

So… I don't know if his goal is to make me fall in love with him or just to make me swoon, but he's succeeding on all accounts. Oh boy.

I can take care of myself, and when I forget to, my family is there to do it for me. But having this wonderful man look out for me, even though his schedule is packed? Well, I won't lie… it touches somewhere deep inside me and tugs at my heartstrings. Tugs at all the strings.

An electrifying energy coils through me while we're at the spa, and it only grows more intense once I'm at home. Alex calls at eleven on the dot.

"How's my girl?"

"Thoroughly pampered. To what do I owe that surprise?"

"You sounded down when we talked the other day, and I couldn't have that, could I? And since I'm not there to work the tension out of your system…."

I giggle into the phone. "Careful, Mr. Alexander Westbrook, or I might want you to stay away just so you can surprise me like this."

"Choosing spa treatments over me, huh? Ouch."

I wiggle under my sheets, sighing. "I'll fess up. Your snuggles are way more relaxing than spa treatments."

There's a pause, and then he says, "Snuggles?"

He says the word slowly, as if checking that he heard correctly.

"Yep."

"I thought you'd choose a sexier activity."

"Snuggles *are* sexy." Clueless man. "You wrap those muscle-roped arms around me, squeeze me to the muscled chest."

"Ah, now I get the picture."

"I can't wait for you to come back, Alex."

"I can't wait to be back, baby."

Alex is scheduled to fly back on Saturday around lunchtime, which is why I put my sneaking skills to good use and convince his sister, Sophie, to let me in his house early that morning. I met her last Sunday briefly, but I didn't have her number.

Obtaining it from Alex required utmost sneakiness, but I managed it without him sniffing me out. I'm *so proud* of myself. *So proud.*

I want to surprise him, bake him one of my specialties as a coming-home gift. And then there's me, of course. I can't wait for him to unwrap me. We don't have much time before we have to leave for my parents' house, but I have full confidence in his ability to blow my mind even in speedy mode.

"You're going to be all right on your own?" Sophie asks as I move around the kitchen. "I'd help you with the baking, but my son has an appointment requiring both parents."

"I know my way around here, Sophie. Don't worry," I assure her.

"My brother hasn't been so happy in a long while. Just don't bail on him when the going gets tough. I'll come after you if you do that."

I stop in the act of spreading flour on the counter. "I don't plan to bail on him."

"No one plans to, but they just do when things become... too much. Even our parents kind of checked out. His life can get overwhelming at times."

"I noticed. But I know how to handle a lot of this stuff, and what I don't know, I want to learn."

Preston's e-mail with instructions flashes in my mind. Overwhelming doesn't even begin to cover it. Almost every aspect of our relationship must be preplanned, to avoid being seen.

And this house... though I can hear the wind blowing when I'm outside, the tall tujas are planted so close together that they block the brunt of it. I bet their purpose goes beyond decoration, to ensure no curious eyes can peek inside here. But jeez... what kind of parents check out when the going gets rough?

After Sophie leaves, I throw myself into my baking project. Once it's in the oven, I clean the kitchen, which looks as if a flour bomb exploded in it. *Yikes*. I'm so immersed in tidying it, that I barely register the front door opening. But when I do, panic shoots through me.

"Can you turn your back and pretend you

haven't seen this? I need two more minutes to finish cleaning."

Instead of showing me mercy, Alex stalks toward me, pulling me into a hot, wanton and dirty kiss. He tastes like coffee and mint, and I can't get enough of him.

"How are you even here?" he whispers.

"Sophie. Since you conspired with my sisters, you brought plotting with each other's siblings to the table."

He holds me close, both arms wrapped around me, pressing me against his chest. Oh boy. He barely arrived, and he's already snuggling me. Can I keep this man? Forever and ever? I really want to keep him.

"What's that delicious smell?"

I grin impishly, wiggling against his body. Yep, all those muscles are just as hard as I remember. "I baked you a welcome-home apple pie. Momma's recipe. And please know, I don't bake that for just anyone."

Alex takes my face in his hands, resting his thumbs on my temples. "Is that your way of telling me I'm special to you, baby?"

The voice of reason urges me to hold back, because this could blow up in my face at any moment. What are the chances of an international star falling in love with me? When he could have any beauty in Hollywood, any runway model? If I'm honest though, the "holding myself back" ship sailed a while ago.

And the way he looks at me? I swear it seems to say that he wants to keep me for good too.

"You are very special, Alex."

"Good. Because you mean the world to me."

My stomach flips back and then flips some more as he kisses my forehead, snuggling me *again*. I don't know if this is official snuggle day or anything, but I soak it all up, right until it's time to take the pie out. Once it's on the counter, Alex reaches for it, but I pat his hand away.

"It's scalding hot. You'll get burned. Wait a bit."

"I don't like to wait when I'm hungry."

He levels me with his gaze, unleashing the full power of his million-dollar smolder. I'm tempted to check if my panties have melted off. They certainly feel on fire. He's not hungry just for pie. *Oh, goodie*. My body has been in a state of semi-arousal since I woke up, in anticipation of sexy shenanigans.

He holds me against him, covering my mouth with his, and by God, this isn't just a kiss. It's the kiss of all kisses. It feels sweeter and hotter than before, more intimate.

He trails his mouth down my neck, one hand slipping under the hem of my shirt. I press my hips into him, almost involuntarily parting my legs.

"Alex," I whisper.

"Fuck, you're so responsive. Those sounds you make drive me crazy."

"What sounds? I'm quiet."

"You try to be, but the way you swallow those

moans... makes me wonder just how much pleasure you can take before you fall apart. Makes me want to test your limits."

A shiver runs through me, and I pull back just enough to look him in the eyes... which are hooded and full of lust.

"Fuck... you want me to test you, to push you, don't you, Summer?"

Well, duuuh.

"I do. But here we are, still talking. Kind of makes me think you don't really mean it."

I'm nearly bouncing on my toes, waiting for his reaction. The flesh between my thighs has turned tender already, greedy for his touch. Whenever I push him, he answers with sexy treats... or sexy threats. *Yum.* Which one will it be now? I have my answer when Alex lifts me over his shoulder, carrying me caveman style all the way to the bedroom.

***

Time is my enemy. It passes too fast when I'm enjoying something, and too slow when I'm dreading something. So of course, by the time we emerge from the bedroom, we're on a tight schedule.

"This is delicious," Alex exclaims, gobbling down my pie like it's the best thing he's ever tasted. In the meantime, his free hand is shamelessly feeling up my ass.

"Hey! My pie demands your full focus. So does my butt. Focus on one thing at a time."

He winks. "I'm great at multitasking. But we should go. I've got to buy flowers for your momma."

"No, you don't."

"It's the first time I'm meeting her. Of course I'll bring her flowers."

I'm definitely keeping him. The world can explode in my face all it wants, I'm going to fight tooth and nail to keep this man.

"Okay. I know a nice flower market on the way. Let's go."

We climb into Alex's car, which has tinted windows. Short of someone jumping in front of the windshield, they can't see who is inside. My thoughts circle back to Tara. Was she really satisfied with my half-assed brush-off? Or is she waiting in the shadows, biding her time?

"I'm trying to picture what it's like to grow up with eight siblings. I'm assuming you don't need friends," he says as we hit the road.

"Ha, you'd think so, but we always had a house full of friends. Some even became adopted Bennetts." At his puzzled expression, I explain, "That's what we call really close friends."

When Alex pulls the car in the parking lot behind the flower market, he turns to me.

"It's best if you stay in the car."

"Sure, no problem. Not being seen together was on top of Preston's list."

Putting on sunglasses and his trusted cap, he plants a small kiss on my forehead before climbing out. It's so weird to see my surroundings through tinted glass.

Running my hands along the plush-leather seat, I smile to myself like a fool, my heart feeling a little too big for my chest. I can't believe I'm with a man who wants to bring Mom flowers. Is it possible that I'm dreaming?

Just when I'm wondering what's taking Alex so long, I hear a ping coming from the bag at my feet. I crouch and take out my phone, turning it screen up.

Alex: Can you lay low? I'm being ambushed by fans, and they'll follow me to the car.

Chapter Twenty-Four

Summer

My heart thumps in my ears, and it takes me a few seconds to realize he literally means for me to lay low.

Panic crawls up my spine, lodging in my throat. Out of the corner of my eye, I see movement in the distance. Alex is hurrying back from the building, surrounded by a crowd. I don't know if there is a reporter among them, but anyone with a smartphone can do enough damage if they get a glimpse of me.

"Okay, Summer. No time to panic. Whip up a plan."

I push my chair back enough so I can crouch down in front of it. Okay, this is good. No one can see me through the windshield… but they can if they peek inside the car when Alex opens the door. The jackets!

Yanking both our jackets from the back seat, I cover myself with them as best I can, hoping it'll look like he's got some sort of package here and threw the jackets over it. Fingers crossed no one looks close enough to realize one of the jackets is for a woman.

My stomach tightens when I hear the driver

door swing open, and Alex's voice booms. "My car is private property. Please step back. I already gave you autographs—"

"Alex, come on, another autograph. I want one on my skin."

"Here, take my number—"

The sound of a door being shut follows, but I don't dare push the jackets off me just yet.

"I'm backing out right now," Alex explains, setting the car in motion. "Just a second until we're out of here."

I count seventy-five seconds until he yanks the jackets off me, throwing them in the back. When his hand comes down on the stick, I notice it's trembling. Anger is etched on his features. I reach out and lay my hand on his. "It's all okay, Alex."

"I'm so sorry."

I push myself up, crawling on my seat. I miscalculate the distance to the window and bang my head against it.

"Owwwww."

"What—"

"I have coordination issues, don't worry."

Sitting properly, I massage the sore spot.

"Does it hurt? I'll pull in somewhere and look at it."

"It's not necessary. Are we being followed?"

"No, those were fans, not paparazzi. Paps would have followed us, but fans don't go to those lengths."

"Okay. I should have gone and bought the

flowers."

"Don't know why it didn't occur to me."

We drive for all of five minutes until we reach the city limit, and he pulls into what looks like the parking lot of an office building. Since it's Saturday, it's deserted.

"This really isn't necessary," I mumble, but show him the side I banged. "See? Nothing happened."

He kisses the spot, cupping my head, and his tenderness reaches to a place deep inside me.

"I'm sorry, Summer," he whispers softly.

"It's not your fault you're so popular you can't even buy flowers without being mobbed. I told you this cap thing is a lousy disguise."

Taking it off, I throw it in the back, which is when I notice the bouquets of flowers. Plural.

"Why did you buy two bouquets?"

"One for you. I saw peonies, and you told me you liked them back at the lake."

"I see you discovered the secret to a woman's heart." My voice comes out laced with more emotion than humor. "Buying her flowers for no reason at all."

"Sweetness… come here." He kisses my head again, on the spot I banged, then trails his mouth to my temple. "I'm sorry," he whispers. "I'll have my security team around more often until the premieres are over. I thought things would be more relaxed here than in LA. Celebrity culture is insane there. But I've let my guard down. I shouldn't have."

"It wasn't so bad."

He pulls back to face me. "How was that not so bad?"

"Okay, so I admit my idea of a quiet Saturday morning wasn't hiding under our jackets from your fans. I... errr, honestly thought Preston was being overcautious with the lists and the protocols. How often do you get mobbed by a hoard of fans? It didn't happen that night during our walk or at the hotel."

"We got lucky during the walk. As for the hotel... people are more laid back when they see me around for a longer period of time because the novelty wears off. But this happens often enough that it may become uncomfortable for you."

His eyes grow sad, which I can't have. Am I shaken, and maybe a little scared? Yep. Do I fear that all this hiding will overwhelm us? Absolutely. And then there's the little fact that his promo tour with Amy will start in three weeks, but that's a can of worms I don't even want to think about.

He needs me to be strong now. Pressing my mouth to his, I kiss him with all I have, then pull back a notch, looking him straight in the eye.

"I'll learn to deal with this. I'm tiny. I can hide in small places. I kind of feel like James Bond. And after we don't have to hide anymore, I'll strut on your arm everywhere, giving every woman in sight the evil eye. I can't wait for that part."

"You're incredible, you know that?"

"Feel free to remind me whenever you feel

like it. I happen to love compliments in any way, shape, and form. But if we don't hurry and arrive late at my parents, there will be no saving your skin, superstar."

***

Alex

Once we're on the road again, Summer talks my ears off, dishing advice about winning over her family.

"Sebastian and Logan will play their eldest brothers' card. No doubt about that. Don't let them scare you."

"I won't."

"Oh, and pay special attention to Blake. He's the youngest of my brothers and likes to pretend he's laid-back. Actually, he might genuinely think he's laid-back. He's not."

"At least Daniel will have my back," I reason.

"Nope, he most definitely will not. You might have been his client, but I'm his sister."

She fiddles with the hem of her shirt, and I reach out to clasp both her hands in one of mine. "Summer, why are you nervous?"

She shifts in her seat but doesn't answer. I wrack my mind for the best way to coax her out of her shell, because I want to know. I don't want her to feel like she needs to hide her fears from me.

"I'll tickle you until you tell me."

"You're driving!"

"We already established I'm great at multitasking."

She chuckles. "No, you claimed that. Out of respect for your man pride, I didn't contradict you."

"You just stamped all over my pride," I inform her. "And you're trying to distract me. Something is eating at you. Tell me."

"I... well, my family is important to me... but we can be a bit overwhelming when we're all together."

"I'm not going to run away, sweet girl."

She's silent for a beat, then leans in to place a quick kiss on my cheek.

"What was that for?"

"Pfft, I don't need a reason to kiss you." Even though her tone is playful, I don't miss the hint of emotion, and I bring one of her hands to my mouth, kissing it. We spend the rest of the drive in companionable silence, and I can't help replaying the scene with the fans in my head.

After the episode, I half expected her to ask me to pull over so she could go about finding herself a date who doesn't ask her to hide under a seat. But she keeps surprising me, with her quiet strength and fierce determination. Still, I know exactly how crazy my life can get, how fast it can become too much. I silence the voice at the back of my head that reminds me Hollywood craziness has a way of wearing out people's patience, driving them away.

Chapter Twenty-Five

Alex

Within five minutes of arriving at the Bennett house, I realize Summer wasn't exaggerating when she said her family is huge. Eight siblings sounded like a lot, but nothing I couldn't handle—or so I thought. Once you factor in everyone's spouses, and the kids... the numbers escalate quickly. Her parents' home is a two-story house on a vast property, but everyone's gathered around the white gazebo in the front yard. Even though I train my memory extensively by learning lines, I forget about a third of the names after the introduction round. The kids, who seem to range between toddlers and primary school, mob me right away.

"Can we get an autograph?"

"Can you really fly?"

"Of course he can. He's a superhero. Can you teach me how to fly?"

"No, me first."

They sputter questions faster than I can answer them.

"Kids, settle down," Jenna Bennett says. "Pizza's ready, why don't you eat before the flying lessons?"

Seeing their little faces all scrunched up as they weigh in pizza against flying lessons is hilarious. Pizza wins.

"Thank you for the flowers. They're beautiful," Jenna says once the little ones sprint to the gazebo, where I presume the pizza awaits. "I'll go put them in a vase."

"Momma, I'll go. I got flowers too, and I'll put those in water as well. They'll dry up if I leave them in the car the entire day," Summer says.

"Sure thing, honey."

Summer takes the flowers from her mother, turning to me. "Did you lock the car?"

"No, it's open."

"Great. I won't be long."

"You have a beautiful place here, Mrs. Bennett," I comment after Summer leaves, and we walk in the direction of the gazebo.

"Thank you. It's far too big for my husband and me, but when the entire family gathers here, it's just the right size. I'm happy you could make it here today."

"Summer talks a lot about you. Couldn't pass up the opportunity to meet everyone."

Jenna smiles, sizing me up the way only a mother can. With just enough severity that you know she's measuring how worthy you are of her daughter.

"How are you liking San Francisco? Summer says you moved recently."

"Yes, ma'am, a few weeks. I wanted to be closer to my sister and her family."

I can practically see Jenna checking off an item on her mental worthy-of-my-daughter list.

We chitchat about Sophie and San Francisco, and why I chose to move here. When we approach the gazebo, Summer's sisters join us too.

"Mom, don't monopolize Alex," Pippa says. She looks a lot like Summer, while Alice resembles their mother. "We all want to talk to him."

"I need to go check on the next batch of pizzas. He's all yours. I'll catch you later, Alex."

I lean against one of the wooden poles of the gazebo, looking between the two of them. I have a hunch I'm about to be cornered.

"Summer wasn't exaggerating," Pippa comments once their mother is out of earshot. "You look even better in real life." Then she presses her lips together, looking around her. "And I have to add that I meant that in a purely objective and sisterly way. No one's hotter than my husband."

Her expression shifts subtly when she trains her eyes on me again. "So, I'm gonna say this outright. You already won about one thousand points with the spa conspiracy, and about another thousand for bringing Mom flowers."

"But that still doesn't mean we won't be keeping an eye on you," Alice weighs in. "Any hint that our baby sister's unhappy, and you'll have your hands full."

I grin. "Summer warned me about your brothers grilling me. She forgot to mention you two."

Alice scoffs. "I'm offended. She thought she'd

show up here with you, and we wouldn't give you the talk?"

"That's how little she thinks of us, huh?" Pippa asks, tsking and shaking her head. A delicious smell reaches us as the wind blows in our direction.

"Pizza's ready," Jenna announces.

"Oh man, the second pizza batch smells even better than the first. Mom is killing me," Pippa comments, rubbing her belly.

I remain just outside the gazebo while the sisters head in, lured by the promise of pizza.

I like knowing that my girl has so many people who care about her, who have her back. I'm so lost in my own thoughts that I don't notice Summer until she steps right in front of me.

"What are you thinking about?" Summer asks. "You're flashing your I'm-super-happy smile."

"I've got a sad smile too?"

"No, but you've got your acting smile—the one you flash when you're required to smile but don't feel like it; you also have the sneaky smile—that's when you're smiling even though you're not supposed to."

Gripping her waist with both hands, I pull her flat against me.

"What are you doing?" she whispers.

"I'm about to kiss you."

"No, no, you can't do that. Everyone's watching, and your kisses aren't exactly PG-rated."

She tries to wiggle out of my grip, but I just sling my arms tighter around her, nuzzling her neck with the tip of my nose. She shudders lightly.

"This is the first I've heard you complain about my kisses."

"It's not a complaint, but your kisses are always at least a seven out of ten on the heat scale, you know?"

I stop nuzzling her neck, straightening up. One glance at her expression, and it's clear she's not pulling my leg.

"No, I don't. Believe it or not, I haven't actually measured the heat level of my kissing."

She smiles sheepishly, her cheeks turning pink. Summer is her own brand of adorable, and she's getting under my skin faster than anyone ever has. Deeper too. I missed her while I was gone, looking forward to our nightly calls more than anything.

"Sooo... I'm thinking I should be your shield," she says.

"What?"

"You know, be a buffer between you and whoever wants to interrogate you. I know your superhero arsenal includes a cape, but that won't help you much here."

"Summer, you don't need to babysit me. Go do whatever you do when you're here. I'll kiss the hell out of you if you don't go, and I'll make it heat level eleven." Whatever that is.

"Fine. Fine. I'm going." Licking her lips, she adds, "But, can you make good on that threat later? When we're alone?"

She knows exactly the effect her words have on me, the adrenaline spiking my blood. But I can give as good as she can.

"I'll make good on it and then some. That's a promise."

Her eyes widen, a light flush spreading on her cheeks. Mission accomplished.

Once Summer heads inside the gazebo, the kids gather around me so fast, I bet they were watching like hawks for me to be alone.

"Mr. Superhero, can you teach us how to fly now?"

"His name is not Mr. Superhero—"

"But the police officer called him that in the last movie."

The group explodes into conversation, contradicting each other, talking at the same time. All I can do is watch them and grin, deciding on the best tactic.

Obviously, teaching them how to "fly" is out of the question. It requires a green screen and CGI.

Early in the superhero movies, I made the mistake of explaining this to kids. The expression on their faces was akin to them finding out Santa Clause doesn't exist.

"Kids, flying's out of the question today. I left the magic cape at home. I'll teach you a few other tricks. But I need another adult to assist me."

"I'll go get Dad," the boy named Will announces. In his absence, I instruct the group to form a semicircle so they can watch what's going on while they wait their turn.

Will joins us, with Sebastian in tow. We shook hands when Summer introduced me earlier today, but I didn't have a chance to talk to him.

"There's no getting out of this, huh?" he asks as Will joins the semicircle.

"Afraid not, but it's not too complicated, and it won't take long."

About one hour later, I'm forced to admit that I'm in over my head. Both my arms feel like they're about to fall off. Sebastian flexes one hand, holds up the other.

"All right everyone, you've each had your turn. That was enough. Alex isn't here to entertain you all day. Say thank you and go back to what you were playing before."

To my astonishment, the kids don't argue... out loud. They mutter under their breaths but accept the dismissal.

"That's some serious group management skill right there," I tell Sebastian honestly.

"I've had plenty of time to exercise. Once they get used to you, it's easier."

He throws the comment offhandedly, but I don't miss the point. Sebastian's sly, but not sly enough. He wants to know if I plan to stick around.

"I look forward to that," I reply. "Though I'm not sure how often I can use the excuse of forgetting the cape before I have to explain that flying is a special effect."

Sebastian whistles, shaking his head. "Wouldn't want to be in your skin when you have to explain that."

"I'll ask Summer for tips."

"You do that. She's excellent with kids."

I'd surmised as much from seeing her interact with the kids at St. Anne's. But I like seeing Summer from her family's perspective, piecing together more details about her.

"Come on, let's go get a drink inside," Sebastian says. "And by the way, Summer told me and Logan about some trouble with the press. If there's anything we can do… Bennett Enterprises has a lot of resources. You can count on our support."

"Thanks. I appreciate that."

It's been a long time since anyone offered me their support. Usually, people approach me looking for something *from* me.

The party's split into several subgroups, which isn't at all surprising, given the sheer amount of people. Several, Summer included, are sitting in the gazebo, another group is huddled around the grill.

Laughter reverberates throughout the yard, and I swear to God, the sound is contagious.

The interior of the house is eerily quiet compared to the mix of voices outside. Sebastian leads me through the foyer into a vast living and dining room.

"Ah, I knew you'd eventually find your way to

the bar," Daniel says from the other end of the room, where a bar has been set up. His brother Blake is with him.

It's a good thing I didn't bet against Summer that Daniel would have my back, because I would have lost spectacularly. As far as brother's duty is concerned, I could take notes.

"Alex, I like you, but if you break my baby sister's heart, you're going to have a big problem on your hands," Daniel says, pointing at himself.

"Two," Blake puts in. "We've got her back."

I nod. "Fair enough."

The rest of the day is a whirlwind of activity, with eating, talking to every Bennett, and yet another round of stunt performance for the kids.

Usually when I meet new people, especially a group as large as this one, I'm on the defensive. But I'm relaxed around this lot. It helps that, aside from the kids, no one gives a damn about my being an actor. I like watching people interact—learn a lot about approaching roles, slipping into other people's skin. And watching the Bennett family paints a picture of a group who sticks together no matter what, who doesn't mind going the extra mile, or balk when the going gets tough. I can see where Summer got that quiet strength of hers.

By the time Summer and I head back to the city in the afternoon, I'm wrung out. But she's smiling ear to ear, holding the peonies I bought her this morning. I'll be damned if I've seen her so happy before.

"Did you have fun?" she asks as I veer the car out of her parents' property.

"I did. Thank you for trusting me enough to invite me here. You know who is actually laid-back? Your dad. He didn't give me a single warning."

"Umm... well, he knows my brothers took the job of intimidating my dates, so he can just lay back and watch."

"So, what's the plan for the next three weeks?" she asks.

"I'll have phone conferences and live events on Facebook I can do from my living room, and other than that, I'm yours. We'll have to stay cooped up in my house, though."

Stolen moments, cooped up in my house, that's all I can offer her right now, and I hope to God it will be enough.

"That's such a hardship, I'm telling you. The place is a small palace."

Yeah, but that palace still has four walls and a six-feet thuja fence surrounding it. Stay inside long enough, and you'll wish to be anywhere else. But especially after the incident this afternoon, I can't risk exposing her. She deserves the world damn it, and I want to lay it at her feet. Which gives me an idea.

"I have a proposition for you. How about a getaway in the Bahamas next weekend? Or anywhere else."

She perks up, her smile even wider than before. Bingo.

"Wait, is that safe?"

"Sure. We'll rent a villa with private beach access, and not venture out."

"You'd really just do that? Whisk me away somewhere?"

"I'd do anything for you."

"Well, I'd love to go. Wow. I haven't been to the Bahamas. I can't wait. Also... I can't wait for you to make good on that heat level eleven kiss."

I laugh, pinching her arm. "You have to work hard for that."

She shifts in her seat, bringing her lips to my ear. I grip the steering wheel tight, making a concerted effort not to take my eyes off the road.

She tugs my earlobe between my teeth. "Hard like this?"

"That earns you a seven, at most."

"You foul creature."

"I know how to play my cards, Summer."

Chapter Twenty-Six

Summer

In the past, whenever I heard actors say "promotional tour," I imagined flashy trips, hours upon hours of relaxing in a hotel spa before heading to interviews. Even the weeks *before* the tour officially starts are packed with phone interviews.

When Preston e-mailed Alex his tour schedule, he shared it with me too, so I know when he's available to talk. He will run a tight schedule from six o'clock in the morning until ten at night. His free time will consist of fifteen-minute windows every two hours. Except for our amazing trip to the Bahamas, he's been working all the time.

"Are these work hours even legal?" I ask as we look at his schedule, curled up on his couch, three evenings before he's set to leave for the tour.

"You sound like Sophie."

"Well, I happen to think your sister is right." She and her family stopped by quite a few times over the last few weeks, and on a few occasions, we *might* have banded together against Alex. For his own good, of course.

"I can't complain. Paycheck's decent." With a chuckle, he adds, "But your indignation is cute."

"Well, I hope they keep masseurs on call for you. Male masseurs."

"So if they send sexy blondes, you'd rather I continue suffering from a stiff neck?"

I consider that for a moment. "I'm conflicted. I want the best for you, but I don't want anyone touching all this." I run my hands over his shoulders, down his chest. "Hey, I've got an idea. I can give you advance massages."

"I like how your mind works." He kisses the tip of my nose. "You little opportunist. You just want to touch me."

I straddle his lap, shaking my head vehemently. "No, those are just fringe benefits. You can't blame me, though. Not really. You display all this muscle before me, what do you expect me to do?"

"I can't believe you're real, and mine. You make me so happy, Summer."

My heart expands in my chest. "Hmm… define *so*. Like this?"

I hold my hands in front of my chest, with just a few inches between my palms. Then I move my hands further and further apart, stealing glances at Alex. "You tell me when to stop."

When my arms are opened wide around me, and I can't possibly move them further apart, Alex hugs my waist, kissing my neck, nipping it gently. I can feel his grin against my skin, and it's contagious.

"More than that," he whispers. My grin widens. "I'll miss you, Summer."

God, the things this man makes me feel. Pure bliss spreads through me, reaching every cell. He moves his hands from my waist up to my breasts, fondling them. I have no choice but to call him out on it. "You're so full of shit. You were accusing me of looking for an excuse to feel you up?"

"Never said I wasn't looking for one too. You're quite irresistible, Ms. Bennett."

"Why, thank you for the compliment, Mr. Westbrook. In case you're trying to bribe your way into my panties, you already had me at *I'll miss you*."

He tugs my lower lip between his teeth, but the ringtone of his phone interrupts us. He grabs it from the between the cushions, and I sigh.

"Preston is working overtime again," I comment.

"He works all the time."

I climb from his lap as he takes the call, putting it on loudspeaker. It seems to be his preferred way to take work calls, but I don't mind.

"Have you seen Amy's Facebook Q&A with fans?" Preston asks without further ado. "She couldn't do more than five minutes before the comment section got out of control."

"No, but I'll take a look now at the comments. Wait a second."

He taps on his phone, pulling up the Facebook app, scrolling. Then Amy's voice fills the room.

"Hey everyone! Welcome to this Q&A session. Just type your questions in the comments, and I'll do my best to answer them."

He mutes the sound, but little icicles pop along the back of my neck. "I'm reading through the comments now. Jesus, they hate us."

"It's not a stretch to imagine it will be worse when you'll be doing promotional appearances together."

"No, not a stretch," Alex answers dryly.

"It would be good for the two of you to be seen together before your first appearance. Take her out somewhere. The more public your outing, the better. It'll make the story of you two still being friends more credible. There's already talk at the studio of pulling back some of the promotional activities. They're already writing this off as a box office bomb."

"Are you kidding me? It's too early in the game to draw that conclusion." Alex rises to his feet, locking his eyes on me. I'm hugging my knees, my stomach tight all of a sudden.

"I'm going to meet with them, try and talk them out of it," Preston says.

"Okay. Thank you. I appreciate this."

The weight of the world seems to be pressing on Alex's shoulders after he ends the call, slumping on the couch next to me.

"Comment section so bad, huh?"

"A lot of fans talk about boycotting the movie. They feel duped that we broke up. Some even accuse us that is was all fake just to sell them the first movie. Which is true… was true, at least in the beginning."

"That's messed up. What are you going to do?"

"I don't know yet."

"You think Preston's right, that you should meet with Amy, be seen together?"

I do my best, but my voice still wavers. Alex snaps his gaze to me.

"I don't want to lie anymore. And it would bother you, wouldn't it?"

A knot lodges in my throat, making it hard to swallow. I avert my gaze, schooling my voice to be strong, steady. These types of conversations always get nasty. At best, he'll say I'm possessive. At worst… I don't want to think about the worst right now.

I try evasive maneuvers. "Doesn't matter."

"Yeah, it does matter. You matter to me. Summer, I can't read your mind."

"Trust me, you wouldn't want to read my mind."

"Try me. Why are you so tense?"

I realize I've been chewing my lower lip and stop. Alex skims his hand from my belly up to my chin.

"Tell me," he beckons.

"Well, you started by faking things last time too… and then it turned real. I know it's about friendship now, but…"

My mom always says honesty and communication is the key to a lasting relationship. In my experience, admitting my fears was the kiss of death. But this is Alex. I can trust him. Drawing in a deep breath, I open my mouth. Here goes nothing.

"The thought of you having to go out with her in private, even as friends, makes me want to scratch something."

"Why was it so hard to admit it?"

I blink twice, shrugging. "Because insecurity isn't cool?"

He takes my face in both hands, kissing my temple. "I don't want cool, Summer. I want honest. I want real. Look at me."

Taking a deep breath, I up my focus to his eyes.

"You're all I think about. When I imagine the future, you're all I see."

Emotions bubble up my throat, even as the surprise of his words leaves me breathless.

"You do?" I manage to croak out.

He nods, more to himself, seeming surprised by his own admission. I read once that feelings have a way of sneaking up on you, growing without asking for permission. I didn't understand the sentiment until now.

He brings his hands to my waist. I rest my palms on his bicep, loving the feeling of his hard muscles under my fingers. He's so strong. All man. All mine.

"I'll tell Preston I won't do it. Being seen with her in public would fuel speculations, and I don't want that. We wouldn't be in this mess in the first place if the studio hadn't used our personal lives as a marketing stunt. I'm not playing that game anymore. I didn't want to do it anyway, and even less now that I know how you feel about it."

He's being so kind, so understanding. He didn't react at all like I expected.

"Why are you so accommodating? You're going to so much trouble for me. I bet there are thousands of girls out there who'd make things so much easier."

"But I want you. I've wanted you since I kissed you the first time. And now we have something, and I don't mind putting in the work to keep it. It's worth it. You're worth it, Summer Bennett. What we have is real and beautiful, and you're precious."

I've never heard a man talk so honestly, state things so simply. He's willing to work on what we have, because it's worth it to him. I'm worth it. I've never heard anything more romantic.

And because my romantic streak is wired to my tear ducts, I blink away tears as Alex starts kissing my neck, skimming his hands up until his thumbs are brushing the sides of my breasts. It's hard for me to think when he does that. Then I don't want to think at all anymore. I want to feel, to touch, and taste. I want to be wrapped up in him. His hands are everywhere. Moving from my waist up my back, down to my hips, cupping my ass.

He peels off my shirt, then my pants and

panties. *Poof!* My bra goes next, and then he presses his hard—and clothed—body against me. The friction of the bulge in his jeans low on my belly shoots sparks of awareness up my nerves. I push him off me, needing a little space from all the testosterone flying around to make a plan of attack. My favorite place for sexy shenanigans is the bed. But it's so far away.

The couch is plush and comfy, and it will have to do. When I grab the hem of his shirt, ready to get rid of the pesky thing separating me from his skin, he stops me.

"No!"

I look at him confused. Amusement dances in his eyes.

My fingers itch with the need to remove his clothes. He grabs my ankles, placing them up wide apart on the couch. I feel so exposed, all naked and spread before him, while he's still fully clothed. My skin burns where he holds my ankles, and I wish he'd touch me in other places, but he doesn't.

"Touch your inner thighs, Summer. Start with the right one, then move to the other."

A shiver of excitement runs through me. What's he playing at? No idea, but that doesn't stop me from playing along. I let my hand drift down my right inner thigh.

"Slower," he says. "Draw it out."

I swallow, fastening the muscles in my belly. I move my fingers toward my center as slowly as possible. My toes curl in anticipation. When I near the apex between my thighs, he murmurs, "Stop."

I do, more confused than before… and more aroused. He pulls his shirt up, tossing it away.

"If you do exactly what I ask you to, I'll remove my clothes, one item at a time."

I nod, drinking in his bare chest. I reach out with my other hand, but he pulls away.

"You're not touching me. Just yourself. Run your hand down your other thigh, Summer."

Knowing he's off-limits drives me insane. All I can do is touch myself, watch him take off his belt, then push down his jeans. When he's down to his boxers, he takes one of my nipples in his mouth, twirling his tongue around the tight bud until my hips buck.

When he pulls back, the hunger in his eyes sends a physical shock through me. I'm more on display than ever. I've been so caught up in him, lured by his promises of revealing more of himself, that I gave no thought to baring myself. On instinct, I clench my knees together. At least, I try to, because he stops me midmotion, kissing down one thigh, eyes locked on mine. Then he stands, takes me in his arms, and carries me upstairs. I kiss and touch every inch of him I can reach, grazing my teeth over his shoulder, biting gently on his neck.

After placing me on the mattress, he pushes down his boxers, then gloves himself with a condom. I watch hungrily, my body aching for him to fill me.

He opens me up, one kiss, one loving and passionate thrust at a time. Despite our wild lovemaking, our gazes remain locked. Our connection intensifies with every second. I'm drunk on it, feel it in every cell. He loves me fast and hard, until I fist the sheets, pulling at them.

"That's it, beautiful. Don't hold back. I want to hear you cry out. Don't hold back on me, baby," he whispers.

I'm pulsing around him, and I'm so close, and still, the anticipation keeps building and building, spurred by his thrusts, his touch, and his sinfully sexy words, which feel as if they came from a place of trust and affection.

I come hard, pulling him with me. We grind against each other until we wring out every drop of pleasure. As he lays with his cheek on my chest, I tightly wrap my arms around his head, semi-aware that I'm smothering him. Scratch that, I'm *fully* aware, seeing how I'm having a little trouble catching my breath too. But I can't help wanting to soak it all in. If I loosen my arms a bit, I think I'd breathe easier. But then we wouldn't have full frontal contact. *Decisions, decisions...*

"Want to shower?" he murmurs.

"Nope, I'm not letting you go. Do you mind?"

"I can think of worse things than being trapped between your thighs and arms."

I pat his shoulder playfully. "For your sake, I hope you can't think of better things. Or if you do, then lie. Lie through your teeth. Except, I'd know you'd be lying."

I feel the corner of his mouth lift against my skin. "You're setting me up for a trap."

"That's right. Leaving you just one option. This is amazing or amazing. Take your pick." I work as much sass in my voice as possible… and it all goes straight down the drain when he flicks his thumb over my nipple.

"*You* are amazing, Summer."

"Oooh, you're so lucky you're good at charming."

"What if I wasn't?"

I don't miss a beat. "I'd torture you," I say, wiggling my lower body so he knows I mean business.

"Woman, do you want to kill me?"

"Nah, merely proving a point to my sexy friend down there."

Laughter reverberates through Alex's chest, shaking my torso too. I finally release my arms—because we're both close to choking, *not* because I've got enough of him—and he rolls off me.

"All my clothes are downstairs," I mutter. "Can you give me a robe? And some panties would be good."

He grins. "New rule for today: no panties allowed in the house today."

"I'll be staying in the yard, then."

"Watch it, or I'll add bras to the list of banned items."

"Why don't you go ahead and ban all clothing?"

"I might do just that."

As he hauls me up from the bed, he wraps his arms around me from behind, planting small kisses on my neck. "I'm not even gone, and I already miss you."

"Oh, Alex." I turn around, kissing his mouth, fashioning a plan of attack for the next three days.

Step one: I shall smother him with enough kisses so they last him while he's gone.

Step two: I shall not make this harder for him by admitting how much I'll miss him too.

And then I'll brace myself for twenty days without him.

Chapter Twenty-Seven

Summer

"Yes, yes, yes. Nailed it!" I clap my hands, feeling on top of the world. I just talked *the* Tate museum into lending little old us a collection. It took me three months to seal the deal, but I can nag like nobody's business. Pardon my French, I meant convincing. Yeah! That's the word. Ha! I could sing for joy, but I don't want the windows cracking from my terrible tunes.

I check my clock and hop off my kitchen counter right away. It's almost time for my daily phone call with Alex.

The live events started two days into his tour, and there's no pussy-footing around it: they're a shitshow. Alex told me that all moderators and presenters have been warned to avoid the topic of their breakup, and still they ask about it.

Fan events are the worst. I watch every single one that's broadcast online. Alex fills me in on the events that aren't broadcast. They don't go any different. I want to make things better, but I have no clue how.

I brainstorm like crazy as I pour extra whipped cream on my hot chocolate. Ten minutes until our call. Eleven o'clock in the evening isn't the best time for such a caloric bomb, but I need reinforcements. I can't be expected to talk to my boyfriend, whom I miss like hell, and not have something hot and tasty to devour. He's been gone for one week, but it feels more like one month.

I curl up in my bed with the hot chocolate, willing a brilliant idea to strike, so I'll cheer him up. He and Amy finished a Facebook live video chat one hour ago with fans, and it had gone about as craptastic as the rest.

My phone rings at eleven o'clock on the dot.

"You know, I was admiring your punctuality in the beginning, but now it's a little scary," I say.

"In some parts of the world, it's considered rude not to be punctual."

"I'll make sure to avoid those parts, then. Are you in your room?"

"Yeah. Just came up."

"But your event finished an hour ago."

"Yeah, we had an emergency meeting with our managers and publicists."

I stop in the act of spooning whipped cream into my mouth, my stomach tightening.

"Oh?"

"The studio is pulling the plug on the rest of the live events and interviews. They only bring bad publicity."

"Oh, Alex. I'm so sorry."

"Well, the good part is my schedule will clear up a bit. I was thinking about hopping on the jet and coming to see you."

My insides warm, and it has nothing to do with the sip of hot chocolate I just took. But something doesn't add up.

"Wait, what? I know your schedule. It doesn't only consist of live events."

"No, but I'll ask Preston to move them around. I'd love to see you. I miss you like crazy. When I go to bed, when I wake up."

My insides warm even more, and I'm so tempted to tell him to stamp all over his schedule just to spend time with me.

"But you're flying to LA next, as far as I remember. You're attending some important shows there. You can't just hop on a plane and—I KNOW—gaaaaah!"

I finally realize what I can do to cheer him up. Unfortunately, I had a whole-body realization—I straightened with a start, jolting my cup. Half its contents landed on my sheet, the other half on my pillow.

"Summer?"

"I messed up my bed, but never mind. I had an idea. I could fly out to LA."

"It'd be easier if I came to you, though. For you, I mean. In LA we'd have to be more careful. There are paps at every corner."

I accidentally sat on the drenched part of the bed and immediately leap to my feet. "We'll manage. It was getting dull around here without any James Bond-ish missions."

"You'd do that?"

"Yeah. Olivia won't be happy that I'm taking off again, but I have so much accrued time that she'll have no choice."

"I'll talk to Preston, if you're sure."

"I'm sure. I'll e-mail Olivia right away, tell her I want time off starting on Wednesday. I could stay in LA until Sunday."

"I'd love it if you could stay with me for the entire tour, but I know that'd be pushing it with the paps, not to mention your job. Summer? This means the world to me."

My insides flutter for the rest of our conversation, and even while I change the bedsheets afterward. I'm going to see him in two days. That's so much better than two weeks.

I'm so proud of the way I just up and offered to go see him. The old Summer would have been afraid he'd think I'm suffocating or clingy, but Alex appreciates it. He appreciates *me*. I don't know that there is a better feeling in the world. LA, here I come!

***

I downplayed Olivia's possible reaction when speaking to Alex, because I didn't want him to worry. But even though I have more accrued time off than anyone else, Olivia scowls and shakes her head when she corners me.

"You want to take time off, again?"

We're on the ground floor of the gallery, in the back, packing up the Monet collection. It's going back to Paris today. I'm in the supplies corner, searching for Bubble Wrap.

"It's just three days, for personal reasons."

"First volunteering, now personal reasons."

"It's unavoidable, plus, I don't have any groups scheduled this week." Even though it's mid-August, and the constant stream of tourists means we have a lot of tours scheduled, Diana and Jacob agreed to jump in for me.

"I get the sense you're not prioritizing your job anymore."

I stop in the act of searching for Bubble Wrap. I'm acutely aware of Diana and Jacob watching us.

"It's my right to take time off," I say calmly. "Since you opened this gallery, I took less time off than anyone else, including you."

Maybe that's the problem in the first place. Olivia is so used to me being here, that she takes the hours I put in for granted.

Olivia plays with the key chain around her neck, standing straight as a rod. "I appreciate all your effort, but this feels so out of the blue."

"I know it's short notice, and I'm sorry about it."

"I hope you'll be more considerate from now on. I see a bright future for you here at the gallery, and I'd hate for you to jeopardize that."

I feel like a child being scolded in front of the

entire classroom, and I won't have it. Especially when I'm the main reason the gallery has a future.

"Don't forget I brought in fifteen of the twenty collections this year. I'm certain my partners would follow me to whatever gallery has a bright future for me."

My voice is as calm as I can muster, but Olivia's eyes become glacial. She glances sideways at the rest of the team. Oh, now she cares that we aren't alone.

"I'll see you next Monday," Olivia says before swirling on her heels and heading out. My colleagues give me a thumbs-up.

"You should run this place," Diana says.

Jacob pipes in, "Or, if you decide to set up your own shop, I'll apply for a job, just so you know."

I smile. Maybe it *is* time to think about opening my own gallery again. I was young, dreamy, and foolish when I tried the first time. Now I have more experience. That I failed once doesn't mean I'll fail again.

Diana rubs her palms. "So, dish out. Why do you need time off? It must be pretty big."

"It's a secret," I tease, already counting down the hours until I'll see Alex.

***

The flight to LA seems endless, even though I have my hands full going through Preston's security list. It's exhaustive... and exhausting. I wrinkle my nose at the smell of food surrounding me. Alex offered to send me his private jet, but it felt excessive, so I declined.

I only ordered a glass of wine. Now I regret the wine, because it isn't helping my concentration.

1. We will check you in under a different name. In case the media gets wind of the relationship, you'll be safe from the paps. You need a room for yourself because Alex will be conducting two interviews from his room.

2. You will be staying on the same floor as Alex.

3. You are not to be seen together ANYWHERE. That means:

—you will not ride the elevator together

—you will not go to the hotel pool, spa, or any other amenities together

—you will not walk out of the hotel together

There are thirty-five "*You will not*" items on the list, and even as I work on memorizing them, I fear we'll slip at some point. I tuck the list in my purse as the plane descends, and tell myself I shouldn't fret so much. Alex has plenty of experience. I'll trust him to guide me.

A driver waits for me at LAX, with a shield displaying my fake name, *Tessa Cavanaugh*.

I wish Preston had left the choice of fake name to me. I would have come up with something much cooler.

The driver rolls my enormous suitcase for me to the car, a black SUV with tinted windows.

Between the fake name and the windows, this feels more like a mafia club than a James Bond mission.

When I climb in the car, I discover a takeout box in the back seat.

"Sir, there's a takeout box back here."

"I completely forgot. It's for you, Ms. Cavanaugh."

I catch myself just in time. I almost asked him whom he meant. I'd better get used to answering to Cavanaugh, and get used to it fast.

The takeout box contains a salmon and salad wrap. I barely take it out when I realize there's a note too.

"*Sorry it was too risky to wait for you at the airport. I'll make it up to you tonight. I know you don't like to eat on planes, so here's a snack to get you by until dinner.*"

I stare at the note open-mouthed. My heart hammers madly as I inhale the wrap. It's the most delicious thing I've tasted. Then again, I have a hunch everything right now will taste delicious. Oh, I'm so happy I flew out here.

I've been to LA many times, visiting my Connor cousins. I plan to see them at least once while I'm here. Given Alex's packed schedule, I'll have plenty of time on my own.

Chapter Twenty-Eight

Summer

My jaw goes slack when the car pulls in front of the hotel. Paparazzi are camping everywhere, their eyes trained on the entrance, their cameras poised.

"Is there a service entrance?" I ask the driver.

"Yes, ma'am. I'll take you there right away."

Five minutes later and countless surprised glances from the personnel, I step into the lobby, where Preston is waiting for me.

"Hi, Preston!" I greet, inflecting a little extra cheer in my voice, because he looks as if he's in dire need of it. Lines so deep mar his forehead, they'll become permanent soon.

He nods curtly, gesturing me to the reception. I look around as we wait in the short line to the check-in. I've been here numerous times with my cousin Valentina, sitting at the coffee tables spread past the lobby area.

They serve excellent pastries. The two of us had often spied the lobby while filling our bellies, in case any celebrity was staying here. Oh, the irony.

"How is—" I begin, but Preston shakes his head.

When our turn comes, I present myself as

Tessa Cavanaugh. The name rolls strangely off my tongue.

"We'll need an ID, please."

I freeze. Of course, they need an ID. What's Preston thinking, asking me to give a fake name? Unless he has a fake ID ready, but that seems far-fetched.

"That won't be necessary," Preston says. "She's on my team."

To my astonishment, the receptionist merely nods, sliding me a keycard.

"Enjoy your stay, Ms. Cavanaugh."

"Are they used to this?" I mouth to Preston as we march to the elevator.

"Celebrities give fake names all the time. The paps still find out, as you saw in front of the hotel."

There are four elevators, but none are on the ground floor, so we wait, Preston tapping his foot, me torn between telling him to stop and hurrying to buy him a pastry. He looks like he needs it. Hell, I need it. The hoard of paps in front is unnerving.

When one of the elevators finally dings and the doors open, I patiently wait for the half a dozen guests to step out before heading in. Then several things happen at the same time.

As I step in, someone calls my name. My *real* name. I pivot on my heels and come face-to-face with Tara Delaware. Oh crap. Guess who won't be fooled by Tessa Cavanaugh?

Preston tries to usher me inside, and she makes to grab my arm. I yank it away, but she still catches the sleeve of my T-shirt between her fingers. The fabric tears from my shoulder as I leap further back.

"You're not allowed in here!" Preston booms.

"Just some gossip. That's all I'm looking for. And right now, the fact that Summer Bennett is here smells like a story, especially if I work in their trip to Tahoe in the article." She holds up the camera, and Preston makes to step in front of me, shielding me, but I wiggle out, going straight for the pap.

"This is private property, and I am not a public persona. The hotel has a no-pictures policy too. You're breaking the law by being in the hotel, and if you take that picture, you'll be breaking another law. My chances of winning a lawsuit against you are 100 percent." I point to the torn sleeve. "This counts as harassment in any court. I don't think you can even afford legal fees, much less damages."

Tara blinks, eyes wide, lowering her camera.

"I thought so," I say through gritted teeth.

"I'll be biding my time, you know. At some point, I will snatch a picture of you outside."

I punch the button to close the doors, and Preston presses the one that will take us to the seventh floor.

"Summer, are you okay?" he asks gently. I realize I'm shaking, picking at my torn sleeve.

"Fine! I'm fine. I can't believe that idiot."

"That was a very good answer. It wasn't even on the list."

I stop picking at the sleeve. It's no use anyway, I'll have to toss the shirt away.

"No, but a few years ago the press was practically stalking everyone named Bennett. They always bank on people not knowing their rights or being afraid to exercise them. Is Alex in his room?"

"Yes. He's waiting for you."

I take a deep breath, gathering my wits about me.

***

Alex

I realize something is off the second Summer and Preston step inside the room. Preston looks even grimmer than in the past few days, and that's saying something, since he's been sulking like he's trying to win an Oscar for it.

Summer walks right into my arms. I melt against her sweet body, then freeze when I see the torn sleeve.

"What happened?" I inquire.

"A pap got in the hotel," Preston answers. "Tried to touch Summer's arm as she was stepping back. But Summer knows her stuff."

"What do you mean?"

"Basically told her I'd sue the crap out of her, because she's on a private property and I'm not a public persona," she explains.

"I'm going down to the reception to file a

complaint anyway. Paps aren't supposed to come inside. Why the hell do they have security for? We have another problem. The pap was Tara Delaware. She knows who Summer is. She won't give up."

I swear, pressing Summer closer to me. "Go and talk to her right now. Promise her an exclusive story."

Preston raises his eyebrows. "What exclusive story?"

"Doesn't matter. Promise her that we'll give her something big as soon as we have it."

He glares. "Exclusive stories are important Alex, you can't just give them away. We don't even know from which publication she is. Could be some fifth-hand—"

"I don't care. I want this issue buried before it escalates."

What I'd like to do is make sure Tara Delaware never gets her hand on another story, exclusive or not. But I get what they say about losing a battle to win the war.

"Fine, I'll go find her," Preston says.

The second Preston's out the door, I lower my mouth to Summer's. I kiss her until I feel the tension unwind from her muscles, and then I kiss her some more, because I can't bring myself to stop. It's insane how much I've missed her.

"I'm so happy you're here," I confess when I pause for a breath. "But this was a crazy idea. We'll get some of my security guys around you when you go out."

"I don't want that. It's just going to attract attention. I can take care of myself."

"I know you can. Still want to keep you in a glass globe or locked up here with me."

"Hmm, you'd have to entertain me all the time, though. Are you up for the challenge?"

"Oh, baby, I am."

"I wonder how you could do that." She smiles, and the world seems to fade around us. Nothing else matters right now: the upcoming box office bomb and the subsequent damage it would do to my career, the paps downstairs. Nothing matters when she smiles like that. *I want to marry this woman.* I've never been more certain of anything in my life.

"What are you thinking?" she asks, tilting her head to study me.

"One week apart and you already can't read me anymore?"

She pinches my forearm. "Tell me."

I don't believe in voicing all my thoughts, especially when I can barely sort through them myself. But there is no denying Summer, so I press my thumbs at the corners of her mouth. "Because I'd do anything for this smile. For you."

A grin spreads across her face. Next thing I know, she jumps me, literally. She laces her arms around my neck and wraps her legs around my middle. I meet her halfway, securing my hands under her ass.

I carry her across the suite, bringing her from the living room to the bedroom. Laying her on the king-sized bed, I run my hands over her arms. My gut twists when I reach the bare skin of her shoulders through the ripped shirt. I kiss that patch of skin, then move back up to her face.

"I'm sorry about this, Summer. Sometimes I can't believe you're willing to put up with all this craziness. Why do you?"

I swallow the next words, kissing her instead, tasting her sweet and sinful mouth. I was about to confess how much I fear she'll wake up one day and decide this is all not worth it.

She takes my face in her hands, looking straight at me when I tear my lips from hers.

"Because you remember I don't eat on planes and send me a snack. Because you buy me flowers for no reason at all, and hold me tight when I'm afraid of deep water." Her voice is raw with emotion as she kisses down my jaw. I push the hem of her shirt upward, lowering myself until I'm level with her belly. I kiss every inch of skin I uncover. I want to uncover all of her. She gazes down at me with so much emotion and desire that I lose my trail of thoughts for a moment. Rising back up, I claim her mouth, kissing her until she fists my shirt, yanking it over my head. We've never undressed so fast.

As soon as I do away with her bra, I take one nipple into my mouth, turning it into a pebble with my tongue. I flick my tongue until she digs her heels into the mattress, crying out for me.

I roll a condom on. Sitting upright, I pull Summer into my lap. I grip my erection at the base, running it along her slit, feeling her quivers every time I nudge her entrance, gobbling up her moans when I tease her clit.

I enter her slowly, stopping to kiss her after every inch I push inside. No matter how much she thrashes, I have the control. When I'm buried inside her to the base, neither of us move for a while. I just hold her, feeling her pulse around my cock.

Her frantic heartbeats reverberate against my chest. Our torsos are flush against each other, my hands palming her ass, keeping her right where I want her. When she starts rolling her hips, I guide our movements, keeping the rhythm as slow as I can stand. I know it drives her crazy, because I'm hanging on to a tether of control too. But the buildup is so much more powerful, and the slow rhythm allows me to kiss as much of her as I can reach. When her inner muscles start to clench around me, she whispers, "Alex, please. Oh, please. Let me come. Please."

She begs so sweetly that it completely undoes me. I swipe my thumb on her clit. She comes within seconds.

I love her through her orgasm, not giving her any reprieve. My insides strum with tension. Every muscle burns and spasms as I ride her harder, until she comes a second time, and takes me over the edge with her.

I hold her tight to me afterward. She's leaning her head on my bicep, her nose close enough to brush my nipple with every breath. It tickles the hell out of me, but I hold it together, not wanting to move her. I love seeing her all spent and worn out because of me. But eventually, I do have to move her so I can sort out the condom.

"Shower?" she murmurs.

"Let's go."

I scoop her up in my arms, carrying her to the bathroom. When we pass by the door connecting us to the living room, she sniffs the air.

"Do I smell fries?" She sniffs some more. "And cinnamon rolls?"

I laugh. "LA's finest, just for you."

"They were here when I arrived?"

"Yep."

"I can't believe you distracted me so much I didn't realize it." She gives me a thumbs-up just as I cross the threshold to the bathroom. "What's the schedule for the weekend? Last I looked, you only had an interview Saturday morning and Sunday in the evening."

"It hasn't changed. I'm all yours in between, Summer."

"Excellent. I have so many plans for us."

I start the shower, getting us both wet. "Is that so? Like what?"

She shrugs a shoulder, soaping me up. "Have a little faith in my abilities to surprise you."

Chapter Twenty-Nine

Summer

"Mmm, stop it," I mutter, trying to block out the voices. Blinking open one eye, I notice the room is bathed in light. With a sigh, I stretch on the king-sized bed, focusing on the voices filtering in from the living room. The connecting door is shut, but I recognize the speakers: Alex, Preston, and Amy.

I search my memory, trying to recall Alex's schedule, but I'm fairly certain he didn't have a meeting planned Thursday morning. With an uneasy jolt in my stomach, I push myself out of bed and hurry to the bathroom to brush my teeth and comb my hair. Crap, I don't have anything to wear. My suitcase is in my room, which is further down the corridor. Yesterday's clothes are piled up next to the bed, and the shirt is too wrinkled to be wearable. I have no choice but to throw on a robe. Not exactly the attire I want to wear the first time I meet Amy, but I soldier on, heading to the living room.

"Hey, babe, I'm sorry, did we wake you up?" Alex asks. He's sitting in one of the armchairs, a tight smile on his face.

"I had to get up at some point," I say, sweeping my gaze to the others. Preston sits in the armchair opposite Alex, fingers laced on top of his head. Amy waves at me from the couch.

"Hey, Summer. I've heard a lot about you."

I relax when I take in her appearance. She's wearing jeans and a hoodie, and her hair is piled up in a messy bun. I walk up to her to shake her hand, which is when I notice her eyes are red and a little puffy. Has she been crying?

"What's going on?" I ask, returning to Alex.

"Box office predictions for *Bree Shannon Finds Love #2* went live last night," Preston explains. "They're down 20 percent even from the studio's worst-case scenario."

"But these are just predictions, right?" I ask, stepping just behind Alex's armchair, resting my hand on his shoulder.

Preston shakes his head. "They're very accurate."

"Everyone in the industry takes them at face value," Amy continues. "And word travels fast. I'd been considering three scripts. This morning my manager got calls regarding two of them. Apparently, they already decided to go with another actress. Translation: no one wants to cast someone with a box office bomb as their leading lady."

I squeeze Alex's shoulder.

"I've heard from the studio this morning," Preston says, looking from Amy to Alex. "They want you two to fake a reunion and keep up the charade for one month until after the premiere. Anything to get fans to shell out money at the box office. You need to be seen in public. The more displays of affection, the better. Alex, you could even fake moving in with Amy. You two know the drill."

Amy rearranges her messy bun. "Sam won't like it, but I was afraid it might come to this."

I go very still, even though my heart's hammering like it's about to leap out of my chest. Did I hear them right? Just like that, they're supposed to stage a reunion and keep up the charade for six weeks? The thought of them kissing slices at me. Preston is right, they know the drill... last time they had to pretend, the fake romance led to a real romance. They were engaged for God's sake.

What if they get carried away with all the fake kisses and fall back in love? A lump settles in my throat, blocking my words of protest.

"No," Alex says quietly. "Out of the question."

I haven't even realized he's laid his hand over mine over his shoulder, squeezing it gently.

"Alex, be reasonable." Preston focuses on our interlinked hands, then snaps his gaze up to me. "Summer, this is business. Surely you understand?"

Clearing my throat, I say, "No, actually. I don't. I think honesty is the only way to go. From where I stand, it looks like the problems started because the studio relied on the fake relationship in the first place."

Amy throws her hands up, her eyes becoming glassy. "Who cares? It's up to us to fix it. We agreed to it in the first place, so it's not like we're innocent.

And if this will fix things, I'm all for it. Do you know how hard it is to get roles once you've got a box office failure of this magnitude hanging around your neck? I don't want to do B-movies for the rest of my life."

Alex interlaces his fingers with mine, brushing the side of my palm with his thumb.

"Look, I'm willing to do anything to bring in more sales. Anything *honest*. The studio knows I don't shy away from hard work. Hard and honest work. I want this movie to succeed as much as anyone else. But I will not lie to the fans. And my relationship with Summer is too important," he says. His words wash over me, melting my worries and insecurities away. He holds my hand tightly, as if he knows. As if he understands. "If you care about Sam at all—"

"Don't pretend you know how I feel," Amy snaps. "Sam understands how this industry works."

"This isn't the time to choose the high road," Preston says calmly. "You don't want to have the reputation of an actor difficult to work with. On top of a possible box office bomb."

"I don't want the reputation of an actor willing to sacrifice his personal life for ticket sales. That's not how I want to build my career."

Amy sniffs, wiping her nose with her sleeves. "You're being selfish. And you're talking like that just because you have another franchise in the works. If you were scrambling for roles like me, you wouldn't have this holier-than-thou attitude."

"Alex—" Preston begins, but Alex cuts him

off.

"This is my final word. If this is why you called this meeting, you're wasting your time. I have a photo shoot in two hours, and I want to have breakfast first."

Alex and Preston exchange a glance, rising to their feet.

"Alex, don't be a stubborn mule," Amy says from the doorway. "You can exercise your newly found ethic compass after we've saved this from becoming a stinker."

Preston doesn't say one thing as he leads Amy out of the room. The second the door closes, Alex guides me around the armchair, pulling me in his lap, bringing his lips to my temple, raining kisses down to my jaw, then further down on my neck.

"Alex, I'm sorry about the box office. How can I help?"

"You already are helping," he whispers. "By being here."

He rubs his thumb across my jawbone, pulling me into a kiss. Oh God, how he kisses me. Like I'm his lifeline, like he needs my strength more than anything else. I give him everything I have, hoping it's enough.

"I felt you go rigid when Preston said Amy and I should start faking it again," he whispers, trailing his mouth down on my neck.

"I'm sorry... I... I want to support your career, Alex. I don't mind hiding from paps or even being chased by them when we eventually go public.

But I couldn't watch you in a fake relationship…."

He stops trailing kisses, snapping his head up until our gazes are level.

"I know. You don't have to explain. Or apologize. I understand perfectly."

"But what if the studio changes their mind about the superhero spin-off? You haven't signed that contract yet after all, right?"

"No, it's all been informal, but I don't like to think in what-ifs. We'll cross that bridge if it comes to it."

"Okay."

He resumes kissing my neck, nibbling at my clavicle. I settle my knees at his sides, wedging them between his thighs and the armrest, kissing what I can reach of him, touching the rest.

"I don't want to go to that photo shoot," he murmurs, unfastening my robe. "I want to stay here with you."

He pushes the tank I've slept in up, baring me to him, feathering his thumbs on the undersides of my breasts, until my nipples harden. Then he rolls each between his thumb and forefinger until I gasp.

"Alex!"

I scramble out of his lap, fastening my robe again. "You don't have time for this, mister. Your photo shoot will start soon, so go. Chop, chop. You can think about this," I gesture to my body, "all day. It'll be your bonus."

He traps me with his molten gaze, licking his lips. I press my thighs together, quenching the sudden ache. To think, I could be feeling his tongue on me right now…. It's messing with my determination to shove him outside the door. Oh goodness, what's a girl to do when Alex unleashes his smolder on her? Surely I'm not expected to resist him. He rises from his armchair, stalking toward me without a word. He pushes my shirt up again, taking one nipple into his mouth, twirling his tongue over it until my toes curl.

"For good luck," he mutters, smiling against my skin. Then he straightens up. Damn. Just when I was going to succumb to the dark side, he decides to behave. Just my luck.

I bare my other breast too, batting my eyelashes at him.

"For the best luck?"

Grinning like the devil he is, he swipes his tongue once over what I'm offering, before covering me.

"Go get them, Westbrook. Charm America with your smolder. I can't wait to have the results in my grubby hands."

"I'll ask the photographer to give me some samples to bring to you. And that smolder? Just know I'll be thinking about you the entire time. Only you."

***

After Alex leaves, I call my cousin Valentina Connor. It's been a few months since I saw her, which is a few months too many.

"Hey, girl," she greets me.

"Val, hey! I'm in LA right now."

"Shut the front door. Since when? Until when? You're not leaving without us meeting, or the bad vibes I'll send you will reach you faster than karma."

I grin. "Relax, Val. Of course we're meeting. That's why I'm calling. I'd love to see all of you. Are Friday dinners still a thing in the Connor clan?"

"Of course. It'll be a thing until we're ninety or toothless, whichever comes first."

"Great. At what time should I stop by tomorrow?"

"Dinner's at seven, but I'll be home at six."

"Perfect. I'll be there at six. See you tomorrow, Val."

The next day, I'm bumbling through shops in search of a gift. The Connors are family, but I don't like to go to anyone's home empty-handed. I love shopping in LA as much as I love taking leisurely strolls. We might still be in California, but LA has such a different vibe than San Francisco, we might as well be on another continent. At least that's how it seems to me. The pace is different than in the Bay area, for one. Plus, the artistic vibe is strong here. I'm about to enter a shop selling hand-sewn tablecloths when Alex calls. Weird! According to his schedule, he should be in a meeting with Preston right now.

"Hey," I greet. "Finally realized they're

exploiting you and you lobbied for a longer break?"

"No, but the atmosphere in the meeting room was so tense, we needed a breather."

"Why?"

"The studio called Preston. They're pulling the plug on the spin-off."

"Oh God." The other shoe dropped freaking fast.

"Yeah. They've read the box office forecast."

My throat tightens. "But that's bullshit. Why are they using predictions for a romantic comedy to make decisions for a superhero franchise?"

"Because there's enough crossover in terms of fans, and because they don't have much else to base their decisions on."

"Why aren't they waiting for the movie in the main superhero series to come out?"

"Because that's an ensemble cast. They're afraid I can't carry a franchise on my own, that I'm not enough of a box office draw without the group. Preston was right about one thing. They've labeled me as difficult. No one wants a diva on their hands."

I fix my gaze on the beautifully sewn rose on one of the tablecloths in the storefront, but I'm not really seeing it.

"You're not a diva for wanting to be in control of your personal life. Where are you?"

"Taking a walk in the hotel's inner yard."

God, he sounds so sad that all I want to do is wrap my arms around him.

"How long is your break? I can be at the hotel

in half an hour, and I can bring donuts. They make everything better. I promise. I can sprinkle a kiss or two as well, you know, for improving your luck."

"No, that's fine. I'm going to walk some more on my own, gather my thoughts, consider my options."

If someone dropped an ice bucket on my head, I don't think my blood would have felt as glacial. Consider his options? What exactly does this mean? Is he considering faking the romance with Amy after all? I'm too much of a coward to ask.

"Tell me how I can make things better, Alex."

"You can't right now. I just need to think."

A hundred-pound weight settles on my chest. Yesterday morning he said we'll find solutions together. Up until now, he's always sought my presence when things went haywire. Why does he want to be alone now?

"Okay. You'll tell me if you change your mind?" I ask.

"Yeah."

"Alex, I'm really sorry about this."

"So am I. Listen, I've got to go. I just wanted to tell you."

"Okay. See you tonight. We're still on for room service at ten, right?"

He has another photo shoot while I'm at Val's, and it should last until nine.

"Of course. Have fun with your cousins."

"Thanks. I will."

Spending time with the Connors is always fun,

but I'm not sure even Val's cooking or Jace's constant teasing will keep me from worrying.

Chapter Thirty

Summer

The cab drive to Val's house takes forever, which gives me far too much time with my thoughts. I fiddle with my phone, itching to call Alex again, to hear his voice, reassure him somehow. But here's the thing: I don't know how to reassure him. No matter how you look at it, this blows. And he said he needs time to think. My being a nuisance wouldn't help at all.

Even though it nags at me that he won't at least let me be there for him, I shove my phone deep in my purse and look out the window.

Traffic is the one thing I dislike about LA. Not that San Francisco lacks in this department, but LA is considerably bigger. So is its traffic problem. I use this as an opportunity to admire the street fashion and art.

When the cab pulls in front of Val's gate, I can't help a smile. Her fence is painted in vibrant blue. A few months ago, it was green. She's always changing something. Val is one of those people who can't stay still for too long.

I push past the gate and up the cobblestone alley snaking up to her beautiful ranch-style house, which is on top of a rather vicious slope.

"I promise I'm going to turn the alley into stairs… eventually. Everyone complains about the slope, including myself. I'm looking for a landscaper, someone who can transform this whole space." Val waits for me at the top, arms open. I walk right into them.

"I missed you," I say.

"Back at you. Come on in, everyone's waiting."

"Oh, but I'm not late, am I?"

"Nah, but when I told them you're joining us, they all came earlier."

Val leads me inside the house, straight to the dining room, where all the Connors are gathered. Well, all minus Landon, Val's twin brother. He's in the Bay area.

We have many cousins, but I've always had a soft spot for the Connors. We're related on my mother's side. Their parents died when Landon and Valentina were freshmen in college, and the two of them came straight back home, gave up their scholarships and took care of their brothers and sisters. Jace pulls me into a bear hug, almost crushing me with those strong arms of his—hazards of being a professional athlete.

"Jace, you can let go now. The rest of us are waiting our turn," Will teases.

"Ah, Mr. Sexy McHottie, always impatient," I say, turning to him.

Their father, an Irishman through and

through, was a mountain of a man, with rugged, handsome features. And the brothers inherited all that allure. There is no other way to put it, the Connor men are hunks, but I officially gave Will the nickname when he visited us one summer and *all* my girlfriends were swooning after him. If they could see him now.

Will scowls, shaking his head. "Can't escape the Sexy McHottie jokes even now."

My cousin Lori clears her throat, eyeing her young son, Milo.

Ooops. I forgot about the kid censorship, but I focus on Milo next.

"Hi! I brought you something." I pull a miniature Ferrari from my purse, handing it to him.

"Wow! Cool."

Lori nudges him. "What do you say to Aunt Summer?"

"Thank you, Aunt Summer."

"You're welcome."

Lori and the third sister, Hailey, pull me into a group hug.

"Wow, I love the smell," I say as a delicious whiff drafts in from the kitchen. "You made red pepper quiche?"

Val winks. "Of course. Thought making your favorite might give you an incentive to visit us more often."

"She cooks Landon's favorite when he visits too," Will informs me. "It's only my pleas for baked Camembert she ignores. Discriminating much?"

Val bumps her shoulder into his forearm.

"We can't have Camembert every Friday, you big oaf. Besides, Jace can't eat all that fat. Not on his meal plan. We can't have our star losing his edge, can we?"

"Oh, I don't know," I say, "I've watched Jace play. I'd say there's no danger in him losing the edge."

Jace nods. "True, but my coach would jump down my throat if I didn't respect the meal plan. I'll make an exception for you, though."

"More proof of discrimination," Will whispers to me conspiratorially.

"Let's set the table," Val announces. "The quiche is almost ready."

Ten minutes later, we're all sitting around the table, enjoying Val's cooking.

"How come you're in LA?" Hailey asks. "Work or pleasure?"

"Both," I say vaguely. I trust them, but the fewer people know about Alex and me, the better.

"Why aren't you staying with me? You always stay with me," Val asks, pointing her fork at me. Oh man, I hate lying.

"We're a group, so it was easier." Which is not exactly a lie, though that doesn't ease my conscience.

"Have you seen Landon lately?" she continues.

"Not as much as I should, considering he's so close. But he's turned into a workaholic." He's always had a solid work ethic, but after losing his wife, the whole thing escalated.

"We know. He's like a robot," Lori complains. "We're working on turning him human again, but are failing in grand fashion."

"Have you tried emotional blackmail?" I suggest. "Always works on my brothers."

"We tried," Val says. "But maybe we missed something. Give us pointers."

Jace grimaces. "No, no, no. Don't do that, or Will and I will be toast too."

The whole table starts laughing. The evening flies by as we rehash old and dear memories. But as nine o'clock approaches, my thoughts flit more and more to Alex. I need a plan of attack to soothe him. Now, I didn't get to be twenty-eight without facing my own shitty periods, but my entire dealing-with-crap arsenal might not be enough for this occasion. Still, some tactics are clear winners.

I excuse myself from the table, heading to the foyer where I left my purse and phone. I want to call the hotel, make sure they have cheesecake with caramel topping ready when I return. A lot of caramel topping.

I have three missed calls from Preston, three from Alex, and a message.

Alex: Can't make it to our date tonight, and we have to cancel the weekend plans. I'll explain everything later. Be careful when you get back to the hotel. It will be crawling with paps. I already talked to Preston about security.

Oh boy, oh boy. What is going on? Swallowing past the unease in my throat, I call Alex, but it goes to voice mail. I try Preston next. He picks up right away.

"Summer, thank God. I tried to reach you. Okay, so here's the new development. Amy and Alex are preparing for a press conference tonight here at the hotel to make the announcement."

"The announcement?"

"Yeah, that they're supposedly back together. I'm so glad you two finally worked that out. It's for the best. These weeks will pass by quickly, you'll see. I'm arranging right now for Alex's things to be moved to Amy's home. It will be tricky to get you two to meet, but we'll manage to sneak you in somehow."

I'm too numb to react for a few seconds. My thoughts freeze, my body feels foreign. Like someone else is standing here, hearing those words. He decided this... just like that? Without even bothering to tell me, let alone consider my feelings?

"Be careful when you come back to the hotel. All entrances are swarmed with paps. Text me when you're five minutes away, and I will send our security guys to sneak you in."

The hotel? I don't want to go back to the hotel. To see Alex and Amy pose for cameras, kiss, hug. To fear that they might fall back in love.

How exactly does Alex think he can explain this to me?

Summer, my career is in a rocky spot. This was the

easiest way out. Sorry for sweeping your feelings under a rug like the assholes before me. Oh, but yes, you're very important to me. Sorry you'll have to endure a few weeks of me kissing Amy and sharing a house with her, but afterward, everything will be peachy.

"Preston, I won't be returning to the hotel. I'll text you an address. Can you send my bag? It's all packed in my room." I need to be surrounded by family right now, by people who care about me unconditionally.

"Sure. That's a great idea, actually. Safer for you and everyone involved."

After the call disconnects, I lean against the wall, working on breathing past the lump in my throat, the tightness in my chest. I don't know how long I stay here, but it must be long enough because Val comes to check on me.

"What's wrong? Bad news?"

"Can I stay here tonight?"

She smiles sympathetically. "Sure. But what happened? The pleasure part of *work and pleasure* didn't work out?"

"Something like that."

"Oh, honey, I've got you covered. I'll treat you to Val's Kit for Emotional Messes as soon as the gang leaves."

"Val, you're my hero."

I'm on autopilot for the next hour or so, until everyone filters out. The second Val and I are alone, I curl up on her couch like a kitten.

"Do you have ice cream?" I ask.

"Nope. Cardinal sin, I know, but if I know it's in the freezer, I just eat it. But I have hot chocolate, whipped cream, and a bottle of Pinot Noir."

"We drank Chardonnay at dinner. Why don't we stick to it?"

Val motions no with her finger. "Chardonnay's for celebrating. Pinot Noir is for commiserating."

"Because Pinot's bitter and sour?"

"You've got it."

I throw my head back, laughing. God, I could hug Val for making me laugh. "Pinot it is. I can't believe you have a system for that."

After setting us both up with a glass, she joins me on the couch.

"Want to tell me what happened, or you just need commiserating?"

"Just commiserating."

"I'm your girl."

"How come you're such a pro at it?"

Val plays with her glass, shrugging. "Practice. You should've seen me and Lori when she realized she's going to be a single parent. I've had my own pity parties too, obviously." She sighs, sipping from her glass. "Some people just stumble onto their happily ever after, and others only find shitty ever after. At least we have Mr. Pinot."

"Hear, hear."

I twirl my glass, watching the wine swish inside. Oh, what I wouldn't give for that cheesecake with caramel topping. I wonder if I can have Preston send me a portion along with my bag, then push the thought away.

Nope, not even cheesecake is a good enough reward to risk Preston giving me more details. I don't want to know. Should I have pushed more today? Gone to Alex even if he hadn't wanted me to? Would he still have decided the same? Could I have changed his mind?

I gave Alex my heart. Why couldn't he take care of it the way I wanted to take care of his? With a lot of love and dedication? Was that so much to ask? My chest burns, and I swear my heart stings, as if someone is drilling and drilling inside it. I blink back tears, sipping my Pinot. I'm so tired of heartbreak, of putting myself out there only to have my heart stomped on. Something must be wrong with me, deep down, I just know it. Why else would my love not be enough? I break out in a cold sweat, even as my insides churn and burn.

"Summer, whatever happened is not the end of the world. You can start over."

I try to muster a smile for Val, but my entire face feels wobbly. I don't want to start over. I wanted to love that man for the rest of my days. And even though my heart feels like it's splitting in two, I can't bring myself to even imagine anyone else but him. Why couldn't he value that?

"Crap, Pinot won't cut it tonight," Val says, inspecting my cheeks, which are stained with tears. "I'm going to run to the store and buy some Ben & Jerry's. My go-to flavor for such occasions is strawberry cheesecake?"

"Oh, that's a good one. But I also love caramel. Buy all things with caramel. And I need hugs. Lots and lots of hugs."

Chapter Thirty-One

Alex

The roar of voices in the hotel's conference room grows deafening when Amy and I step inside. The clicks of cameras form a constant stream that rises above the voices.

The reporters only grow silent after we take our places at the table. I glance sideways at Amy. Her hands are shaking in her lap. My nerves are strung tight too, but this is the only way forward. When the sound technician announces the mics are ready to go, I clasp the one in front of me, bring it to my lips. Amy gives me a thumbs-up, her smile tight.

"Good evening, everyone. Thank you for showing up at such short notice. Amy and I appreciate it. We've called you all here to address the rumors that have been flying around lately. They've been overshadowing all the events Amy and I've attended, whether together or separate. It's been overshadowing our work on *Bree Shannon*, and that's a shame. We want to put an end to the speculations, give you information right from the horse's mouth."

I'm not looking at anyone in particular as I speak, my gaze simply sweeps through the crowd. I'm definitely not looking at Preston.

"Two months ago, our breakup made tabloid rounds, but the truth was, we'd been over a long time before that."

I nod at Amy, who grips her own mic tightly and begins to speak.

"We'd been trying to make it work for months, but we were struggling. We fell out of love gradually."

Preston waves his hands from the back of the room, but I purposefully ignore him. No one will stop the conference while Amy and I keep talking.

"Not only that, but we fell in love with other people," she continues, her voice stronger. "There was no cheating, no lies. We just weren't meant for each other."

The crowd erupts all at once, firing off question after question. I talk until my throat feels like sandpaper, regurgitating the answers Amy and I agreed upon beforehand. This could be career suicide for both of us, but it's a risk I just have to take. No more lies. All the spin-offs in the world aren't worth these lies. Summer is right. Honesty is the best policy. I'm doing this for her, and for us. I don't want us to have to hide anymore.

I barely convinced Amy to go along with me. We both perused our contract with the studio to make sure we wouldn't be outright breaking it, but the execs will be livid nonetheless that we've taken matters into our own hands, going directly against their directives.

The conference lasts well into the night. Once

the shock of the announcement settles, everyone wants to know who the significant others are.

"Mine is an actor," Amy says coyly. "Alex here went after a civilian. And she's very lovely."

I won't reveal Summer's name before talking this out with her. Amy gives me an honest smile. Despite our spotty history, I'm grateful to her for doing this, even though this isn't her favorite option.

After I pledged my case, she said, "Well, you won't budge on the fake romance things, and my career is in the toilet as it is. I suppose this can't get worse. But Preston said he's trying to talk the execs into reconsidering your spin-off. They won't give it another thought after this."

"It's a risk I'm willing to take," I assured her.

We didn't tell anyone from our teams what we were planning to announce so no one could stop us.

"We need more details. Who are the lucky ones? Amy? Alex? Come on, one of you has to budge."

I smile mysteriously. "Nope. I have to prepare my girl for going public properly."

"Aww, did you hear. He called her *my girl*," someone says in the back.

On and on it goes, and after it ends, I head straight to my floor, flanked by bodyguards and avoiding Preston. I know exactly what he'll tell me, and I'm not in the mood to hear it. I'll deal with the fallout in the morning. I suspect said fallout will include extreme paparazzi attention and an explosion in interview requests.

It's why I told Summer to drop whatever plans she had for the weekend. No way would I be able to protect her from the press. I stop by Summer's room first and knock at the door, but no one answers. Maybe she's waiting in my room. I swipe the keycard, pushing my door open. The room is dark. Switching on the light, I walk from room to room, but she isn't anywhere. Did she decide to stay at her cousin's overnight? I did warn her the hotel would be crawling with paps. If I'm honest, it's safer for her to stay away tonight, but I need her warmth tonight of all nights.

My career is hanging by a thin thread, but it doesn't matter if I have her. Where is she?

Sitting on the empty bed, I pick up my phone from the nightstand. I didn't carry it with me in the conference room. I have a plethora of missed calls and messages, including one from Summer.

Summer: I can't be with you through this, I'm sorry. I hope everything works out for you.

My fingers turn icy against the plastic case of the phone. *She's sorry? She can't be with me through this?*

My chest constricts as I try to make sense of this. I check the time of the message. She sent it midway through the conference. Did she realize the press attention she'll get once we go public and decided it was too much after all? That she could do without all that in her life? That being with me was not worth the hassle?

Jesus, she can't mean this, can she? I thought... she seemed to love me. Was I projecting?

Wishing I wasn't the only one who felt so strongly?

Well, even if she did have feelings for me, they were clearly not strong enough to last if she decided to give up. The ache in my chest obstructs my breath.

I've had so many friends walk out on me due to the complications of my fame. Even my parents distanced themselves. But Summer deciding what we have is not worth fighting for stabs deeper than the rest.

Chapter Thirty-Two

Alex

A knock at the door interrupts my thoughts.

"Alex, we need to talk," Preston says. I open the door right away. Verbal sparring with Preston is just what I need to take my mind off Summer. Preston stomps into the room dragging his hands down his face.

"You're trying to kill me, aren't you?" he asks.

"No, murder isn't on my to-do list. Voluntary or not," I deadpan. Preston's collar is darkened with sweat.

"Why didn't you tell me what you were going to announce?"

"Because you would have tried to convince me not to."

Preston throws his hands up in the air. "Damn right I would have. But there's no use crying over spilled milk right now. You knew everything you were risking and still went through with it."

I sit, sprawled on the couch, watching Preston pace like a lion in a cage.

"Now we need to make the most of this. All eyes are on you. Maybe if we turn this into positive publicity, the studio won't have your ass. I've already had five high-profile interview requests."

"Perfect, book them."

Preston takes out his phone. Tension seems to bleed away from him while he types. After finishing, he whips his head up.

"You'd better not leave your room tonight. The paps are everywhere. A crowd of fans gathered too. We'll have to sneak you out tomorrow through a service entrance, or you'll be mobbed. Good thing I've already sent Summer her bag."

"What? When?"

"She called me when the conference was about to begin. I explained it would be safer if she didn't return tonight, and she asked me to send her bag. Obviously, since she thought you and Amy were going to live together for the next few weeks—"

My spine stiffens. "Why would she think that?"

Preston stares at me. "That's what I told her. That's what I, and everyone else, thought the conference was about."

"Tell me exactly what you told her and what she said." I push myself to my feet, taking in two deep breaths.

"I told her you were going to announce that you're back together with Amy, and I was making arrangements to have your stuff moved into her house. I told her it'd be better if she didn't come to the hotel tonight because the paps would be all over the place, and she agreed, asking me to send her bag. This is all moot, I suppose since she now knows you didn't."

But I know better. I could bet anything Summer hasn't even tuned in to watch. Not if she thought I was about to announce a "reunion" with Amy. I understand the message now. Fuck, I can't even imagine what she must be thinking. I can count on one hand the instances when I wanted to throttle Preston. This is one of them.

"I need to leave the hotel," I say.

"You can't do that, Alex. There is no way for you to get out of the hotel without being followed by paps."

My mind is racing. I need to talk to Summer, but I can't lead the paps to her. I'll call her. Except, she must be sleeping. It's past midnight. I'll wait until the morning and whip up a plan.

Preston and I end up not going to sleep at all. Preston's phone rings with request after request for interviews. His e-mail inbox is overflowing too. The media never sleeps. We adapt my schedule with every call, and the next two weeks will be spent traveling across the country. I'm not looking forward to it. Overnight, three fans and a pap attempt to sneak up to my floor. That's why I wanted to move out of LA. Celebrity culture is out of control here.

Toward five o'clock in the morning, things slow down. I gaze out of the window. I have a direct view over the back entrance of the hotel. There are fewer paps out there. Experience has taught me that this is the magic hour, when most head home for a nap, or just to get a coffee. In two hours max, they'll all be back and on high alert. This is my window of opportunity.

I turn to Preston. "Arrange a car for me."

"Your plane leaves before lunch. You have plenty of time."

"I want to see Summer first."

"Alex—" he begins to protest, but I cut him off.

"I'll be gone for the next two weeks. I'm not leaving before seeing my girl first and talking to her face-to-face. There are fewer paps out there. You know where she's staying, right?"

"I know where I sent her bag, but there's no guarantee she's still there. Maybe she went to a hotel."

Nah, I know Summer. She likes being with her family. I'm sure she spent the night at her cousin's.

"Have a car ready in ten minutes. I'm taking all the bags with me. I'm going straight to LAX afterward."

Ten minutes later, I stride through the dim garage of the hotel and climb into the back seat of a gray Toyota. The car should be inconspicuous enough. It doesn't have tinted windows, which poses a risk, but it'll draw less attention.

"Hey, Mike," I greet the driver, handing him a slip of paper with Summer's address. "Let's get out of here without making a fuss."

"Hard thing to do with all those wolves out there waiting for you, but I'll do my best."

Today's disguise isn't my cap, but a newspaper. I hold it open close enough, so my face isn't visible from the sides. My stomach knots when the car lurches forward, then up the ramp leading out of the garage. When the car is horizontal, Mike hits the gas hard. I sink against my seat as the car propels forward.

"We have a pap car behind us," Mike announces.

"Just one?"

"Yes."

"We need to lose the trail before reaching the highway."

Left, right, left again. Into a passage, then out of it and down a labyrinth of streets. Our detour takes almost an hour, and my temples are pounding from the adrenaline coursing through me, but it pays off. We lose the pap car.

"Great job, Mike."

"Thank you, Mr. Westbrook."

I relax a little, pressing my fingers to my temple, moving them in a circular pattern. When my phone beeps, I expect to find a message from Preston, but I'm pleasantly surprised.

Summer: Are you awake?

I wasn't expecting her to be up so early.

Alex: Yes.

I call her at the same time she calls me.

"Any chance you deleted my message last night without reading it?" she quips.

"I read it. Talked to Preston too. I know what

he told you. Neither Amy nor I shared with our teams what we were going to announce, so they'd assumed we were going along with the studio's plan. I'm sorry I didn't tell you the plans, but you didn't pick up your phone, and I didn't want to put all that in a message. I couldn't wait for you to return to the hotel to talk to you about it, we had to act fast. But I'm sorry, I didn't handle that well. Are you at your cousin's?"

"Yes. Why?"

"Because I'm on my way. We had a pap car behind us, but we lost the tail. I'll be there in…"

"Three minutes," Mike tells me.

"…three minutes," I repeat into the phone.

"Oh, shit. I didn't tell Val about you. She'll freak out. She'll fangirl. But she's trustworthy. She won't tell anyone." She talks so fast that I barely catch her words.

"Baby, relax. It's okay. I won't stay long. I need to get to LAX, but I wanted to see you this morning. Set things straight."

"Yes, Preston e-mailed it to me. I saw just before I texted you."

"We just pulled into your cousin's street."

"I'll come open the front gate."

A few seconds later, the car slows to a stop. Shoving the phone into my pocket, I look around before climbing out, but the street is deserted except for a few parked cars, so I head to the front gate, which opens right away.

"I told my cousin, but I don't think she's had

time to process it," Summer whispers as she lets me inside the yard. A tall brunette approaches us, grinning widely.

"Alex, this is my cousin Valentina. Val, this is—"

"Alexander Westbrook," her cousin says, looking between Summer and me before letting out a squeal. "Oh my God. Oh my God. You were talking about Summer last night at the conference?" She turns to Summer. "You've been holding out on me. I can't believe this. Oh my God. My lips are sealed, though. Don't worry."

I smile, even though I'm getting impatient. I want to be alone with my girl.

"Valentina, right? Not to be rude, but I don't have much time. I need to leave for LAX soon, and I want to talk to Summer alone."

"Yes of course. I'll just… find something to do." Valentina nods vigorously, then climbs the steep slope of the yard, entering the house. I take Summer's hand, leading her to the small wooden picnic table at the foot of the slope.

Then I cup her face in my hands and kiss her with all I have until we both come up for air. "I'm sorry I didn't tell you about the plan," I say, still out of breath. "I should have found a way, but there was no time. I wasn't thinking straight. I had no idea Preston would jump to conclusions before seeing the actual conference. I would never have gone for the fake romance, Summer. I promised you I wouldn't."

"I know, I'm sorry. It's just that… when we

spoke yesterday afternoon you sounded so distant, and I… I know I was overthinking it, but it felt like you were pushing me away a bit, wanting to deal with it all on your own."

I press my forehead against hers, breathing in her sweet scent. Did I do that? Admittedly, I've always had the tendency to push out everyone when shit hits the fan, focusing on finding a solution.

"It wasn't my intention to shut you out. I'm sorry I made you feel that way. Sometimes I get lost in my own head when things get rough, but I promise I'll do better. I'm a work in progress, baby, but you mean so much to me. You're so amazing and so important to me. Don't doubt that. I need you to promise me one thing too. That you won't believe again that I'd do anything that could hurt you. I need you to trust me."

"I know. I do. But Preston said it, and he knows everything that's going on. And I know how important your career is to you. I thought… well… I thought that when it came down to it, you'd do anything for it."

Including walking all over her feelings. I can't even imagine what she went through last night. My sweet girl.

"I'm sorry about the text. Were you mad at me?" she asks.

"Yeah, I was. Because I thought I'd lost you, and I love you too much to let that happen, Summer."

"Oh, Alex… I love you too. So much."

I kiss her again, and I don't let her go until I feel her melt against me, and she sighs in my mouth. I need to reassure this amazing woman that she's the most important person in my life. I need to show her.

"I'm so glad you came to see me," she whispers. "You need to be kissed and smothered with love before you leave. I can't do that over the phone."

My Summer. Always looking out for me.

"When will we see each other? Your schedule for the next two weeks looks packed."

"It is, but I'll fly straight home after it's over."

"When are you flying to Chicago? I saw that your first interview is there."

"Take off is scheduled in two hours. I was thinking about leaving part of my security team with you—"

"I don't need it. You didn't name me. I'll be fine, Alex. Just fine. Don't worry about me. Concentrate on the interviews. And by the way? I'm so proud of you for laying it all out like that, for doing things on your terms."

I smile. I knew Summer would understand. She's probably the only one who does.

"Thank you."

"Have you heard from the studio execs yet?"

"Preston did. They're pissed off. If they saw me as difficult before, now I'm their least favorite person. I'll try to turn things around during these interviews."

"I know you will." I kiss her again, until she feels it in her very bones that she's *the one*.

Chapter Thirty-Three

Summer

The week after my return from LA drags on forever. Olivia is on edge, snapping at everyone. I heard that in my absence, she yelled at Diana, who let slip that if I ever open my gallery, she'll work for me even for free. As a result, I'm her least favorite person. The idea has been brewing in my mind for a long time, more so after the confrontation with Olivia last week.

During my breaks, I look online for spaces to rent, make lists of galleries I could work with and artists I'd like to feature. On a particularly reckless evening, I even pull up my old business plan template. Could I pull this off? I *do* have more experience. And lately, I found the courage too. Seeing Alex take risks has been rubbing off on me. He makes me want to dare more, to reach for what I want.

I've been feverishly watching his appearances. The fans adored his and Amy's interview in LA. I can't quite understand why, but Preston says it's probably because they have two fresh happily ever afters to latch onto.

Gossip magazines still blast snippets of it.

There is no word from the studio regarding the spin-off. Whenever someone asks Alex about his secret love, he smiles mysteriously and says it wouldn't be a secret if he spilled the beans.

What with his back-to-back appearances and flights this week, we've only had time for short, quick conversations. I'm in a half mind to fly to New York, where his next appearance is. He needs love and pampering, and it's hard to do that from a distance.

He needed me that night after the conference. Was I there to shower him with love and reassure him that his career won't go up in flames—or that I'll be there for him and support him even if it does? No, I was not.

What if he thinks we might not be meant to be together after all?

I try to push that thought away, but fear is a sneaky thing. I push it out the door, but it comes barreling back through a window, which prompts my sisters to whisk me to a spa on Saturday morning.

"You look like you need some girl time and pampering," Pippa declares. I told them what went down in LA when I returned, and they've been watching over me like mother hens ever since.

"I'll never say no to that."

Alice nods vigorously. "We're going for manicures, pedicures, massage, facials. The entire shebang."

"Do you also need cookies? Cupcakes? Should we go all-out with tiramisu?" Pippa inquires as we climb into her car. "We need to estimate the seriousness of this."

"I'm conflicted," I say honestly. "But there's no way we can go wrong with cupcakes, right?"

"Done," Pippa says.

Alice takes her phone out of her bag. "I'm calling my cook to tell him to make us a fresh batch."

"Alice!" I admonish. "Your cook's shift starts in one hour."

She smiles sweetly. "It's a sisterly emergency. And he knows better than to say no."

Oh man, some sisterly love is *just* what the doctor ordered. I love them to the moon and back for spending this day with me.

They drop me back at home late in the afternoon, and I fiddle some more with my business plan. When the alarm on my laptop rings, I scramble for my remote. Alex's segment on one of the top national late-night shows begins in a few minutes.

My heart rate picks up when Alex appears on screen. He takes my breath away every time.

"Alex, you've caused quite a stir," the host, David, says. He's one of my favorite presenters, with a spot-on humor and old Hollywood type of charm. "You're the fans' golden boy again."

"So everyone tells me." He turns to look straight at the camera. "I hope it gets back to the studio." Turning to look straight at the live audience in the studio, he holds his hand in front of the mouth, mimicking an amplifier. "Spread the word, guys. Spread the word."

"Still giving you trouble, eh? I've heard there is a petition for your spin-off to be approved. Received three million votes."

Alex holds up his finger. "And counting! Thank you for all your support, folks."

The presenter leans forward, clasping his hands together, a crooked grin on his face. "I've got to ask. You've been mysterious about it, but I still have to ask. America is dying to know. Who won Alexander Westbrook's heart?"

Alex turns to the audience again, fake whispering. "Who will tell David I can't say? He won't invite me again if I tell him to his face to mind his own business."

The audience roars with laughter.

"Do you think she's watching?" David asks.

"Come on, man. You're putting me in a rough spot. If I say yes, she'll think I'm a self-absorbed you-know-what. If I say no… well, I actually don't know what she'd think."

David leans back in his chair, crossing his arms over his chest, a thoughtful look on his face. "True. I don't know what my wife would say either, and I've been married for twenty years. Women's minds are a mystery, huh?"

"The struggle is real, David. But hats off to them for keeping us on our toes."

I grin, clutching a couch pillow to my chest. Surely that's a good sign?

David tilts his head. "I'll try another angle. You can't tell us who she is, or where you met. But tell us about her. What made you fall for her?"

Oh, oh, oh! I shift to the edge of my couch, swallowing hard once, twice, hoping to overcome the rhythmic thumping in my ears.

"She's fun and stubborn. I don't know exactly when I started to fall in love: when I realized how sweet she is, or how fierce. But I haven't stopped falling since."

David whistles, clapping his hands. "I think if we opened the window now, we'd hear America release a collective swoon."

Yes, yes, they would! I'm swooning loud enough for the entire country.

"What would you tell her if you knew she'd be watching?" David asks.

The camera focuses on Alex's handsome face, and he flashes my favorite smile. The one he shows only when we're alone. I grip the pillow tighter, my ass nearly sliding off the couch as I lean forward in anticipation.

"I'd tell her that she has my heart. I can't wait for this tour to be over so I can head straight to her. I miss her every day. And I'd be the luckiest guy if she married me."

Messages pop up on the screen of my phone before I even have time to react.

Alice: Have you just been proposed to on national television?

Pippa: OMMGGGGGGG yes!!! I'd call, but I don't want us to miss anything else he has to say.

Val: BRING OUT THE CHARDONNAY!!!!!

"Way to raise the stakes!" David exclaims. "Folks, this is how a superhero proposes. On primetime TV."

The audience cheers and whistles, and as the camera focuses on them, they wave, sending kisses.

Whoa. Did he really propose? Is this really happening, or is it just a figment of my imagination? Wishful thinking, because I've dreamed so much for Alex and me to be forever? My heart grows in size, and I have an overwhelming urge to hug someone, preferably Alex. My eyes are damp with tears, but there is no one here to see, so I don't bother to wipe them.

This terrible, terrible man. Look who's talking about being kept on his toes.

I turn my attention to the TV again, but David and Alex have already moved to another topic. I lie on my couch curled up, hugging two pillows to my chest, smiling like a fool.

Alex calls forty-eight seconds after the show is over. In my haste to answer, I somehow manage to reject the call. My hands are trembling a tiny bit as I call him back.

"Sorry, I pressed the wrong button," I explain.

"What are you up to?"

It takes me a second to realize he doesn't know I've been watching.

"I watched the show." My eyes sting, happy tears swelling to the surface. The problem with these pesky tears is that it doesn't matter if they're happy or sad, I still get that weird knot in my throat. As I try to swallow it, a snotty sound reverberates from my throat and nose.

"Summer, are you crying? Why are you crying?"

"Because I love you. I love you so much, and I… I didn't know if that was enough," I admit, sandwiching the pillows between my knees and chin.

"Babe, you're mine. Even when you're scared or have doubts, you're mine to love and take care of. I love you more than life, Summer. You have my heart, and you'll have it for the rest of our days. I can't promise you it will all be rainbows and sunshine—"

"I don't want you to promise me that."

"But I do promise we'll work through everything together. We'll be a team, and we'll make it through every challenge."

"You're so romantic," I whisper.

"I propose in front of the entire country, but you think this is romantic?"

My entire body yearns for him. I need to feel the warmth of his arms around me, his lips on mine.

"Both are romantic, Alex. That was the fairy-tale version. This… this is real."

"So you're saying yes?"

"Of course I'm saying yes. Did you plan this? Saying it on TV?"

"Not exactly. You've only ever known real love and trust from your family. I think I only realized that last week after the ordeal with the conference. I wanted to do something big so you don't even have a one percent doubt about how I feel. So when David pushed, I thought, here's my chance to go all-out."

I close my eyes, smiling from ear to ear. How can he know I needed that? Even I didn't know it. "Alex, I wish you were here so I could snuggle the living daylights out of you."

"Snuggle? I go all-out, and it only earns me a snuggle?"

"I might throw in a kiss or two. I'm *not* saying where."

He chuckles softly, then asks, "When would you like to go public? You'll have a mob out your front door, so I'd rather be there with you."

"Would it help with the box office if we went public now? Every media outlet is bursting to know. Positive publicity would bring more fans to the ticket counter." The *Bree Shannon* premiere is next week.

"That doesn't matter."

"I'll take it as a yes, so I say we go public as soon as possible. I can deal with the press, Alex."

"Stubborn woman. What am I going to do with you?"

"Well, apparently you want to marry me, so I think you secretly like it."

"I will not confirm that."

I grin. "I notice you're not denying it either."

"I've got to keep a few aces up my sleeve, future wife."

My grin widens. "It'll be my pleasure to discover them one by one, future husband."

***

The next day, I'm on pins and needles as I arrive at my parents' house. Mom called yesterday after the show and insisted I stop by to spill all the details. My sisters announced they're joining us too. As is habit in the Bennett clan, it became a big affair, so now the entire family is getting together for some steaks and gossip. When I pull into their yard, I realize everyone else is already here. Whoops, did I remember the time wrong? I'm fairly sure we agreed on one o'clock, and I'm usually not late.

Everyone is milling around the gazebo, where two grills have been set up. When I'm close enough to see who is who, my heart goes pitter-patter. Sophie is here, with her husband and son. My parents are in the gazebo... with Alex.

"Our girl's here," Pippa calls as I walk up the steps to the gazebo.

"What are you doing here?" I ask Alex.

Dad pats his shoulder. "Came to do things by the book, ask for your hand."

Oh my God.

Mom hugs me, kissing my cheek. "You've got yourself a great man, baby girl."

She lets go of me and, together with Dad,

walks out into the yard, leaving me and Alex alone in the gazebo.

He steps right in front of me, taking my hands in his, kissing them.

"I wanted to make this special. Surrounded by our families." He lowers himself on one knee, taking out a small, dark red jewelry box with the Bennett Enterprises logo embossed on it. He opens it to reveal a beautiful white gold ring, with a large princess cut diamond in the center and three small sapphires on either side.

"Summer Bennett, will you be my wife? Will you be mine to love and cherish every day?"

"Yes, yes I will."

I hear someone sniff behind me as he pushes the ring on my finger, then stands and takes me in his arms, kissing me softly.

"And they were all in on this?" I ask him.

"Yes, we were," Alice chirps from somewhere behind me. "Well, about today, not the TV thing yesterday."

"Alex and I have been plotting ever since you returned from LA," Pippa adds. "But I had to keep the secret."

"I can't wait to call you my wife, Summer Bennett," Alex says. "I love you."

"I love you, too, Alexander Westbrook."

Chapter Thirty-Four

Three months later

Summer

Choosing only one or two flower girls and boys from my nephews would have started a small war, and as such, I had an entire brood of flower kids. Everyone who can walk on their own two feet received a basket. All the girls are wearing princess dresses, and the boys miniature suits. The youngest are still a tiny bit unsteady on their feet, but I figured they'd be walking on sand, so no biggie even if they fell. Not one of them even wobbled on their feet.

They're still carrying their baskets inside the restaurants, even though their jobs were over once they spewed flowers on the carpet we rolled out on the beach.

Alex and I decided on a destination wedding. After we went public three months ago—Tara Delaware got the exclusive story first—things became a little gaga. On the bright side, the publicity helped *Bree Shannon Finds Love #2* rake enough at the box office for the studio to greenlight Alex's superhero spin-off.

I've always wanted a beach wedding, but with

all the media attention, we couldn't do that in San Francisco, or the place would be crawling with paps.

"I still can't believe we've flown everyone to Hawaii," I say to Alex. We're sitting at the bride and groom's table, watching our guests. The room is beautiful, decorated in shades of champagne and gold, with twinkle lights adorning the ceiling.

"I wanted you to have your dream wedding." He kisses my hand, smiling mischievously. I can't believe this gorgeous man is my husband. "You're beautiful, Summer. I love your dress."

"Thanks."

I don't just love my dress. I *love, love, love* it. Nadine, Logan's wife, designed it, and it couldn't be more perfect. She wrote down every single request I had, and I was half expecting her to tell me I'm crazy, but instead, she held up a finger and announced, "I know just what you want." The result is a stunning mermaid-shaped dress with a lace pattern crisscrossing the skirt. The bodice is asymmetric on one shoulder, made of strips of intricately braided silk and lace.

"I can't wait to take it off you," he whispers.

Of course, that's where he was going with it. Typical. But then again, I've been harboring thoughts of tearing that tuxedo off him all evening. Great minds think alike, right? "I can't wait to make love to you, wife. I can't wait to love you for the rest of our lives."

He leans in closer, feathering his lips over mine.

"Remember! Keep the heat level under five," I say breathily.

"I did a great job at the ceremony, didn't I?" he counters.

"You did." He was the perfect gentleman. Decent kiss. Too decent. Too gentlemanly. "And the entire time, I wanted to climb you."

"Watch it, or I'll use this as leverage tonight."

I grin. "*Excellent* plan, husband."

The DJ taps the mic, announcing it's time for my speech. Alex went first, and he charmed the room from the get-go. He didn't even seem to break a sweat, while my palms are already clammy. I'm not great with speeches, but I want to make one tonight.

"Are you ready?" Alex asks.

"Not one bit."

"I've got you, Summer."

I stand up, picking up the mic from the table, where Alex put it after his speech, and clear my throat. Yikes. Here goes nothing. I just have one rule. No tears.

"Thank you all for being here today and celebrating with us. I know flying across the country on such short notice wasn't easy for some of you."

"Girl, you could've gotten married on the moon, and we'd be right next to you," my brother Blake calls from the table nearest to us.

"First, I want to thank some very important people for making me into the woman I am today. Mom and Dad, you're the best, seriously. You've been our rock, always." I sweep my gaze to my eldest siblings next. "Sebastian, Logan, and Pippa… growing up, I looked at you for guidance as much as I did to Mom and Dad. I couldn't have asked for better role models. You have done so much for our family. I don't know how to repay you, except by meddling into your lives the way a baby sister should. I hope you don't mind, because I plan to keep doing it."

Oh shit, I detect glassiness in Pippa's eyes and feel tears swell in my own. *No, no, no.* I'm not even half done. I still have to keep it together for a bit.

"Alice, when I was ten and people asked me what I wanted to be when I grew up, I used to tell them, *I want to be Alice when I grow up*. Everyone thought that meant I want to copy your fashion style. But I just wanted to be as kickass as you are."

Alice is fighting a sniff. Pippa looks up at the ceiling, flaunting her palms in front of her eyes, as if trying to dry them.

"We should have taken the waterproof mascara," Pippa complains. I think she meant to whisper, but since the room is silent, her words reverberate through the space.

"You girls aren't wearing waterproof mascara?" I inquire, hoping I'm misunderstanding.

"I thought the risk of turning into raccoons will motivate us to keep it together. Bad idea. Bad, bad idea," Alice mutters, then draws in a deep breath. *Yikes.* On I go with my speech. I turn my attention to the first pair of twins.

"Christopher and Max, thank you for teaching

me the value of pranks. Life at Casa Bennett would have been dull without them. Never lose your humor. We need the next generations of Bennetts to take after you."

Lastly, I turn to the younger pair of twins. "Blake and Daniel, you were my partners in crime, but also my silent protectors. Yes, I know all about those times you sabotaged my dates in high school and after I returned from college. I know you thought you were smooth about it, but you really weren't."

They flash me sheepish grins, not looking sorry in the slightest.

"Well, thank you for doing it. Every sabotage brought me one step closer to Alex." I glance at my husband, who stands up the moment I utter his name. "I love you more than I can say. But I'll be happy to show you every day."

As everyone starts clapping, I lower the mic, gazing up at him. "I promise to always have a smile for you and to believe in us."

"We're going to have a wonderful life, Summer."

He pulls me in a long, passionate kiss. Heat level?

Though the roof.

Epilogue

One year later

Summer

I can't stop watching them. I'm half hidden by the doorframe, drinking in this moment of bonding between father and daughter.

Alex sits in the armchair next to Libby's bed, and our daughter is sleeping soundly on his chest. He sang to her right until her little eyelids closed. For a week, this has been the only way Libby would fall asleep, and we need her to take her morning nap before we leave to go to my parents' house. I promised myself every day that I wouldn't spy on their special moment, and every day I failed.

I hold my breath when Alex rises to his feet, returning Libby to her crib.

The day Alex first held Libby, who looked like a red and wrinkled burrito against his enormous body, I fell in love with him all over again. Being on the receiving end of his affection is pure bliss, but watching him with Libby fills me with a different kind of joy altogether. My heart grows in size every time he plays with Libby, or kisses her forehead, or just holds her. I try to duck behind the door, but it's too late.

"You've been spying again," he says as he pulls me out of the room.

I search my mind for a real excuse, as I have all week—I've come up with some stinkers such as "I was just passing," or "I thought I heard something," or "I needed something from my room"—then decide to own up to it from the get-go.

"Guilty." I lifted my arms, lacing them around his neck. "But you both look so adorable! I just can't help it."

He brings his hand to my cheek, pressing his thumb on the bow of my upper lip. Then he kisses me there, and when he pulls back, my breath catches.

Sometimes he looks at me with lust, sometimes with tenderness, and sometimes, like now, I see something in his eyes I can't quite decipher, but it tugs at all my heartstrings. He angles my face up, kissing me deep and hot.

Lowering both hands to my hips, he guides us backward down on the corridor. I chuckle when I realize where he's taking us.

"I'm already dressed for my parents' party. What do you think you're doing?"

"If I get my way, I'll be making love to my wife in a few minutes. And we both know I always get my way."

I narrow my eyes, attempt to glare… and fail. I'd point out how smug that assumption is, but he does get his way when it comes to activities of the wicked and hot variety.

It isn't my fault that the man is hotter than sin though. Or that I grow more susceptible to him as time goes by.

Okay, so maybe that *is* my fault, but I can't own up to that, or I'll never hear the end of it.

I pull him in for another kiss, sighing against his mouth. He makes sure to close the door to our bedroom once we're inside. "You look beautiful, Summer."

"It's a new dress." Pink chiffon, with a trim bodice and a layered skirt. "I managed to buy it in my old size." I twirl once and, when I come to a stop, notice Alex has moved closer. He's right in front of me.

"You're beautiful in any size, Summer."

He brings his hand to my belly, caressing it, the way he used to do when Libby was inside. He even made up a song for her, and she kicked the first time when he sang it—even if it was terribly off tune, but I didn't have the heart to point it out. "Our Libby grew in here. She came out strong and healthy, like you."

He kisses the tip of my nose, then each of my eyelids. One of his hands goes to the zipper.

Seconds later, my dress is pooling around my feet. Then he spins me around, placing both my hands on the bedpost. He pushes my panties to one side, stroking me until my thighs quiver. Then he slides the panties all the way down, tracing the back of my thigh with his tongue, and I grip the bedpost tighter. My hips arch when he slides inside me, just the head, rubbing it against the tender flesh until I'm out of my mind turned on. He hugs me from behind, flattening my back against his shirt.

"I love you so much. Sometimes I wake up in the night and look at you and still can't believe you're mine. I'm the luckiest man on earth."

"Alex…."

My voice trails away as he pulls out of me, and we move to lie on the bed. He climbs on top of me, loving me fast and deep until I pull at the bedsheet with both hands. He covers my mouth, kissing my sounds of pleasure before giving in to his own release.

"I love you more every day, Summer. How is that possible?"

"I don't know," I whisper. "It's the same for me." I run a hand through his hair, then pull him closer. "I love you so much."

***

Libby wakes up ten minutes before we're set to leave. Through a miracle, we actually do make it out the door in time.

Once we're in the car, I check my phone to see if anyone has written in our family chat group. Considering the sheer number of people in it, I always have to catch up.

My e-mail inbox is hopeless these days. I have no clue how the public got wind of it, but it's cluttered now.

"Oh, look. I just got the seven hundred and forty-fifth request to post a pic with you and Libby on social media."

He smiles. "They'll wear you down eventually, babe."

"Nope, the two of you are for me. Just for me. I'm territorial like that."

"I love that you are."

I found out I was pregnant with Libby two months after we married and one month after I opened my gallery. We'd planned to wait a while longer before having children, but we were over the moon anyway.

Needless to say, things got a bit out of hand after she was born. Most days I'm still trying to figure out my ass from my elbow. But when Alex looks at me with those molten green eyes and says, "Babe, we're in this together," I remember that life isn't about perfect. It's about figuring it out together, every step of the way. I don't know what I would do without him, or my family. My parents hover over Libby every chance they get, and so do Alex's parents. The desire to be closer to their grandchildren outweighed their fear of Alex's fame, so they moved to San Francisco a few months ago. They're working on mending their relationship with their son.

Things are mad at my parents' house when we arrive, but that's nothing new. Mom and Dad had to extend the gazebo because it was too tiny for all of us.

Not, of course, that everyone attending today will fit inside. My parents' wedding anniversary events are usually a crowded affair, but for today's event, every single adopted Bennett seems to have shown up, as well as all of our cousins. A soccer match is already being planned. Business as usual in the Bennett clan. Mom takes Libby into her arms as soon as she sees us.

"You won't give her back to me until I have to feed her, right?" I tease.

"You have her all the time," she coos. Mom is very sweet that way. Whenever a newborn pops into our family, she's all over the baby.

"That tip for the tummy ache worked like a charm, Mom. Thanks."

"Anytime, sweetie."

Alex tucks me into his side as Mom heads with Libby to my dad.

"You know what? I think Libby needs a brother or a sister. Or both, really," he murmurs.

"Oh no. I knew it. Your dad gene has been unleashed."

"What are you going to do about it?"

"Put the leash back on for another few years. Unless you can convince me otherwise."

Now, see? Why in the ever-loving hell did I say that? I just gave him free rein to use his persuasion techniques on me, and I know for a fact I don't stand a chance against half of them.

"Oh, sweetheart. If it's persuasion you need, I

can give it to you in spades."

I gulp, as he wiggles his eyebrows. And so begins my downfall. With a wiggle of eyebrows and a sly smile.

"Alex, the man of the hour," my brother Logan says, walking up to us. "You know what I've got to ask."

Alex looks past Logan to where my nieces and nephews are huddled together, in the spot where Alex usually shows them his latest stunts.

"Yep. Duty calls," Alex says. He touches his lips to mine, just barely, but his hand moves in little circles at the small of my back. It's our newly developed secret language for, I want to kiss you until your knees go weak, but can't in present company.

Well, I'll be happy to report that even this chaste brush of lips makes my toes curl. God, this man is sex on a stick, I swear.

After Logan whisks him away, I head over to Sebastian and our cousin Landon Connor, who are chatting next to the gazebo.

"You two look like you're plotting something," I say when I catch up with them.

Landon clutches his heart theatrically. "Who, me and Sebastian? We're always on our best behavior."

I roll my eyes. "Oh, yeah. I know. Oldest brother syndrome."

"Hey, I did convince the entire Connor clan to fly here for the anniversary. Doesn't that earn me any points?" Landon challenges.

I cross my arms. "You've got some cheek, Landon Connor. I know for a fact that your siblings are looking for any opportunity to spend time with you, you undeclared workaholic. That probably tipped the balance in favor of them flying here more than your persuasion skills."

Sebastian whistles. "Ouch. You got caught in Summer's crossfire, cousin. If I were you, I'd run."

Landon laughs. "Who says I'm undeclared? Workaholic and proud."

Hmmm... Landon has been lonely for too long, and that's just unacceptable. Such a waste of a hunk. And I'm not just saying this because he's my cousin and I'm biased. Half of the single female adopted Bennetts eye him with thinly veiled interest. The other half doesn't bother with the veil. That's solid proof, right there. All our Connor cousins are single, which is a damn shame. To meddle or not to meddle? That's the question.

Valentina waves at me, crossing the yard and stealing me from our brothers. She hooks an arm around mine as we traipse around. "So, how are we doing on that emotional blackmail plan?" I inquire. She and I agree Landon needs a swift—and very loving, of course—kick in the butt to get things... moving. Obviously that requires a lot of plotting.

"I'm making progress. Slowly, but surely. I think the first step is getting him out of that office, convince him he needs a longer holiday. After that, the sky is the limit."

I grin. Val is smart. "I like that plan."

We chat until my parents ask us all to come closer to where they're standing, near the entrance of the house.

"I think they're going to hold their speech," I say, clapping my hands. I love my parents' anniversary speeches. They're always so full of wisdom, I feel like I should take notes or something. Valentina goes to look for her sisters, and Alex joins me with our daughter in his arms. And cue the heart flutter.

"What?" I ask, realizing he's watching me closely.

"I like seeing you smile. I promise to give you a reason to look at me like that every day."

"You already do."

The yard falls silent as Dad begins to speak. His hand is around Mom's shoulders, keeping her tucked into him.

"Thank you all for joining us today. It's a special day for Jenna and me. We like celebrating like this, surrounded by the people dear to us. Our family has grown exponentially in the past years, and we couldn't be happier. We've been pestering them to give us grandkids for a long time, and now they're everywhere. Our children have been blessed to meet their soul mates. Ava, Nadine, Eric, Emilia, Victoria, Nate, Clara, Caroline, and Alex: thank you for being part of our family. Seeing our children so happy makes us happy, and we're lucky to have you all. At every anniversary, I get asked at least ten times how

Jenna and I made it so far. First, I have to thank my wife for putting up with me every day."

I swear to God, Mom blushes. Dad kisses Mom's hand, then holds it in his. He still looks at her like she can walk on water, even after all these years.

"He has his bag of tricks, you know," she says. "Still makes me coffee every day."

Dad nods thoughtfully. "I wouldn't want to face you on a day you haven't had coffee."

Several people, myself included, laugh. Yep, Mom's need for caffeine runs through the family's veins. The laughter subsides as Dad continues.

"But Jenna and I weren't married for so long without experiencing our own share of rough patches, so here's my advice: Even when things are hard, hang onto each other. Don't turn away or try to put on a brave face. If you're lucky, the person at your side will also be your best friend. Don't hide from them. Remember to tell them how much you value and respect them. You think they might know, but sometimes they just need to hear it. And don't forget to laugh and love together."

Everyone claps as Dad raises a glass to toast. In pairs, we all clink glasses with them.

The entire day, I feel like I'm walking on a cloud, surrounded by both my old family and my new one. When it's time for Libby's afternoon nap, Alex just sits on the bench under one of the enormous trees in my parents' garden, and Libby sleeps happily on his chest.

I smile, shimmying close to my husband.

"She sure likes sleeping here," he says.

"Takes after her momma. My girl sure picked a great napping spot."

I kiss the top of Libby's head before brushing my lips against Alex's, soaking in all the love and warmth of this moment. I'm going to make him a happy, happy man for the rest of our days, using the same simple rules our clan lives by: laugh hard, love harder, and always look after each other.

THE END

Other Books by Layla Hagen

The Bennett Family Series

Book 1: Your Irresistible Love (Sebastian & Ava)

Sebastian Bennett is a determined man. It's the secret behind the business empire he built from scratch. Under his rule, Bennett Enterprises dominates the jewelry industry. Despite being ruthless in his work, family comes first for him, and he'd do anything for his parents and eight siblings—even if they drive him crazy sometimes. . . like when they keep nagging him to get married already.

Sebastian doesn't believe in love, until he brings in external marketing consultant Ava to oversee the next collection launch. She's beautiful, funny, and just as stubborn as he is. Not only is he obsessed with her delicious curves, but he also finds himself willing to do anything to make her smile. He's determined to have Ava, even if she's completely off limits.

Ava Lindt has one job to do at Bennett Enterprises: make the next collection launch unforgettable. Daydreaming about the hot CEO is definitely not on her to-do list. Neither is doing said CEO. The consultancy she works for has a strict policy—no fraternizing with clients. She won't risk her job.

Besides, Ava knows better than to trust men with her heart.

But their sizzling chemistry spirals into a deep connection that takes both of them by surprise. Sebastian blows through her defenses one sweet kiss and sinful touch at a time. When Ava's time as a consultant in his company comes to an end, will Sebastian fight for the woman he loves or will he end up losing her?

AVAILABLE ON ALL RETAILERS.

Book 2: Your Captivating Love (Logan & Nadine)
Book 3: Your Forever Love (Eric & Pippa)
Book 4: Your Inescapable Love (Max & Emilia)
Book 5: Your Tempting Love (Christopher & Victoria)
Book 6: Your Alluring Love (Alice & Nate)
Book 7: Your Fierce Love (Blake & Clara)

The Lost Series

***

Book 1: Lost in Us (James & Serena)
Book 2: Found in Us (Jessica & Parker)
Book 3: Caught in Us (Dani & Damon)

***

Standalone USA TODAY BESTSELLER

Withering Hope

Aimee's wedding is supposed to turn out perfect. Her dress, her fiancé and the location—the idyllic holiday ranch in Brazil—are perfect.

But all Aimee's plans come crashing down when the private jet that's taking her from the U.S. to the ranch—where her fiancé awaits her—defects mid-flight and the pilot is forced to perform an emergency landing in the heart of the Amazon rainforest.

With no way to reach civilization, being rescued is Aimee and Tristan's—the pilot—only hope. A slim one that slowly withers away, desperation taking its place. Because death wanders in the jungle under many forms: starvation, diseases. Beasts.

As Aimee and Tristan fight to find ways to survive, they grow closer. Together they discover that facing old, inner agonies carved by painful pasts takes just as much courage, if not even more, than facing the rainforest.

Despite her devotion to her fiancé, Aimee can't hide her feelings for Tristan—the man for whom she's slowly becoming everything. You can hide many things in the rainforest. But not lies. Or love.

Withering Hope is the story of a man who desperately needs forgiveness and the woman who brings him hope. It is a story in which hope births wings and blooms into a love that is as beautiful and intense as it is forbidden.

AVAILABLE ON ALL RETAILERS.

***

Your One True Love
Copyright © 2017 Layla Hagen
Published by Layla Hagen

All rights reserved. No part of this book may be reproduced or transmitted in any form, including electronic or mechanical, without written permission from the publisher, except in the case of brief quotations embodied in critical articles or reviews.

This is a work of fiction. Names, characters, businesses, places, events, and incidents are either the products of the author's imagination or used in a fictitious manner. Any resemblance to actual persons, living or dead, or actual events is purely coincidental.

This book is licensed for your personal enjoyment only. This book may not be re-sold or given away to other people. If you would like to share this book with another person, please purchase an additional copy for each person you share it with. If you are reading this book and did not purchase it, or it was not purchased for your use only, then you should return it to the seller and purchase your own copy. Thank you for respecting the author's work.

Published: Layla Hagen 2017
Cover: http://designs.romanticbookaffairs.com/

***
Acknowledgements

Publishing a book takes a village! A big THANK YOU to everyone accompanying me on this journey. To my family, thank you for supporting me, believing in me, and being there for me every single day. I could not have done this without you.

<<<<>>>>

Printed in Great Britain
by Amazon